❧ THE ❧
ANNA PAPERS

BY ELLEN GILCHRIST

೧ THE ೧ ANNA PAPERS

A NOVEL BY

Ellen Gilchrist

LITTLE, BROWN AND COMPANY

BOSTON   TORONTO   LONDON

FIRST PAPERBACK EDITION

The characters and events in this book are fictitious.
Any similarity to real persons, living or dead,
is coincidental and not intended by the author.

The author is grateful for permission to include the following previously
copyrighted material:

Excerpts from "Adultery," copyright © 1966 by James Dickey. Reprinted
from *Poems 1957–1967* by permission of Wesleyan University Press. First
appeared in the *Nation*.

Excerpt from *Ernest Hemingway, On Writing* edited by Larry W. Phillips.
Copyright © 1984 Larry W. Phillips and Mary Welsh Hemingway. Reprinted
with the permission of Charles Scribner's Sons, an imprint of Macmillan
Publishing Company.

I FALL IN LOVE TOO EASILY by Sammy Kahn and Jule Styne, © 1944
(renewed 1972) METRO-GOLDWYN MAYER INC. All rights assigned to SBK
FEIST CATALOGUE PARTNERSHIP. All rights controlled and administered by
SBK FEIST CATALOG INC. All rights reserved. International copyright se-
cured. Used by permission.

"Elegy" by W. S. Merwin from *The Carrier of Ladders*. Copyright © 1970
W. S. Merwin. Reprinted with the permission of Atheneum Publishers, an
imprint of Macmillan Publishing Company.

Excerpts from "Love 20¢ The First Quarter Mile" from *New and Selected
Poems* by Kenneth Fearing. Reprinted by permission of Indiana University
Press. Copyright © 1956 by Kenneth Fearing.

Library of Congress Cataloging-in-Publication Data

Gilchrist, Ellen, 1935-
    The Anna papers.

    I. Title.
    PS3557.I34258A79 1988   813'.54   88-12994
    ISBN 0-316-31316-5 (hc)
    ISBN 0-316-31320-3 (pb)

10 9 8 7 6 5 4 3 2 1

RRD VA
Designed by Robert G. Lowe

*Published simultaneously in Canada
by Little, Brown & Company (Canada) Limited*

PRINTED IN THE UNITED STATES OF AMERICA

For Rita, for Tom, for Jim

"Love is also a good subject,
as you might be said to have discovered."

— Ernest Hemingway, in a letter
to Scott Fitzgerald, 1925

ɔʊ Contents ɔʊ

❧ THE ❧
ANNA PAPERS

৩৯ Prelude ৫৯

ৡ৯ A MAN AND A WOMAN are alone in bed. It is very
dark outside, a pitch-black night with no stars. New
Orleans, Louisiana. Nineteen hundred and seventy-
three. July. The very heart of summer. An air conditioner hums in a far room. Outside the open window a
thousand crickets and tree frogs are making a raucous
din. An outrage, an uproar of cicadas and crickets and
tree frogs, the hum of the air conditioner's motor. A
record player is playing Bach, Bach played on a twelve-
string Martin guitar. A candle is burning on a table
beside the bed. The air is full of the sound of love, the
smell of love, the taste of love is all over her lips and
breasts and hair. His arm is across her body. He rises
above her and shakes his head.

"Jesus Christ. Who's been making love to you?"

"Nobody," she says. "I'm married. Married people
don't make love. They make deals."

"God, that's so cynical."

"No, it's just true. And he won't be home for a month,
so don't remind me of it."

"Where's he gone?"

"I told you. He's in England on business. And he

always fucks around on me when he's gone or when he's in town, so what difference does it make? Don't worry about it."

"I want you to go to the coast with me as soon as I finish my exams." He shook his head again and lay back down beside her and was still. He was waiting for an answer.

"Where would we go?"

"To my mother's place. There's no one there all summer. She's in the Orient."

"Then I'll go. I'll do whatever you want me to. I love you. I told you I loved you, Pointer, why can't you ever believe that when I say it?"

"Because you're married. You just want something to do while he's gone."

"I do not. . . . Come here. Get close to me. My God, this is so good I can't believe it." And she pulled him over on top of her and began to make love to him again. His body was so beautiful and young and strong. He was so angry, so crazy, so intense. She had seen him one afternoon on a tennis court at the club and asked who he was and then she had stood beside the court watching him play for almost half an hour. She was very beautiful and very rich and very spoiled and she knew that if she stood there and watched him he would begin to desire her. It didn't occur to her to wonder if what she was doing was bad or good. She had seen something she liked and she wanted to find out more about it.

He stopped in the middle of the match and poured water for himself and his opponent. As he raised the cup to his lips he caught her eye and he kept on looking. She moved one leg in front of the other leg and lowered her head. She took a yellow tennis ball and bounced it a few times with her racquet and caught it. When he went back to the baseline to begin the new game, she took her rings off and stuck them in the zipper lining of her tennis bag. There was a white spot where the rings had been and she held her hand out to the sun to begin erasing it.

"Should I go on home?" she asked her cousin, Rhoda Manning, who was in the dressing room. "Or wait around?"

"Wait around," Rhoda advised. "This is no time for games."

"Games work."

"Yeah, I know. But they aren't worth it. Waste too much time; besides, everyone always sees through them."

"They work even when people see through them."

"Then do whatever you want to do." Rhoda finished combing her hair, tied a white terrycloth headband around her head and picked up her bag to leave. "I'm staying," Anna said. "He's the best-looking man I've seen around this town in years."

"He's just a law student."

"So what? You can't have everything in one man." The women parted and Anna went up to the balcony overlooking the courts and ordered a glass of tea. She propped her legs up on the rail and thought about how nice the day was and how lucky she always turned out to be. How the universe always gave her what she needed, whether or not she deserved it, the universe just kept on supplying her with goods.

"What are you thinking about?" he said.

"I was thinking about how much I love to make love to you."

"What else?"

"About the first time I saw you. How beautifully you were playing. You were beating the shit out of Maynard. Even when I started watching it didn't faze you."

"I thought you were gorgeous. I asked Maynard who you were. I almost choked when he told me. I had just asked your husband for a job about a week before. He turned me down by the way, so go tell that to your Freudian." Pointer moved his body to accommodate hers and she turned her back to his chest and cuddled up inside his arms like a child. He went on. "Do you always get what you want, Anna?"

"Yes. I mostly do. I'm lucky. Terribly lucky or else I just want things harder than other people."

"Wasn't there anything you couldn't have that you wanted?" He ran his hand down her side, he caressed the soft roll of flesh around her waist, he caressed her little stomach, he caressed her thigh; his hand was warm and soft, like a woman's hand. Tender, a tender man when his desire was satisfied. He wasn't really interested in the conversation. He was interested in the quality of her skin. She had miraculous skin, the softest skin he had ever touched.

"I wanted a baby," she said. "But I couldn't have one."

"And you've had three husbands and you still couldn't get pregnant?"

"I could get pregnant. I just couldn't carry them, couldn't keep them alive. I don't like to talk about it, Pointer. It makes me sad. I'm going to get up and blow out that candle and close the windows. Those goddamn cicadas are like a rock band. Did you ever hear them so loud?"

"I can smell the honeysuckle out there. It's wonderful. Leave it open."

"It's mock orange too. And a night-blooming plant next door. I've forgotten the name." She disentangled herself and walked across the room and blew out the candle. She took a silk dressing gown from the bedpost and put it on. "I'm going to get a drink. Can I bring you anything? Water? Brandy?"

"Are you going to see me tomorrow night?"

"Yes. And any other time you want me to." He held out his hands to pull her back into the bed but she left

the room and walked down the long dark hall to the
kitchen, past the antiques from her grandmother's
house, past the bench from her first husband's grandfather's farm and past the paintings they had bought
together and the photographs from the second marriage
and into the kitchen which was painted white and royal
blue, the Virgin's colors. She was thinking about the twin
fetuses. She was thinking about her womb and its seeds.
She was thinking about Pointer's come inside of her and
how many days it had been since she had last menstruated
and how many months it had been since she had seen the
obstetrician who did the last operation and how many
times she had had her fallopian tubes blown out and how
much it hurt and how wonderful it was to make love by
candlelight to someone who had never seen her be sad.

She reached up in a cabinet and took down the brandy
and filled two gold-banded brandy glasses that had been
a gift from her first husband's uncle and carried them
back to the bedroom.

"I don't know what we keep doing wrong," she said,
handing him a glass. "I don't know why things don't
work out."

"Because we're crazy," he said. "Come on, Anna, get
back in the bed and help me get some sleep. I've got an
exam at nine in the morning."

She put her glass down on the table and turned back
the cover and climbed in beside him. "You're right," she
answered. "We're all crazy. Crazier than loons or lem-
mings or wild geese or fish schooling. Doomed and
crazy. Doomed to mess each other up and help each
other sleep. I love you." He moved beside her and together they fell into a lovely remorseless, charmed sleep.

The evidence for telepathy is overwhelming. Anna's
husband called an hour later. The phone was ringing
and ringing in the dark house. She picked up the extension beside the bed.

"Hello."

"Anna. It's me. What are you doing?"

"What do you mean? I'm sleeping. It's the middle of the night here. Where are you?"

"I'm in London. I want you to come over here. I'm lonely for you."

"I can't do that. I have to play in a tournament next week."

"Fuck the tournament. I need you. Listen, there's a doctor over here who's doing miracles with babies. Transplants. I don't know what all he's doing, but you should see him."

"No. No more doctors. It doesn't work. My body kills babies. I don't even care anymore."

"You do care. And I want you. I'm lonely for you. I want you with me."

"I can't help it. I can't come over there now. I don't want to fly. I hate to fly across the ocean. I'm sleepy, Jodie. I was sound asleep. I'll call you when I get up. Where will you be tomorrow morning my time?"

"Never mind it then. I was hoping. I thought we were married, Anna. I thought I meant something to you. I thought I could call up my wife and ask her to come over and keep me company while I make a living. Dumb old me."

"Don't be that way. I'm working. I've got a dozen deadlines to meet. I'm two months late with a book. You know that. Come home if you hate it there." But he had hung up the phone without saying goodbye and Anna replaced the receiver and rolled back over and patted Pointer on the arm until they both fell back to sleep. In her dreams the lost children of her womb lined up across the tennis court to accuse her of killing them. Her husbands were together on the balcony looking down and watching. She sighed in her sleep and reached down into her tennis bag and Pointer appeared and told the children to go away and took her arm and led her into the snack bar to get her a drink and a grilled cheese sandwich.

It was a long night. It was a night Anna would always remember. Twelve and a half years later, on a cold November morning, as she stuck a cyanide tablet in her mouth and walked off a pier into the Atlantic Ocean wearing a fur-lined Valentino jacket with a hood and a pair of knee-high leather boots, leaving behind a man she could finally really love and leaving behind the Pap smears and blood tests and tissue cultures that said she was going to die anyway and soon and in plenty of endless disgraceful boring cruel pain, on that day, on that morning, as she walked out onto the pier holding the pill in her gloved hand, as she passed the last boat tied to the pier and looked up into the cold cloud-covered sky, for some reason all she was thinking about was Pointer and how silly and human and vulgar and funny he had been. What dreadful questions he was always asking and how selfish he was and what a terrible social climber and what a divine tennis player and how the sun had beat down on them all summer when they played doubles, when together they beat the shit out of half the couples at the New Orleans Country Club and how they had moved out to Metairie and even gotten in the car one afternoon and gone up to Jackson, Mississippi, to play a senator and his girlfriend in a match. She remembered Pointer's hand on her thigh and his dick inside her the first time she ever fucked him and how wild and selfish he had been and matched her selfishness and nobody needed to be ashamed of themselves and she stuck the pill in her mouth and walked on off of the pier.

❧ I ❧

Anna

∽ 1 ∾

∽ ARLINGTON, Texas, County of Tarrant, summer, nineteen hundred and eighty-three. Anna was spending a week at a spa in Texas. On the first afternoon of her visit, her old friend Dr. Carl Jancke came by and took her blood pressure and examined her. It was a formality, a prerequisite of the spa.

"Have you had a mammogram lately?"

"No."

"When?"

"Never."

"Pap smear?"

"No."

"That's unwise, Anna. Not worthy of you."

"Well, I don't need a Pap smear. I won't get anything."

"How about coming by my office tomorrow?"

"Hell, no. I came in here to get the fat off my back. Not to have medical examinations."

"Okay."

"I don't need a mammogram, Carl."

"One out of eleven women die of breast cancer. One out of eleven."

"Don't scare me."

"Okay. I won't."

"I'll do it when I get back to New York."

"Promise."

"I promise."

"Good. God, you're a good-looking woman, Anna."

"Thank you. It's the genes." She gave him a hug, but not a promise of anything to come. And of course she never got the mammogram or the Pap smear. Anna didn't like anyone touching her unless she was in love with them.

Sloan-Kettering Memorial Hospital, New York City, New York, late fall, nineteen hundred and eighty-three. Anna was reciting a poem written by Sappho in the fifth century B.C.

"You know the place; then leave Crete and come to us, waiting where the grove is pleasantest, by precincts sacred to you. . . ."

Anna leaned close to her friend, the cold cheek, the cold sheets, the dark eyes of her dearest and most treasured friend, the kindest of all mentors, sweet, sweet memories of kindnesses given and received, cards, letters, calls in early morning hours. Anna continued reciting the poem because Joel had asked to hear it. The other people in the room moved back. A nurse waited by the door. Outside the window rain fell on New York City while Joel Norris died to Anna's voice, her hands in Anna's hands. She was sixty-three years old and she had spent the last two years of her life being tortured in hospitals and she had died anyway.

"Oh, God," Anna said, and turned to the others. Her editor was there and his gentle wife and two women she vaguely knew. Joel's nephew stood by the window. He would be Anna's agent now. Their eyes met. Their grief made them friends. Then Anna took her editor's arm and they went out into the hall to make the phone calls.

"I wouldn't die like this," she said, as he fished in his

pockets for the quarters. "No one will ever make me die in a hospital."

"You aren't sick, are you?" He turned to her and took her arms. "Anna, is something wrong with you?"

"Nothing that isn't wrong with all of us. I'm getting old. I forget names. I don't heal. My immune system isn't as good as it used to be. I don't heat up. Let me use the phone. I want to call Philip."

"Is that still going on?"

"Only when my best friend dies. Nothing will ever be the same now. Nothing will heal."

"You ought to go to the doctor. Go up to Boston and let Carlyle look at you . . ."

"And then?"

"Stop fucking Philip. He won't leave Caroline. He never will."

"I'm not trying to get him to."

"Yes you are." He was so solemn. He knew her so well. He read the goddamn books in manuscript. There was nothing to hide. No reason to hide anything, and besides, Joel was dead.

"She was perfect," Anna said. "They don't make them anymore. Et cetera. Now I will be crying when I call him. Fuck it all, Arthur. Fuck death."

"Anna."

"Yes."

"Don't call him. Go with us to dinner and stay with us tonight. We have to call all the others. Don't call him."

"I have to, Arthur. Don't listen." She put a quarter in the slot and called the married redhaired baby doctor who was her lover. She gave a number to an answering service and in a minute the doctor, whose name was Philip, called her back. Anna turned her back to her editor and began to talk. When she hung up she took her editor's arm and held it. "I'm going to see him now. And I'm leaving New York. For good. Very soon."

"Anna, please don't go."

"I'll call you tomorrow, Arthur. We'll go together to the funeral." She let go of his arm and walked down the hall to the elevator. Leaving behind the tortured, starved, worn-out, distressed, dead body of her dearest friend. Into the stars with you, Anna said to herself. Dust unto dust and after dust to lie, sans song, sans singer, and sans end. Who knows what waits out there?

Two hours later she was in Philip's arms in a room in the Plaza Hotel. "Everything seems so fragile," she said. "In the face of that I guess we at least get to spend a night together every now and then. You can stay all night, can't you?"

"I can stay all night. I'm in trouble over you, Anna. I think it's going to get worse. Because after this nothing will happen." He held her very close to him, her body was enclosed in his. He counted the seconds of his sadness and his happiness. He was enlarged and diminished and broken and made whole. It made no sense to him but he came when she called him. It did not happen often now.

"I love you to the breadth, depth, height. I love you whether I see you or not. If I don't see you I still love you. Remember that." She leaned over him and kissed his forehead, his eyelids and earlobes and the hollow places of his neck. Then she got out of bed and turned on all the lights and came back to him and made love to him like a cheerleader of love, like a panther of love, in view of being alive, of breathing without pain, in the light of being cognizant and alive she took the married man along and they made love.

Sometime during the night Anna hit her arm against the bedside table and it bled. She washed it off and tied her scarf around it. When she woke he was looking at it with his glasses on.

"Don't look at my arm," she said. "I cut it."

"How?"

"I hit it on something. I'm very thin-skinned lately. I told you that. It's hereditary. My grandmother was like that. She always had Band-Aids on her wrists when I was little." Anna stuck her arm under the sheet. "Stop looking at it."

"Are you taking estrogen?"

"Hell, no. What for?"

"It might help your skin." He reached under the cover and took her arm and looked at it again. He was puzzled by it. She seemed so healthy, so alive. It didn't fit in.

"Would you like me to suck your dick?" she said, rolling over to the other side of the bed. "Or not?"

"I would like you to take care of yourself and live a hundred years."

"Well, I probably won't. There's something wrong with me." She sat up very straight with her legs out in front of her. She leaned down along her legs, a show-off yoga move. "I know I'm mortal, that's the problem. I can talk myself into anything. I might decide to die." She waited until he looked worried. "I might die to punish you. Would it work?" He wasn't laughing. It wasn't working. For a moment Anna thought she might tell him what was wrong, then she talked herself out of it.

"You believe anything I say. You are wonderful, Philip. I apologize but it's so easy to do that to you. I cut my arm on a sharp place in the bathroom in the night. It's nothing. I was serious about sucking your dick, however. I really meant that part." She pulled him over close to her and kissed him on the mouth instead. Gave him her old Greta Garbo, Marilyn Monroe kiss that she had practiced on her brothers when she was twelve. The French kiss to end all French kisses. Anna had taught it to all the Hand children, who had practiced it and perfected it in the garage with their McGruder cousins. It was some kiss.

The funeral took two days to arrange. Writers Joel had represented from the Coast and people from Washington and relatives from Philadelphia all came to New York City and went in taxis to a church on Park Avenue and read things they had written and spoke in low voices and buried what was left of their friend. When the funeral was over, Anna went back to her apartment and sat on the bed and waited for the married man to come and tell her goodbye.

This is it, she decided, the way the weather turns around, the thing we run from and never diminish, the long friends, the hosts of the dead, their legions have claimed Joel and will claim Philip and claim Arthur and Mother and Daddy and my sisters and brothers and me. What a fucked-up system. And while we live, no way to know each other, no way to connect. Misapprehensions, uneasy truces, loss.

Then he was there and she forgot about systems and misapprehensions and death and took her married man to bed.

Anna was walking around the Upper East Side of Manhattan. One last long walk before the movers came and took her things out of the extravagant apartment and moved them back to the mountains. One whole day to walk up Madison Avenue and down Fifth Avenue and across Park Avenue and over to Second and Third. One last day to eat deli food and buy shoes and boots and sweaters and look in windows and breathe the strange miraculously clean air of New York City. She was in a good mood when she left the apartment. She was wearing comfortable shoes and a long navy blue raincoat with a hood. A bright yellow

scarf and dark blue leather gloves. She had a handful
of money and credit cards stuffed in a pocket of the
coat, a comb and a lipstick. It was nine in the morning
when she left the apartment, meaning to spend the
day walking. At ten she was sitting in a chair in an
internist's office waiting her turn to talk to him. She
had passed his office and walked on, then turned
around and trudged back and opened the door and
asked the receptionist if she could see him.

"What's wrong? What's bothering you?" He stood up
behind his desk when she came in. He had left someone
who needed him when the nurse told him she was waiting. She looked at her hands, stared at the floor, then
lifted her eyes.

"I think there's something wrong. Like I'm dreaming
I'm sick. It's probably aging."

"Are you going through menopause?"

"No. I don't think so."

"We'll schedule you for a physical."

"I can't do that. I'm leaving town. I just wanted to talk
to you. I want you to charge me for this, William."

"We'll see. Well, take off your clothes and let me have
a look." He giggled. He was a really delightful man.
Skinny, freckled, blond. Anna giggled back.

"I can't today. I have an appointment. I just wanted to
stop by."

"Is something specific wrong? I'll tell you what. Let's
have lunch. Tomorrow or the day after?"

"Tomorrow. I'll call you later." She stood up. He
came around the desk. He walked her to the door. She
told the receptionist goodbye. She went home and called
Philip. Then she called and canceled the lunch with the
internist. It was twelve noon. She told the maid how to
pack the things in the bedroom. Then she went down
the elevator and out onto the street and began to walk
again. No doctors, she promised herself. No checkups.
No hospitals, no operating rooms, no chemicals, no

nothing. *Nada, de nada, de nada.* Keep walking. You are not sick. There is nothing wrong with you. You are not sick. There is nothing wrong and nothing that needs fixing.

She was on Madison Avenue. A shop window was displaying beautiful cotton dresses made in China. Thick cotton in black and beige and white. Beautiful simple designs. Anna went inside and tried on the dresses. She mailed one to her youngest niece in North Carolina. Then she bought two beautiful scarves and mailed them to the girl in Oklahoma who might also be her niece. She bought a gold barrette and tied her hair back with it. She bought a silver barrette and mailed it to her sister Helen. Spending money like a drunken sailor, she told herself. Living like there's no tomorrow.

Philip was alone in his office in the late afternoon. On the wall behind him were the degrees that said he was a doctor of medicine, a healer of mankind and a scientist. That means I am supposed to stay close to the ground, he decided. I am supposed to be able to tell fact from dream, my wife from Anna, my desire from my career, my ass from a hole in the ground, my dick from my head.

I can't do any more today. The computer is going to cost half a million dollars and Steiner is going to quit and I'm not going to operate after this year. I won't do it. Half of them die anyway.

He got up and walked into the bathroom and looked at his face in the mirror. His freckles and his handsome face.

I let it get away, he decided. The one we wait for. She's right. We are all crazy. Let them blow it up.

He walked over to the desk and unlocked a drawer. He took some money from a bank envelope and stuck it in his jacket pocket. He turned off the lights and left the room. He was forty-six years old and his dick didn't get as hard as it used to get and he didn't sleep as well and knowing why or pretending to be resigned didn't change a thing.

He walked over to the East River and watched the water for a while and then he went on home to a woman he hadn't ever loved very much and they had dinner and watched some television and went to bed.

༄ 2 ༄

༄ CHARLOTTE, NORTH CAROLINA. In nineteen hundred and forty-two when Anna was born, right in the middle of the Second World War. And in nineteen hundred and forty-four, when her sister Helen came to join her, then James and Niall and Daniel and Louise. In the old Victorian house on Shannon Street, an old house painted sky blue with white gingerbread and shutters and trim, where the Hand children lived and grew and had their rooms and hid in the attic and the tower. The yard, where the playhouse was, a replica of the blue house and painted a darker, brighter blue. A playhouse with a real wood stove and a real sink with running water and rugs made out of their old dresses and sweaters, loomed by Mrs. Randall, who lived down the street and drank cough medicine to feed her madness and her art. Anna could look down at the playhouse rugs and see Helen's old yellow playsuit or Niall's red sweater or Daniel's Sunday coat. Later, when she wrote books she would think of those rugs and what they were made of and what they meant.

The yard on Shannon Street, the paved driveway with the basketball hoop above the doors to the garage, the incessant thump of Daniel's basketball and Niall's and James's, which was quieter and went through the hoop without a sound.

The neighborhood of Shannon Street, where the Hand children played Prisoner's Base at dusk, after dinner, with the McGruder children and the Purcells and the Havertys and the Wilsons and the Cranes. With the earth growing dark, the moon and stars coming out, the planets, as Lannie McGruder called them, planets, he would say, think of that when you feel sorry for yourself. You'll be up there when you're dead.

The children would run all over the neighborhood, hiding in bushes and each other's garages, hiding in pairs, trembling with excitement, their hands touching in the spidery corners of sheds. It would grow quiet. They would begin to sneak in, one at a time, daring whoever was It. Anna was the one who could wait. She would come tearing in at the last moment, when all the rest were prisoners, screaming, Here I come, here I am. She would come tearing in on her long legs and beat everybody to the base, even Phelan Manning, when he would be staying with his grandmother. Phelan, the terrible and powerful and exciting Phelan Manning. He would take Helen with him to hide in the Purcells' tool-shed, run his hands up and down her legs. After he did it the first time she shaved her legs with a razor she stole from her father, the only thing Helen ever stole in her life. Phelan Manning, a boy you would steal for, if you want a key to his personality.

Anna could outrun Phelan. She was eleven months older than he was and it was her territory. She lived on Shannon Street twelve months a year, year after year. Phelan only lived there in the summers and when his father was overseas or later for two years because only his grandmother could stand to have him around when he was seventeen. Anna could outrun him and when he was It, when he had captured all the other children and dragged them into the garage to sit on the prisoner boxes, when Helen and Daniel and James and Niall were captured and defeated, caught and shamed, they would sit with their hands on their knees and gaze out at the darkness falling all over their yard and all over Shannon Street. They would sit with their hands on their knees and wait for Anna to come tearing in from under the basketball hoop or from behind the garage. Here I come, she would be screaming and Ole ole in free, which meant, Everyone is free, all in free. The long hair she never let anybody cut and her long arms and legs and her famous brown safari shorts her uncle George sent her from Nigeria, screaming, Ole, ole in free. Who will save her brothers and sisters now? Chained to their jobs and their husbands and wives and ex-wives and children and habits and ideas and fears, closed and open doors and spidery corners. Who will save the Hand children now and set them free?

∽∾ 3 ∾∾

∽∾ QUANTUM JUMPS. Anna as a child. If she ever was a child. She was so serious, so old for her age. In her dark blue uniform skirts, her starched white blouses. How the sisters praised her. Little Mother Superior they called her behind her back. Her brothers and sisters went to find her during recess, told her what had happened, asked her what to do, checked in.

Then, when she was fourteen, she demanded to be put in a public school. Her parents caved in. She had made all A's. She tested in the highest percentiles. She said she had to go to a public school and her parents caved in and she was lost to the Church. The sisters grieved over that. They had thought she had a calling.

"I will always think of you with love," she told Mother Elizabeth. She had gone to say goodbye and thank the sisters for the education they had given her. "I will always think of you and give you money when I grow up if I can." She stood before the abbess. She was tall for her age, graceful and tall. Wearing her dark blue uniform skirt and white blouse, her hair tied back with a string. In those days it was her signature to be as plain as possible. She never enlivened her uniform with ribbons or pins or scarves. Even at fourteen she had a sense of herself as someone special, someone who could possess visions and make them manifest.

"We had not thought to lose you so soon." Mother Elizabeth searched the girl's eyes.

"I know you thought I had a calling," Anna said. "Well, I don't. I want to live in the world, one bigger than Charlotte. I want to go out and see everything that's going on."

"I hope it pleases you." Mother Elizabeth was smiling. Everything was very still. Outside the windows spring was cool and vital and new. A line of Bradford pear trees marched from the window to the gate, their brilliant white shook at the sky. A shaft of light fell from the window onto Mother Elizabeth's hands. Anna picked one of them up and kissed it. She kissed the soft pale hand very gently, feeling the veins beneath her lips, then she handed it back. "You should not have the girls kneel in the gravel at the Feast of Saint Mary," she said. "It is not a good thing to do and hurt my knees so much and Helen cut hers. I do not believe that Jesus wanted children to cut their knees and there wasn't any gravel long ago when He lived. He put the names of flowers into the Bible and I saw a book with all the flowers from the Holy Land, real flowers pasted in it. It belonged to my aunt. You should concentrate on things like the flowers, not when He was nailed to the cross or kneeling in the gravel. The Stations of the Cross are terrible things to look at."

"Is this why you are leaving us?"

"No, but it is part of it. I like it here, where things are very old and feel like part of the earth, but out there, at the public school, are other things I need to know. So I won't get caught up in one thing. Like my mother. She does the same things every day. I wrote down what she did every day for six days. The same things every day.

Like a snail going in a circle. A person should have a different life, with different things to do."

Then everything was quiet and when they spoke again it was in polite assurances and goodbyes and when Anna was gone Mother Elizabeth called in Sister Martha Teresa and told her of the conversation and they considered calling Mr. and Mrs. Hand and speaking with them but decided against it. The other children were still in the school. It would not do to create a problem.

So Anna went to the public high school and was the editor of the yearbook and directed the senior play and was the class poet and the valedictorian and had six different boyfriends every year and could not love them very much. You are made of ice, her friends told her admiringly. You never love anyone enough to get hurt.

"I get hurt," Anna said. They were playing Truth in the living room. Anna and her sister Helen and two friends of Anna's from the public school, Dixie Lou and Janissa. Helen still went to the convent school, none of her friends would ever be named anything as silly as Dixie or Janissa.

"When?" Helen asked. "When did you get hurt?"

"I get hurt when people do stupid things I can't understand. When Michael Wheaton came down here to see Ben and never wrote me back a letter. I got hurt over that."

"He's twenty-two years old," Helen screamed. "He's in med school."

"So what?"

"Medical students don't write to high school girls."

"Well, you said I didn't get hurt and I told the truth. Why are we playing this game?"

"Because there isn't anything to do in Charlotte in the summer. It's a stupid game, you're right." Janissa got out a package of Pall Malls and lit one. She leaned back on her elbow. "So where are you going to college?" she asked. "Have you decided?"

"She's going to the University of North Carolina because that's all Momma and Daddy can afford." Helen was sorry it was true. She had wanted the stars for Anna. Vassar or Radcliffe or Berkeley.

"Daddy wants us near to home," Anna said. "He hasn't been well lately. He doesn't want me to go far away."

"She has a scholarship," Helen said. "She could have had one anywhere she wanted."

"I want to go to Chapel Hill," Anna added. "I am going to be very happy there."

Anna met her first husband at Chapel Hill. She was a freshman and he was the senior captain of the ROTC. He chose her to be the sweetheart of ROTC and she marched with the cadets at football games. Wearing a smart gray uniform and huge yellow and green chrysanthemum corsages, she marched up and down the field beside the captain and on the basis of that she fell in love with him and they were married the month he graduated from college. He was a cold young man with little to say that interested her but the perfection of the courtship swept her along. His name was Carter and he had an uncle in Charlotte who hired him to help run his real estate business and Anna quit college and came home to Charlotte to live. She was nineteen.

"I know how to read," she told her friends. "I'll be happy learning things my own way." The newlyweds moved into a duplex apartment six blocks from Anna's parents and the next year Helen Hand married Spencer Abadie and moved half a block down the street.

Anna was pregnant at Helen's wedding. She was radiant with it. Never before or after in her life was Anna as beautiful as the months she carried that little boy. She carried him for six and a half months and lost him in a car on the way to the hospital emergency room.

She went crazy. She was twenty years old and she was disconsolate. She thought she had done something wrong. She lay in bed and went over every step she had taken since the moment she learned she was pregnant, every cigarette she had smoked, every potato chip she had eaten, every walk she had taken, every car ride, each time she and Carter had made love. The priest started coming around. Anna hadn't been to church in two years. Now she went every day. Also, she began seeing an old Freudian named Wilton who gave her bottles of the new tranquilizers, lithium and Valium, and when she complained that they made her sleepy he gave her bottles of Dexedrine and then phenobarbital to make her sleep off the Dexedrine.

Helen gave birth to her first child a year later, a little girl named DeDe. That consoled Anna somehow. She quit the Freudian and stopped taking the pills and began to see her sister Helen. She would get up every morning and send her husband off to work and then go over to Helen's house and hold the baby.

Then Anna got pregnant again and again and again and again and again. Bloody miscarriages each time, the last two in bed. In the meantime Helen gave birth to Kenny and Winifred and Lynley.

And all those years the thought of becoming a writer never entered Anna's head. She had written poetry all her life and she wrote it now, poems she gave to other people and poems she kept for herself. But she never thought of giving her life away to words. Anna wanted to have a baby and keep it alive. There were six miscarriages during those years, although Helen always said it was seven and Mrs. Hand, Senior, thought it was five.

There was a divorce finally and Anna moved back into her parents' house and had her fallopian tubes tied so no more babies could be conceived to die. And then she met a poet and really fell in love and married him and when he died in a car wreck she pulled an old Royal portable typewriter out of a closet and set it up on a wooden card table in a sewing room and began to write. And all those years, from the time she was a small child until her death, she thought of herself as a fortunate person with a charmed life, blessed and indulged, lucky to have lived in a good place in the best of times. "If I looked out my window in the spring I saw twenty pear trees in full bloom and in the fall oaks and maples and in the winter the architecture of a dozen different species of trees," she told the married redhaired baby doctor once and many years afterwards he drove alone down the street where she had grown up and lived and was amazed at how ugly and ordinary it all seemed.

ᔌᔑ 4 ᖉᔌ

ᔌᔑ "YOU AREN'T immortal, Anna," the married red-haired baby doctor told her, when he found out she hadn't seen a doctor or had a checkup in years.

"I don't know. I might be. No one in our family dies of anything but strokes. Strokes in their nineties. I think you will your death, anyway. When you're ready. Don't talk about it." She swung her long hair back from her shoulders and held a glass of wine up to the light. "The observing system," she added. "Changes everything. Actualizes an aspect. Oh, well, forget that. You want to see a play if there's time?"

"The Royal Shakespearean Company is doing *Lear*. We could see that if there are tickets. Shall I call?"

There had been tickets and they had gone together to the play and sat very close holding hands until their palms were sweaty and then continuing to hold hands because neither of them wanted to be the one to pull away, and afterwards Anna had been quiet, thinking of her father. "I am like Cordelia," she said. "In my family I'm the one that tells the truth. My father secretly likes it, I think. I'm so far from all of them now. It's a shame."

He took her home and stayed the whole night and was there in the morning and when he left the sun was barely up in New York City and the day was ruined for work.

That afternoon she went to see her old psychiatrist, to tell him goodbye before she left the city.

"I will be closer to them there," she told him. "To Helen and James and Niall and Daniel and Momma and Daddy. The mountain house is only eighty miles from Charlotte. And there's something else, a girl in Oklahoma I have to do something about. A child that might belong to Daniel. Well, that's a long story. You don't have time for that now."

"Of course I do. Tell it to me."

"Daniel married an Indian girl when he was pretending to be a hippie. He was only nineteen or twenty. I can't remember. Anyway, he was out in California at a hippie commune and he married a Cherokee Indian and brought her home to Charlotte but she only stayed a few weeks. She ran away because Momma and Daddy were snotty to her. Everyone was. Even I was, I think. I can't remember. Everything was so confused back then. Anyway, LeLe, my cousin on the West Coast I've told you about, LeLe and I have reason to believe the girl died having Daniel's child and her sister raised it. The child has written to me. She's fifteen years old. I have a picture of her. She looks like us. I need to do something about this soon." Anna was curled up on the psychiatrist's sofa. She had forgotten he was there. She was thinking of the letter she had received the week before and Daniel's silence and disbelief.

"Anna."

"Yes."

"Where did you go?"

"Okay. Well, anyway, it's interesting and will give me something to think about in the mountains. I want to go and see her. I want to take Daniel and go and see if she's ours."

"I think that might be your brother's decision."

"I know. You're right. It's just that she wrote to me first. Because of the books. Her English teacher assigned her one of my stories and she started wondering about the name. They called her by our name. Why I don't know since they never told us about her, if she's ours."

"I think you better leave it to your brother."

"I know. I can't stop mothering them. I think they're mine."

"Why don't you write about them instead?"

"I always am. What else does a writer know? The day Helen was bit by a dog. The night Daniel was burned, how hard we all worked to keep Niall from failing, how sick Momma was after Louise, the kitchen and the huge stove Daddy had put in and how we all cooked all the time. Funny that I never cook anymore. Never make a sauce or a soufflé."

"You were your mother's right hand. You told me that one day. Do you remember saying that?"

"I used to rub her back while we waited for the babies to come. We would listen to Beethoven as the last days went by. The Sixth Symphony. Do you know, to this day, if I hear that music I want to rush down to a hospital and look at the newborns."

"Get back to work as soon as you can, Anna. You know where the satisfaction is. You've told me."

"I know. Well, it will be okay for me in the mountains. This didn't work out for me up here. Taxicabs and stretch limos and television people, the married man. It was not a good idea."

"I'll miss talking to you." He stood up, the hour was almost over.

"I will miss you too." She sat up, rearranged her clothes, thought she might kiss him goodbye, touch him before she went away. She smiled at the thought and liked him better and looked up and they laughed at the things that had passed between them and the things that had not and Anna gathered up her coat and pocketbook and took her leave.

Anna spent the next year in the Carolina mountains, in a house she had lived in with the poet. And did something she had never done. She had two lovers at the same time. The redhaired married baby doctor in New York City. He was the one she yearned for, dreamed about, tried not to think of, kept no pictures of, letters from, souvenirs of any kind. She talked to her close women friends about him as though he were a character in a movie or a play. She thought it was very very funny that she had fallen into this trap. Oh, it was hilarious, wasn't it? And her compadres and companions would agree, it was a riot.

The other man was young. Violent and proud, brilliant and talented and poor. He was a carpenter and built houses in the mountains where she lived. When she called him he came, driving up in his baby blue pickup truck and swinging down out of the cab as if he owned the world. He would walk into her house and take her straight to bed. "You been doing any yoga?" he would say.

"Yes," she might answer.

"Let me see," and he would pull her to him and run his hands down the fine clean muscles of her back and legs. He never asked if she had other men. He never asked her where she was when she wasn't with him. They went out to eat and killed time and made love and talked about themselves. He wanted to go back to school and get an engineering degree but he didn't know where to begin. He wanted to be older and marry Anna and fuck her all night every night but he only told her that he loved to fuck her. "You always make me hard," he said. "You make my dick so goddamn hard."

She was fascinated by the young man, whose name was Adam Halliday. He had captured her imagination from the start. She would lie in his arms after making love and wonder why she didn't marry him after all, take him on, take care of him, be the mother he had never had. Then she would remember herself walking in the snow in New York City with the redhaired married man and know the heart can never be sounded. Looking for love in all the wrong places. No, not looking. Finding. Anna's problem was finding. Love found her out and told her there are things we need that we cannot have.

Strange lonely creatures that we are. Besides, the young man would remain young and Anna would grow old and a young woman would come along and who would set herself up for such a blow.

She had left New York City and returned to the mountains in the late fall. The sugar maples had done their golden dance and then their red one. Winter came in a moment. There was deep snow and sleds and Adam built huge fires in her fireplace and they slept on futons before the fire and ate thick country stews and she helped him fill out the applications to Auburn and Georgia Tech and Vanderbilt. In April he received a scholarship and they got drunk for three days to celebrate. In May he left for Nashville for summer school. It did not make Anna sad to lose him. She had lost her desire to possess anything. He asked her to go with him, to be his wife or mistress or anything she liked but she would not go. She kissed him goodbye and sent him off to school and began to make plans to close up her mountain house and go home to Charlotte, North Carolina, to make her peace with her family.

"I'm coming home." She called her mother and told her to find her a place to live.

"There are some wonderful new apartments not far

from us. On a lake. You can live with us and have an office there."

"I can't live with you, Momma."

"Why not?"

"I might want to sleep with someone."

"Oh, Anna, don't say that."

"Line up a realtor. I'll be there in the fall."

"Your father will be so pleased."

"Tell him to get out his maps. I want to know everything he knows about rivers. I want to write about all the rivers of our state."

ജ 5 ൝

ജ THERE WAS one last book to write. And the summer to be lived through. She worked on the book in a desultory manner, writing odd disjointed pieces at strange times of the day, dating them like journal entries, although they had nothing to do with the days on which they were written. They were pieces of the past, a history of obsessions, endowments, angelizings, as Phelan Manning once called falling in love. But Anna wasn't thinking about the men out of her past. She was thinking about the married redhaired baby doctor. She woke up thinking about him and she went to sleep thinking about him and she dreamed of him. How strange desire is, Anna thought. If you would ask me why I needed him I would reply, So I could look at the freckles on his hands. Reckless reckless reckless. Stop. Soon I will leave and go home to Charlotte and this will dissipate and go away. I have to learn to control my mind. No. Examine it, that's all you get, Anna. All you get to do is watch. Then watch.

She made a list of the things she was thinking about:

1. The married redhaired baby doctor.
2. The girl in Oklahoma.

3. The box of coins Phelan and I buried at Summerwood for a joke.
4. Why the skin keeps peeling off my fingers when I type. Key to relationship between physical and mental. Be sure to call Collis Garen at the university and tell him about it.
5. Write to Adam. Call Adam. Introduce Adam to woman he can breed with. Stop wanting to control Adam or anyone.

She was trying to think of number six when the phone rang. It was Philip calling from Washington.

"I had to come down here for a consultation. It's an hour's flight to Asheville. Can I come there tomorrow?"

"No. It wouldn't do any good. It makes things worse."

"We wouldn't have to make love. We could talk. I want to see you, Anna. I'm lonely for you and I can't sleep and I'm worried."

"Then divorce your wife."

"Oh, Anna."

"Goodbye." She hung up the phone and took it off the wall jack and walked outside and put it in the firewood shed. "The very heart of loss. The very heart of loss."

The next day was Thursday. A glorious spring day. Small fledgling birds and chipmunks, rabbits and squirrels, honeysuckle, all the flowers of late spring. Anna walked out across the stone porch and down the stone stairs Adam had built for her and down across the lawn where rabbits watched her without moving and on down past the swing and the rose trellis to the garden Adam had planted the summer he stayed with her. She stopped by the garden thinking of him. How good to have fucked a man who could always make her come. Make me come just walking into a room, she thought, lapsing into the language of the black women who had

nursed her when she was young, the soft laughing language of the Gullah natives. Make me come just thinking about it, she decided. Adam or the land. Wide fields
and strong black faces, mornings, evenings, afternoons,
the river, days with no time, body all hot and starched
dresses wilting on my fat little waist, pot liquor and
cornbread and black-eyed peas, butter melting in my
hands. Bruden and Lannie and William Claire. I've got
to go and see them when I get home. See how they're
doing, if they need anything, where their children go to
school.

Make me come. I never said that to the married man.
Never had to. It was all so hurried and desperate and
intense. Anna knelt in the damp moist soil. She picked
rosemary and thyme and mint. She picked six violets
and holding the little bouquet she walked back to her
house and picked up the phone and called the number
he had given her in Washington.

"Please come to see me. I'm sorry."

"Are you sure?"

"I'm sure."

"I'll be there this afternoon."

"Let's be happy. Can we be happy?"

"We can try."

He came on a plane to Asheville and she drove him to
her house. A house of wood and stone and glass, fur-
nished haphazardly with bits and pieces of all the lives
Anna had led. A handmade rug of many jewel-like blues
and greens. Wicker chairs from a beach house. Philip
dropped his bag on the rug and turned to her, waiting
to see what she would tell him next. She had already told
him that the culture was dead, that no one in the United
States could read, that there were no heroes, that she
had stopped smoking, that her lost niece was writing to
her, that Bill Bradley would make a good president, that
Knight-Ridder had bought the Charlotte newspaper,

that fission releases the energy that gives matter its form, that she was tired of the West Coast and wasn't going there anymore. That she was moving home to write a memoir.

"I love thee," she said now.

"I love thee," he answered and they went into the bedroom and lay down upon the bed and cuddled up with their clothes on. "You smell so wonderful," she said. "Like yourself and no other. Lewis Thomas says we might do the whole thing by smell and not know it. Pheromones. But you know all that."

"No, I don't."

"Make love to me as though you would never have to leave. I want it to be different and not frantic and hurried and sad."

"It is frantic and hurried and sad. I've been waiting to fuck you for three days."

"Then fuck me." She took off her blouse and then her brassiere and then her slacks and underpants and she tilted her head to one side and waited for him to get in bed. He walked over to her bookshelf and took down a book and held it in his hands. Then he replaced it on the shelf. "I don't know what to do."

"Come to bed. It will come to you."

She dreamed about the lake where she had spent weekends with Adam. It was October in the dream. The leaves were gold and red and burgundy and the wind caught them and whirled them around and Anna thought they looked like coins. Treasure spread out on the floor of the woods.

"We will be here always," Adam said. "Now we never have to leave."

"But, the married man is here. He's in my house. I have to cook breakfast for him."

"No, he's all right. You can't get there now. It's too far away. We are here, Anna. This is where we are." He smiled at her. He was wearing a brown plaid shirt, old blue work pants, lace-up boots. He held out his hands. They were on an island in the middle of a river. On the shores the life of man went on but on the island it was only Adam and she. "What will he think if I don't go back?"

"He will think he got what he deserved." They went into the tent together and lay down and the darkness descended and the river began to rise.

When she woke up the married man was sitting on the side of the bed looking at her. "Stop worshipping me," she said and they giggled and got up and made thick black coffee and cinnamon toast and carried it out to the stone steps and ate breakfast watching the birds and squirrels and chipmunks. Rabbits sat on the lawn as if they owned the place. "This goddamn place is turning into a rabbit farm," Anna said. "No one lived here for four years before I came back. There must be a warren under here with a hundred rabbit families. How did I end up running a rabbit, squirrel, chipmunk, jaybird refuge?"

"Why would you leave here and go back to Charlotte? That's the question. Why move into town? It's not good to keep moving around."

"Because I need to be nearer to them. I have to have someone to love, so I'm going to try my family. Feel out the source. My sister Helen says I look for love in all the wrong places. Maybe she's right. Besides, I have to make my peace with Daddy."

"I could stay in a house like this forever and never want to go anywhere else." He leaned back on the steps. His arm was resting on a huge piece of limestone that Adam had struggled for days to move into place.

"My young lover built these steps. When I thought that would get me over you."

"You're outrageous."

"No, I'm not. I'm just trying to make you jealous."

"It's working. Let's see. Who have you told me about since I got here? The college president, the old boyfriend who's a big game hunter, the dead husband, the young lover." He drank his coffee. They leaned on the stone. Anna's new pale peach nightshirt fell across her thighs. Her body was soft and naked and furious and hot.

"You want to make love," she said. "Or not?"

On Monday morning Philip left to go back to New York and Anna was no different than before. No sadder or wiser. She packed a few moving crates, papers and books to take to Charlotte. At noon she called her editor in New York. She had been thinking about the dream.

"I think I'll do it," she told him. "Write that book you thought up. The Tom Jones thing."

"Wonderful. What made you decide that?"

"I don't know. I had a dream. It seemed maybe I could learn something from it. I'm going home to Charlotte. Did I tell you that?"

"Good, I've been worried about you. All alone in that house up there."

"When I get settled I'll start the book. As soon as my hands are well."

"What's wrong with your hands?"

"Some allergy. Maybe to paper. It gets worse when I type. I thought I told you that."

"You've been sick all year."

"I have not. Why do you say that?"

"You should see a doctor, Anna. Go get a checkup. You've had a series of things."

"There is nothing wrong with me. I think this skin thing is a nervous reaction. I mean, think about it, it gets worse when I type. Well, I could do this Tom Jones thing. It would be fun to try it."

"Listen, come up here and see us. We miss you."

"I think I'll fall in love with you."

"Please don't do that."

"I was only kidding. Well, I'll send you some pages when I get something going."

"Anna, get a checkup."

"I might." She hung up the phone and walked around the kitchen, dropping things in cartons, wrapping up pieces of pottery in kitchen towels, thinking about the book.

I could do it. If I just started with the very first one and wrote it all down. If I started when I was eighteen and one night I let Danny Trunbadge stick his penis in the very opening of my vagina and he had an orgasm and then he stopped and we put our pants back on, we were in his car, it was graduation week, and he said, Anna, this could make you pregnant. We must get married. The next day he bought me a ring and I wore it all summer until I was sure I wasn't going to have a baby. Then I gave it back.

No, it started before that. It started with that blond boy in the tenth grade and every night for two weeks we went out and parked on a country road and he would rub my vagina through my underpants. Then he would stick his finger around the edge of my underpants and put his finger in my vagina. Oh, God, it felt so good. I never wanted to quit. The hours flew by. My wonderful little Victorian vagina. Oh, spring.

Finally, one night he said to me, Anna, you touch me too, and I said, Of course not, and he said, Well, listen, if you think I'm going to keep coming out here night after night and rubbing your pussy without getting anything in return, you're wrong. So that was the end of that until three years later when my brother's roommate tried to rape me.

Anna picked up the phone and called her editor back. "I'll definitely do it," she said. "I'll definitely write it. It will be a kick."

"Get started then, and, Anna, see a doctor."

"I have all the doctors I can stand this year, thank you."

"Are you still seeing Philip?"

"Only when I can't help it."

"Well, I've got to go. People are waiting on me."

"I'll send you some work soon. I may start writing about rivers."

"What does that mean?"

"Nothing. Goodbye. I'll write all summer, then I'm going home to live."

There was one last thing Anna needed to do before she left for Charlotte. She needed to resolve the problem of Daniel's daughter in Oklahoma, needed to clear it up, like an unpaid debt, she kept saying to herself. Only how could a child ever be a debt, she would reply, a child is the thing itself, the whole entire meaning of the tribe, nation, species, the branching out, the seed. The one thing that was denied to me that I can never forgive or understand. And now this girl appears on the horizon of my life, of the life of this family, and we all just sit here and don't do a goddamn thing, as if another child is nothing in a family with so many children and generations. But this girl is something brand-new, a whole new set of genetic materials mixed with ours, genes that may have come across the Bering Straits thousands of years ago, genes from Asia. But that is meaningless, all of that is nothing. The real thing is that here is a child for me, this one could be mine and I am doing nothing about it. It's up to me to force this issue, or else, why am I thinking about it all the time, and why is that letter she wrote to me still lying on my desk, why don't I put that letter away? What am I waiting for? Daniel? I am waiting for Daniel to do it and it's clear he isn't going to. He won't even talk about it when I call him. He evades the issue. He pretends it isn't true.

Finally, on a day in August, Anna went for a long walk and came to rest beside a stream that ran along the southern boundary of her property. It was a gay little stream called the East Lurie by folks in those parts. The stream was unusually high for this time of year, pouring down a fall of gray rocks beside the place where Anna had stopped to lean against a tree.

She was talking to herself, arguing her points. I will call him again this afternoon, she decided, and tell him I am going to do it. I'll say, Daniel, enough is enough. We have to go and see your daughter. If you don't want her, I do. I want her. I am going to go get her and bring her home. I love her. I love the idea of her. It's done, Daniel. I'm going to do it and you can't stop me. Please don't stop me.

Anna lifted her head. An oriole was preening itself on a branch above her. It all seemed so simple, so easy to do the simple fearless human thing. Get on a plane and go and see the girl. A girl who made straight A's. A gene carrier par excellence. A face that stared out of the photograph that looked exactly like her own. Olivia. Olivia Hand. Anna watched the oriole and the light on the water. She lay her hands upon her groin and felt the old remorse and then the emptiness was gone and she was filled with elation instead, the absolute clarity of believing she knew what to do.

When she got home she called her brother Daniel and told him. "I'm coming home to live," she said. "Did Momma tell you?"

"We're glad, Sister. We want to have you here."

"Daniel."

"Yes."

"I want to know Jessie. That's why I'm coming home. I need her to fill out my life. Helen's and James's children, too, of course, but especially Jessie, because she's yours."

"I'm glad to hear it. She loves you. She's right here, you want to talk to her?"

"In a moment. Daniel, there is something else I want to do."

"Okay, what is it?"

"I want to go to Oklahoma and meet Olivia. I want to see her, Daniel. I want you to go with me, maybe Jessie too. We have to confront this. We can't pretend this isn't true."

"I can't do that right now, Sister." She felt his voice change. Of all her brothers and sisters Daniel was the one she understood most. Daniel was so spoiled he never bothered to mask an emotion. "Don't mess into this, Anna," he said. "That is my problem out there in Oklahoma and if something needs to be done about it, I'll do it."

"It's our problem, Daniel. It belongs to our family. She's my niece as much as she is your daughter. She is carrying my genes, the same as Jessie."

"What makes you so sure she's mine? I don't know where Summer went when she left here without telling anyone where she was going."

"I'm going to go find out. Besides, have you looked at that photograph I sent you?"

"They sent me one."

"She wrote to you again? Why didn't you tell me?"

"She's written three times. I'm the one she wants to see, Sister, not you."

"Then let's go. It's time to go. We should have gone the minute she wrote to us. What does she think? What must she think that her own family won't come to see her and won't know her? She's your child. My God, Daniel. I can't believe you're acting like this."

"I don't want to go opening up a can of worms. I'm up to my ass in problems this year, Sister. I'm about to lose the business and I've got my hands full with Jessie. I don't need anything else right now."

"Then I'll do it. I'll do it for you."

"Don't do it, Anna."

"Well, I'm going to." She could hear him breathing, getting mad, the thing that used to bring on the asthma and drive them all insane with fear when he was small, when he was a little towheaded boy they all adored. "Daniel," she said.

"I can't talk about it anymore right now. Jessie just came in. I'll call you back in a minute. Don't leave." He hung up and Anna stalked into the kitchen and opened the refrigerator door and began to eat things. She ate three celery stalks and then half a carton of cottage cheese. Then she shut the refrigerator door and took a bottle of gin down from a shelf and poured herself a drink. She drank the gin while she thought of arguments to use on Daniel.

When he called back she was ready. So was he.

"I'm going out there, Daniel. I'm going to see this child."

"If you want a baby, go adopt one, Anna. Don't go messing around in my life."

"It isn't for me. It's for her. It's because she asked for us. She is asking for us, Daniel. She wants to know who else she is."

"You don't know what she wants."

"I'm going to find out and I think you should go with me."

"Then go ahead, goddammit. Jesus, Anna, I don't know if I want you moving down here or not "

"I'm going. It's our duty to go and meet her." The line went quiet. There was not a sound. Maybe they dropped the bomb, Anna thought, then she said, "Daniel, are you there? Please don't hang up on me again."

"I'm here."

"Well, say something."

"You want to talk to Jessie? She wants to talk to you."

"Daniel, don't be mad about this."

"Don't go out there, Anna. Here's Jessie. She wants to talk to you." There was the sound of the phone dropping on the counter, then footsteps, then Daniel's daughter, Jessie, the beautiful outrageous clotheshorse and rotten spoiled only child of the youngest Hand brother, picked up the phone with her carefully manicured fingers and prepared to make sure that yet one more human being worshipped her. She had been the subject of a five-year court battle between her mother and father, with both families joined in the battle including both sets of grandparents and any family friends who could be stampeded into testifying that either or both parents were fit or unfit. In the end Jessie's mother had gone off to London with her boyfriend and the Hands had retained custody of their youngest and most beautiful child. Jessie was now worth about two hundred thousand dollars in lawyers' and court fees. When Daniel looked at her he thought she would have been worth ten times that price. Anything that might harm her in any way or alter the life he was attempting to achieve for her was a threat to Daniel, a threat to the years he had fought to keep her. The jewel in my crown, he called her. My only jewel. When he had received the letter from Olivia telling him that she was also in the world he had been terrified. All the letter meant to him was that there was something that might inconvenience or harm Jessie. He had held the letter in his hand, remembering Olivia's mother, the violence and passion of her nature, remembering the knife she had carried in her backpack. He imagined Summer Deer, showing up suddenly in Charlotte, in her old hippie gear, armed to the teeth and ready to give some drugs to Jessie.

Daniel picked the phone up from the counter. "Anna, don't do this to me. Here's Jessie, she wants to talk to you."

"I'm going out there, Daniel. I have to go."

"Then to hell with you. You always do anything you

like, don't you, Anna. Because you're the only person on
the planet that matters. Right. Here's Jessie, she's waiting." The phone rattled. Then the voice of Anna's
youngest niece came on the line.

"Aunt Anna, it's me."

"Angel, I adore you. I'm coming home to hear you
play the piano every minute of the night and day."

"When can you get here?"

"Next week or the week after that. I have to drive and
bring a bunch of junk in the car. Maybe I'll throw most
of it away."

"Are you bringing your piano?"

"Of course. My little spinet."

"I have to go to school now. I'll see you when you get
here. Hurry up!"

"As fast as I can. I can't wait to be there. It's the best
idea I've had in ages."

"Why did you have it?" Jessie asked. The question
surprised Anna. "Oh, honey, because I'm lonely," she
answered. "I'm so tired of being alone."

"We'll have a good time," Jessie said. "There's lots to
do here."

Anna hung the phone up, then stood with her hand
on it, thinking of them, her wild barbarous family, their
passions, rivalries, obsessions. I will never write another
word if I am around them, she decided. Well, what the
hell, I've written all the books I need to write. I can live
literature and drama as they do. Who will I be in Charlotte this year? What role will I get to play? The one who
found the lost sheep? The one who went to Oklahoma
and brought them back a child they don't have any use
for? Little Mother Superior, imposing my will on them
as usual. Maybe I should go back to New York instead.
Be Philip's mistress. Get laid on Wednesday afternoons
like a good American working girl. To hell with it. This
hasn't got a thing to do with that. This is real life. This

is a child who carries my DNA in every cell in her body and I am going to go and see her tomorrow morning if they have a plane.

Anna walked across the room. Turned on the stereo. Joshua Rifkin playing Scott Joplin filled the little wooden and glass house. The early morning light was everywhere, reflecting on the panels and windows and the copper pots and ferns. Anna called the airport, then she called a number in Oklahoma and a woman's voice answered and then a girl's.

"I'd like to come and see you tomorrow if I may," she said. "I think it's time for us to know each other. I am dying to see you, to tell the truth. Could someone come and get me tomorrow if I flew to Tulsa?"

"Oh, yes. My aunt and I can come. Oh, Aunt Anna. I will love it so much if you come here. Will my father come with you?"

"He can't right now, Olivia. His business is in trouble and he can't get away. But I'll be there. You'll have to start with me." Anna closed her eyes, called up everything she knew about Daniel, his sweetness, tenderness, honor, dignity. How unlike him to be afraid of life, afraid to know his own child. It was incomprehensible.

"What time can you come?" Olivia asked.

"I have a reservation on a plane that gets to Tulsa at two twenty tomorrow afternoon. United Airlines flight four forty-three. Listen, I look like my pictures and I'll have on a navy blue skirt and a khaki jacket."

"I'll know who you are. I bet I could tell no matter what you're wearing. How will you know it's me?"

"I'll know," Anna said. She pictured the child with a whole tribe of Cherokee Indians surrounding her. "Oh, honey, I can't wait to get there and see you. What an adventure you are for me."

"We'll be waiting," the girl's voice said. "I'll be waiting for you."

*   *   *

Anna hung up the phone and began running the peeling ends of her fingers across her blouse, making small tears in the silk, oblivious of the skin on her fingers or the damage she was doing to the blouse. She was thinking of the sequence of events that had led to this moment.

In the spring of 1968, her brother Daniel was twenty years old and living in San Francisco smoking dope and trying to learn to be a hippie. He was a terrible hippie. He was too neat for the job. No matter how stoned he got he still kept getting up and emptying the ashtrays and washing out the Coca-Cola bottles. He had only been in San Francisco a few weeks when he fell in love with an eighteen-year-old girl with a braid of black hair that reached her waist. Her name was Summer Deer. It was not a hippie name, as Daniel thought at first. She was a Cherokee Indian and her grandfather was an elder of the Cherokee Nation. Like her counterparts all over the United States, like Daniel himself, she had run away to join the flower children, dreaming of a new world and perfect freedom. Six hours after they met Summer Deer and Daniel were in her room smoking Arkansas Razorbud marijuana and making love on a pallet of hand-loomed blankets. A month later they were married, in a wedding ceremony in Golden Gate Park attended by fourteen of their friends and several hundred other people that neither of them knew. For a wedding trip they spent six days taking hits of lysergic acid diethylamide. When they woke up from this weirdness, Daniel was scared. His years as a law-abiding child came back to haunt him and he called home for money to fly to Charlotte with his bride.

They arrived there in the middle of the national DAR convention, which Mrs. Hand was helping host. Summer Deer stayed ten days in the Hand house amidst the horrified stares of Daniel's relatives and the guarded kindnesses of Anna and Helen and James and Niall and

Baby Louise. On the evening of the tenth day she sat for several hours in a locked bathroom holding a knife in her hand and waiting to open her veins. Finally she put the knife away in her backpack and bathed instead. As her hands slid down her legs she thought perhaps she would go downstairs and kill some of the Hand children. The thought sustained her and she got out of the bathtub and dried her body very carefully and lovingly and dressed in her jeans and shirt and sandals and picked up her backpack and climbed out of the bedroom window onto a porch roof. She sat on the roof behind a chimney until it was dark and then she climbed down an oak tree and walked out of the neighborhood and found the highway and began to hitchhike to her home. She was in Memphis, Tennessee, when she began to suspect she was pregnant. She went that night to a dilapidated movie theater near the Memphis State campus. They were playing an old film with Olivia de Havilland and Summer Deer cried in the film and decided if the baby was a girl she would name it for the actress who had unleashed the tears in her heart. She wept into her popcorn and wondered how hard her grandfather would beat her when he learned of her shame.

Olivia was born seven and a half months later on the reservation in Tahlequah, Oklahoma, with two midwives and Summer Deer's mother and grandmother and sister Mary Lily in attendance. Summer Deer labored for two days to deliver the child. But without success. When the midwives sent at last for the doctor in Tulsa, it was too late to stop the bleeding and pints and pints of Summer Deer's beautiful red blood ran out upon the bed. By the time Olivia was born Summer Deer was lost in a dream that had nothing to do with birth. "You will call her Olivia," Summer Deer told her sister. "And you will never let her go to those people. Promise you will never let her go there, but she may bear his name. It is

written on a paper for you to see. A marriage paper that
we signed." Summer Deer passed a hand very softly
across the body of her daughter and closed her eyes and
left the world of men and women and birth and death.

The Cherokee honor the words of a dying man or
woman, and so, although it seemed absurd to them to
name a child a word that denoted nothing of either the
heaven or the earth, they named the baby Olivia as
Summer Deer had asked and they took the marriage
certificate and the letters from Daniel that had been
forwarded from California and never answered and put
them in an unlocked wall safe behind a calendar in the
grandfather's room.

By the time Olivia was nine years old she was in the
habit of opening the safe and looking in the envelope
that contained the marriage license and her father's
letters.

Dear Summer,

I know you are mad at my folks but I didn't do anything to you. Please write and tell me where you are. I
want to see you.

Daniel

Dear Summer,

I am sending this to Jimmy because I called him at
Elsie's and he said maybe he knew someone that knew
where you were. We are married in case you forgot.
Please just let me know you're okay. My mom says to tell
you she liked you a lot.

Love, Daniel

Dear Summer,

My dad called the Indian reservation in Oklahoma
where you said you were from but they never heard of

you. If Jimmy gets this to you please call me up right
away. It's important.

Love, Daniel

Dear Summer,

   I have gotten this girl in trouble and we have to get
married pretty quick. She is the daughter of my dad's
business partner. I guess you can see I have to talk to
you as soon as possible. I know damn well you are getting these letters. This is mean as shit not to call me. My
dad's lawyer says he can go on and get me an annul-
ment, have the marriage declared illegal, since we were
stoned. I guess I'll do that.

Love, Daniel

After Summer Deer was buried in the Indian burying
mound on the Illinois River, her family went home and
had a meeting. They passed the baby around from arm
to arm. Finally, it was decided that Mary Lily would raise
the child. She was the youngest of Summer Deer's surviving brothers and sisters and too fat to attract a man of
her own so it was decided that she should be the mother
of Olivia. The natural forlornness of Mary Lily's nature
lifted as she looked down into the child's bright face.
The family were Roman Catholics in this generation
and Mary Lily took the infant in her arms and went to
the parish church and knelt by the statue of Mary,
amazed at the bounty of God.

࿆ 6 ࿆

࿆ ANNA SLEPT on the plane to Tulsa. She had been up since before dawn, dressing, watering plants, writing a letter to Daniel to explain what she was going to do. Tearing the letter up, writing another one, finally calling him, waking him at seven. "I'm on my way. She's meeting my plane. You could come and meet us. It's never too late to be a man, Daniel. I can't believe you've gone pussy on me in my old age."

"You called me and woke me up to tell me this."

"You should have heard her voice when she asked if you were coming to see her."

"Anna, I told you not to do this."

"I'll be in Tulsa, Oklahoma, at two this afternoon. You could fly there in your plane. You could bring Jessie."

"Are you drunk, Anna?"

"No, but I'm alive, I'm still alive. How about you?"

"Don't make her any promises, Anna. I guess you've just gone crazy on us for good, is that the deal?"

"I'll call you when I get back. Daniel, you'll be glad I did this."

"Goodbye, Sister. Thanks for waking me up." He

hung up the phone and Anna finished packing and walked out into the beautiful morning and got into her car and started traveling. She drove down the gravel road leading from her house and turned onto pavement and began to drive into the morning sun. It was eight o'clock when she left her house. In six hours she would be there.

She slept on the plane. Slept and dreamed. She could see the zygote splitting, the map of chromosomes. The paired genes, if only three or four pairs were in each niece or nephew that might make a whole. The books are there, she told herself, half-waking. The books count. No, they are only books, only paper bound in paper and strips of tape in some computer in Boston or New York. Imitations of life, the final reality is living children, a living child, the sine qua non of all history. The books are what I could do, all that I could do. This girl in Oklahoma might be the one who has my brain, my strange old brain. Also, my terrible ambition, the way I feel about cripples, the meanness of me. No, it was only because I was the oldest, and so the leader by fiat, like a queen bee, fed the most ambition, the most attention, the most expected and demanded of me. How could I have stopped, known where to stop, there was always another brother or sister to lord it over, keep in line.

Anna opened her eyes, woke from her wordy dreams. The plane was climbing through thick white clouds, marvelous clouds, a marvelous bumpy ride.

She fell back asleep and dreamed of Daniel putting fish in all the bathtubs of the house on Shannon Street. Get those fish out of here, she was saying. You will give the children germs. Anna took the fish out of the bathtub, scalded them in the sink and set them out to dry for dinner, then told the maids to clean the bathtubs.

When she woke again the plane was landing in Atlanta and she got off and found the connecting flight to
Tulsa and began to think about what lay ahead. All I am
doing is coming to see her, she told herself. I won't
promise her anything or speak for Daniel or speak for
the family or apologize for them. This is Olivia and me,
nothing else. To do my own self-righteous, thrill-seeking
stuff, nothing else. So I can brag to Philip about my
goodness. An excuse to tell him something. Why do I
think I need an excuse to love him?

She took out a notebook and began to write. "I
boarded the plane to Tulsa," she wrote. "And went off
to see what I could see. None of my business. None of
my goddamn business. Sticking my nose in Daniel's
business, into Daniel's child. This girl belongs to him
and to an Indian girl I wasn't even nice to, wasn't old
enough or wise enough or free enough to be nice to. I
wasn't even nice to your mother, I might begin by saying, now I am growing older and I am childless, manless
after all those men I loved or failed to love and now, in
this last-gasp effort to create meaning where there is
none, here I am. It looks pretty good, doesn't it, your
famous aunt coming out here to look you over. Since I
can't have what I want taking anything I can get. Here
at the Last Ditch Carleton it's just one little displacement
activity after another. Oh, hello, Olivia, hello, hello,
hello."

The girl was standing by the rail in a white dress, so
delicate and beautiful, so open and inviting, a wonder
of a girl, a girl anyone would want and need and be
proud of.

"You look wonderful," Anna said. "You look so wonderful. Are you alone? Where is your aunt?"

"You look wonderful, too. You don't look like your
pictures. You look different." She reached for Anna's

handbag and they embraced, excitedly, strangely, pleased with the moment.

"Where's your aunt?" Anna said again.

"She thought we might want to be alone for a while. She's outside."

"How kind of her. Well, let's get my suitcase, then go somewhere where we can talk. Start telling me everything." They walked together through the airport and down to the baggage claim. Twice Anna stopped walking and turned to look at the girl, marveling at the resemblance, amazed and trying to be cautious. Do no harm here, she was thinking. Be careful of this child.

"There's not much happening in Tahlequah," Olivia said. "Unless you like to go to ball games or like to ride. I guess you could say it's just summer, winter, spring, and fall." She was holding Anna's handbag and now she swung it around in front of her and held it with both hands. She looked so much like Jessie it was uncanny. Like Jessie, like Daniel, like Louise, and somehow, most of all, like Anna herself. "I wish you could stay a few weeks, then you could see what I do," Olivia went on. "It's hard to tell anybody what you do. I just keep going to school and thinking about things and about college and, well, you know, about everything." She looked down the walkway, at the receding backs of the passengers who had been on Anna's plane. "I think about you," she added.

"Oh, honey, that's so pleasing to me. I can't tell you how glad I am, that you do, that we are here, together." Anna took back her bag, put it over her shoulder, took Olivia's arm and began to walk toward the baggage claim. "I'm sorry your dad couldn't come. He should have come with me."

"It's okay."

"It's not okay. Tell me about your school. What do you study now?"

"It's terrible. I argue with the sisters about everything. I don't believe any of that junk they're pushing. You don't either. I can tell by your books."

"You wrote me that you were unhappy with them."

"I want to quit and go to the public school but my aunt doesn't want me to."

"I did it," Anna said."I quit a convent school and went into town to high school. What does your aunt say?"

"I almost talked her into it, then she changed her mind. The priest tells her there are drugs in the public schools, as if they weren't everywhere." Bags began to roll past on the conveyor belt and Anna found hers and they went out through the glass doors into the bright blue skies of Tulsa. Then Olivia's aunt Mary Lily was there, appearing as if from nowhere, wearing a stiff gray suit with a pink blouse. She moved close to Olivia, worried, hovering.

Anna took the woman's hands, kept holding them. "I want you to know we thank you for taking care of this wonderful child for us, for making her strong and wonderful."

"Oh, I'm not giving her away."

"I'm sorry. That was the wrong thing for me to say. Look, let's don't be embarrassed by things we say. None of us has ever done anything like this before. Let's go get some lunch somewhere and celebrate. This is a day to celebrate." Anna put her arm around the woman's shoulder, moved in, as her Zen master had taught her, allowed herself to be as vulnerable as she dared. "Let's go do some talking."

They went to a small seafood restaurant and ate salads and Olivia talked about her school and her teachers and her classes. The more Anna looked at her the more she liked her. She seemed so clear, so level-headed, so right. The aunt was sad and fat and Indian. The aunt's a slave, Anna decided. The aunt is the slave and this kid is the princess. But benevolent. She's a benevolent despot. Olivia stopped in the middle of a sentence and gave her aunt a smile.

"So I want to take honors next year, don't I, Aunt Mary Lily?"

"She does very well in her work. They like her work. She helps the teachers with the other ones."

"Is it going to be all right for me to stay with you? I could get a motel room."

"Oh, yes. We want you with us. You can stay in her room."

The check came. Anna paid it and they gathered their things and walked out into the heat of midday in Oklahoma. They got into an old Pontiac and began to drive. Anna was sitting in the passenger seat. Olivia was in the middle. Mary Lily was driving. The child's legs were outlined beneath her skirt. The skirt was thin white cotton with small violet flowers. Her legs were so long, so tender, so perfect. Anna touched the child's hand where it lay upon her leg. This moment, she told herself. This moment in this old Pontiac with this wonderful child, this strange Indian aunt, this car, this day, this sunshine on these leaves.

They left Tulsa and drove out of town on a narrow, two-lane highway that curved down through the hills of the Indian territory, headed for Tahlequah, where the Trail of Tears ended for the Cherokee. Mary Lily turned on the radio. The whiny voice of Willie Nelson filled the air, a ballad about lost love and tequila.

"Don't play that," Olivia said. "I know Aunt Anna doesn't want to listen to that song."

"I love country music," Anna said. "One time I had a fight with a boyfriend to that song."

Mary Lily turned the dial, clearly embarrassed. A Christian station came on, advertising Christ. Olivia reached over and turned the radio off.

"So you all are Catholic," Anna said. "How did you become Catholic?"

"Our mother was a convert," Mary Lily said. "Nearly everyone else around here is Baptist. I raised Olivia in the Church but she's not faithful now. Children don't do anything now, it's not only her."

"I go," Olivia said. "I'm just sick of the school. It's too small. It's not good enough."

"There's the beginning of Indian territory," Mary Lily said. "When you cross this river. Everything on this side. If you have time we'll take you to the museum."

"I'd like that," Anna said. "History interests me."

"Some of it is pretty boring," Olivia put in. "Unless you like arrowheads. Did you know my mother?" she added. "You said something in one of your letters about her."

"I knew her when she came to North Carolina with your dad." Anna paused. "I think she was very unhappy there. Well, you know that."

"What did she look like?"

"Very beautiful and different from anyone I knew. She wore her hair down her back in a long braid. She and your daddy were just babies. They had been in California at a hippie commune and they were pretty wild. We were all sorry when she left."

"And was my father sorry?"

"I don't know. Yes, I think he was. But then he got involved with a girl and she got pregnant with your sister, Jessie. They were so young, Olivia. So very very young."

"I tell her that," Mary Lily said.

"I want to see my father."

"Of course you do," Anna said. She and Mary Lily looked at each other in the rearview mirror. "And you will."

"Why doesn't he want to meet me?" Olivia was very still as she said it. She repeated it in a louder voice, as though gaining courage by the sound. "Why won't he come to see me? I thought he would be with you. All morning I thought he would be here too."

"Because of Jessie," Anna answered and knew she should not have said it. She went on, saying it whether she should say it or not. "I think he believes it will harm your sister. He had to fight a long court battle to gain custody of her. He's irrational where she's concerned."

"I wouldn't have any way to harm my own sister." She twisted her hands together, the fingers wound into each other. "How could I hurt her? I want to know her. I want to know her as much as I do him."

"She doesn't know about you. No one has told her yet. He hasn't told her."

"Maybe I will tell her then." Olivia stopped twisting her hands. Mary Lily heaved a sigh and speeded up. Olivia went on. "She is my sister. Maybe I will write to her. If he doesn't like me enough to even meet me, why should I care what he thinks about anything?" Mary Lily shook her head. They turned a wide curve, then down a series of sharp curves and into a valley. Beautiful black fences stretched out on both sides of the road. They passed barns that matched the fences, then a pasture with roan and dark red horses. One very new colt stood beside his mother. Mary Lily slowed the car. "That's Baron Fork Ranch," Olivia said. "I worked there one summer, helping with the horses. Mr. Spears owns it. Oh, that colt is so sweet. What a sweet colt."

"I can ride," Anna said. "And your father loves to ride. When you come to see us, you can ride the old horses we grew up on. I guess they'll be pretty tame after Indian ponies."

"She had a buckskin last year," Mary Lily said. "He was a good horse."

"He died in the winter," Olivia said. "He foundered. We had boots on him for six months but he couldn't get well. He hated them so he died. I haven't had the time to get another horse. I was too busy with school." Mary

Lily started to say something, then stopped herself. They went on past the brown fences of the horse farm and beside a pasture where white egrets were scattered like fluffs of cotton on the green grass. A sign advertised float trips on the Illinois River. Another warned of speeding and drunk-driving fines. They went down another series of steeply banked curves. Mary Lily drove the old Pontiac at top speed down the curves, then turned onto a gravel road.

"We only live two more miles," Olivia said. "We live this side of town." The road ended in a clearing with a small house surrounded by trees. Smoke was coming from a chimney and a man and a woman came to the door and walked down the steps and stood waiting, hand in hand.

Mary Lily parked the car beneath a tree and they got out and Anna was introduced to Olivia's grandparents. Their names were Little Sun and Crow Wagoner and Olivia told Anna later that they were seventy-two years old. Their surviving children were scattered now around Arkansas and Texas and Oklahoma. Only Mary Lily and one son were left in Tahlequah. The grandmother showed Anna around the rooms of the house. Then Olivia took Anna to her own room and put her suitcase very carefully down on a blue wicker bench beside her bed.

"This is a bench Aunt Lily ordered from Dallas, Texas," she said. "It had a dressing table with it but I don't have room for it now. Because I have to have my desk. It's made of mahogany. My grandfather made it himself. Do you like it?" She stood beside her desk. It was very neat, the books stacked neatly in a pile. Anna's books were above the desk on a shelf.

"I bought them one at a time with my own money," Olivia said. "Are you like that, Aunt Anna? Like the people in those books?"

"I used to be. But not anymore. I don't know what I'm like now, Olivia. It has been a strange year for me." She watched the girl's face. "I am sad now, for the first time in my life. Perhaps people my age become sad, maybe that's what all those metaphors about falling leaves mean, fall and winter and so forth. Anyway, I don't want to give in to things like that, or . . ." Anna paused. "Perhaps from now on I have to borrow life from younger people. Could I borrow some from you?" Anna was sitting on the bed. Olivia sat down beside her and took her hand.

"You can have anything you want from me. I'm still happy. I know a lot of people who aren't happy, who think everything is going to go wrong, but I'm not that way. I think I'll always win at things. I mean, I have a winning nature, like girls you write about. Like Kathy, that girl in those stories who won't let anything get her down. I like her the best of everyone you write about."

"So do I," Anna said. The girl's hand was strong and brown upon her own and she thought of how she had held her grandmother's hand, how the fine old skin and sharp knuckles had seemed to print her grandmother on her hand.

"I couldn't make your father come with me," Anna said. "You must not be harmed by that, Olivia. It isn't only Jessie. Something is stopping him from knowing you, some old sadness or memory of your mother or memory of when he was young and wild. I don't understand it. He's a wonderful man and someday you'll know him. For now, I guess you have to be content with me." Olivia looked down, then shook her head as if she had no answer to that. Anna slipped off her shoes and jacket and curled up on the bed. She was so tired, she was overcome with tiredness. If I get some sleep I'll know what to say, she thought. I will know the best thing to say. "Shall I cover you up," Olivia asked, "so you'll be warm?"

"That would be nice," Anna answered. "That would be lovely." The child pulled the cover over Anna's legs, then bent down and took Anna's shoes and lined them up beside the bedside table. Nothing Olivia had expected to happen had happened. Almost nothing at all had happened.

Anna slept for many hours without moving. Without moving her hand from underneath the pillow, she slept away the days that had led her there. For a long time Olivia sat on the rug and watched her sleep. Then she got up very quietly and went out into the living room.

"Your aunt does not look well," her grandfather said. "She is pale. Has she been sick?"

"She doesn't like to fly on planes," Olivia answered. "She hates to fly. It makes her tired. She may sleep a long time so don't make any noise."

In the kitchen Mary Lily bent over the pot of soup she was cooking. She was counting to herself as she chopped and sliced the onions and tomatoes and peppers. She had a habit of counting when there were things that bothered her that she could do nothing about. The aunt was here. It was the beginning. The man would come to get Olivia. She sliced a carrot. Stopped counting. Brightened up. Perhaps he would take her too, take her away from work and paying bills. Yes, Mary Lily thought, he cannot have the girl without us too. All of us. He must take us all.

It was dark when Anna woke. She sat up in the little bed and looked around the room. Anna felt tender toward the room, disarmed and tender. She stretched her arms and legs until the stiffness left them, then got up and washed her face and hands in the bowl Olivia had left for her on a table. She put on a clean blouse and went out to join the others.

They ate dinner at a table beside the kitchen. Anna

answered the grandparents' questions and listened to their talk about the weather and the food. Every now and then she would look at Olivia and they would smile at each other. It was all very tentative and strange. Mary Lily served the soup. Then the phone rang. The grandfather answered it and handed it to Anna. It was Philip calling from New York.

"How did you know where I was?"

"You left it with the service. What are you doing, Anna? Where are you?"

"I'm not really sure. No, I'm in Oklahoma, visiting my niece, the one I told you about. She's wonderful, by the way." Anna smiled at Olivia. "She looks like me."

"When are you getting home?"

"I don't know. Tomorrow maybe, or Monday. I'm not sure."

"Call me when you get back. I want to talk to you."

"All right. I almost called you from Atlanta. I don't know why. I just wanted to talk to you, to tell you what I was doing. Anyway, I'm glad you found me." She said goodbye and handed the phone back to the grandfather. "That's the man I am in love with," she told Olivia. "I don't know why he called me here. He never calls me up."

"She doesn't like them calling her," Mary Lily said. "She won't talk to them half the time."

"Who?" Olivia said. "Who are you talking about?"

"The boys that call. The ones that call you up. Like the Tree boy that rides for Spears and them."

"That's crazy," Olivia said. "Why did you say that? No one calls me up." She turned to Anna. "There isn't anyone around here I'd have anything to do with."

Mary Lily got up and went to the stove and began stirring the soup. "I could give you more if you want it," she said to Anna. "Yours is getting low."

"Thank you," Anna said. "I'd like some more. It's very good."

"It's venison," the grandfather said. "It's good for you. Better than beef. It's good meat."

"It's wonderful," Anna said. "It's the best soup I've ever tasted." Mary Lily took Anna's bowl and filled it and handed it back to her and Anna thanked her and took up her spoon and drank the soup.

In the morning they had corncakes for breakfast. With blackberry preserves and thin weak midwestern coffee.

"We could go riding," Olivia said. "I know a guy that's got horses we can borrow."

"I'd like that," Anna said. "If you'll lend me some clothes. Or anything to cover my legs."

"You can wear my boots," Mary Lily said. "If they will fit you."

"We'll find you something to wear." Olivia laughed. "Imagine my famous aunt wearing my clothes." She led the way to her room and Anna began to try on boots. Olivia's were too small and Mary Lily's too wide but the grandmother's fit nicely. Anna tucked a pair of blue jeans into the tops of the boots and pulled a white shirt over her head and stood before them for inspection. The boots were very old and beautiful, of handmade leather with thick heels. The grandmother stood in the doorway, smiling because her boots were of use. "Thank you," Anna said and met the woman's eyes, seeing darkness there and light and things she had no words for. Then, suddenly, seeing Summer Deer, standing in a doorway of the Hands' dining room, with that look upon her face.

They borrowed Mary Lily's car and Olivia drove them out of the yard and back down the road to the highway. She drove like her aunt Mary Lily, at top speed with a sort of cheerful abandon. Anna reached for the seat belt, which was broken.

"How'd you get to be such a good driver?" Anna said. "You couldn't have been driving long, but I guess things are different in Oklahoma."

"I've had a permit for two years, because we live on a farm. They've always let me drive. They let me do anything."

"I noticed that. Why do you think that is?"

"Because I'm the last one. Because my momma is dead. Because Aunt Mary Lily is fat and doesn't have any men to love. Besides, I make good grades. They think I'll do good and get a good job. My uncle's kids are always in trouble. They don't even go to school half the time."

"Do you want me to meet them while I'm here? The rest of your family?"

"No." Olivia was silent then and Anna kept her own silence and they drove along the curving two-lane highway in the early morning stillness. After a while they crossed a fork of the Illinois River and turned down a side road and into a gate with a sign that said, RODEO INTERNATIONAL. THE CHEROKEE RODEO, OPEN SEPTEMBER 5 TO NOVEMBER 20. SEE US RIDE.

Two men were beside a stable worrying over the hoof of a pony. Olivia stopped the car and spoke to them.

"Kayo's in the office," they said. "Go on in."

"We want to borrow some horses. You think he's got time to fool with it this morning?"

"He's always got time for you." The men smiled. A third man appeared, a tall man with huge broad shoulders. He came out of the door of a trailer beside the stables. He walked to the car and opened the door for Olivia and then for Anna.

She's using him, Anna thought. She's using her stuff to get this guy to do her favors. That's wild, how would I tell Daniel about this. Is she fucking him? She's just sixteen. She wouldn't be fucking yet. Still, who knows, they could be doing anything now.

Kayo took them back to the stables and Olivia chose the horses she wanted.

"What have you been doing?" Kayo said. "You haven't been around in a while."

"Nothing," Olivia said. "I've been busy at school."

"You still seeing Bobby Tree?" She blushed and he went on, turning to Anna. "She's got the hotshot rodeo star around here in love with her. Kid went all the way to the finals in the National High School Rodeo last year."

"I'm not seeing him," Olivia said. "I don't see anybody."

"Not what I hear." He laughed out loud and stuck his fingers into the pockets of his tight denim pants. A boy appeared, leading the saddled horses, a black-and-white mare and a palomino. Olivia pulled herself up on the palomino's back and lifted her shoulders and the horse was still. She didn't even use the reins, Anna thought. My God, this kid will eat Jessie for lunch. What am I doing? What have I done?

Kayo offered her a leg up and she accepted it and lifted herself onto the mare and they began to ride, down a path leading from the rodeo grounds and across a pasture and into the woods behind it, following a path that was barely wide enough for the horses. Olivia led the way. I bet she could ride that goddamn horse without touching the reins, Anna thought. God knows who this girl is or what she is capable of, but who gives a damn, she's part of us, she's part of me and I like her and am excited by her. *And this is what happens next.*

They rode for several hours, along paths which wound down between trees and along a sluggish brown stream that was a tributary of the Illinois River. Now

Olivia was quiet. Now she did not look like Anna or Daniel or Jessie or anyone in North Carolina. She had entered an ancient reverie. She stopped several times and led Anna's horse by the bridle, around parts of the path where the horses had to tread carefully. Once she stopped by the stream bed and dismounted and allowed her horse to drink. She helped Anna down and watered Anna's horse. And all this time they said very little to each other. There seemed to be nothing that needed to be said.

The path led uphill finally and back to the pasture and Olivia picked up the pace and they trotted the horses back to the barns. They dismounted and talked awhile with the grooms and then got into the car and were quiet again. This is how it's supposed to be between people, Anna decided. And if I don't start chattering or asking questions she won't have to either.

They drove back to the house. The sky was overcast now, a front was moving in, bright blue along the edges with shades of gray pushing against the blue.

The road wound down between hardwood trees and tall scraggly pines. Huge black aeries adorned the bent tops of the pines. Crows the size of shoeboxes flew from tree to tree, calling their raucous calls, announcing the approaching storm. Olivia drove with one hand. The other hand was draped across the back of Anna's seat. Anna watched the movements of her fingers on the wheel, the lift of her chin, the long bones of her legs. And watching Olivia she began to desire Philip, terrible desire, ancient desire. Outside the windows the crows flew from tree to tree.

That night, when Anna was in bed, Olivia came in to tell her goodnight. The rain that had been promised was falling now, beating upon the roof and the windows of the house.

"Turn off the light," Anna said. "And sit beside me in

the dark." Olivia turned off the lamp and Anna reached for her hand. "So you don't care anything about this boy who likes you? This famous Bobby Tree they keep talking about?"

"I like him all right. I just don't want to marry him. If you go with someone all the time around here you end up marrying them."

"Why is that?"

"I don't know. It always happens, though. I see it happen."

"So why don't you want to marry him?"

"Because his folks live in a trailer park. I can't even stand to go over there to say hello. No matter how great he is. He still lives in that trailer park."

"What do you want, Olivia? For yourself."

"I want a good education and a job and a place of my own. My gym teacher took me up to Tulsa to visit this friend of hers who works for IBM. She has a new car and this really nice apartment and she can travel all the time. They send her everywhere."

Anna held the child's hand, the child's perfect hand lay in her own. What was there to say that would do no harm of any kind? "Whatever you do will be wonderful," Anna said. "Even this Bobby Tree might be less dangerous than you imagine. All these people seem to think he's pretty special." She paused. "The world is very wide, Olivia. So much of it is good. One part is not more wonderful than another."

"I guess so," Olivia answered. "But it seems like it. I bet North Carolina is better than this little hick town."

"You will come and see for yourself," Anna said. "You have my promise about that."

The next day Olivia and Mary Lily drove Anna to the airport. While they were waiting for the plane Olivia excused herself to go to the ladies' room and Anna was alone with Mary Lily.

"Is there anything we can do for you?" Anna said. "Anything you need?"

"We always need money. You can see, we live quite simply. Tell him to send money for her." The woman looked down. "I did not want him to know about her. But since he does, I thought he would want to send us money. I make all the money alone. It's not enough for the things we need."

"How much do you need?"

"For three hundred more a month we could live in town. It would be easier for her there. She could go to the school she wants. I don't want her on the school bus. They say things happen."

"Then I'll see what I can do. I'll send you money myself. But I can't talk to him about it. He needs to see her first, to see that she is his."

"It is painful to her that he won't see her. Well, if we had money the other thing would be all right."

"His business has been in trouble. The economy is in trouble and it's hurting him. I'm sure it will be all right about college, though. Don't let her worry about that." Anna looked at her watch. She felt disloyal, split.

"Tell him to see her."

"I tell him every chance I get, ever since I found out." Olivia was walking toward them, was almost within earshot. "Of course you need more money," Anna said. "I'll tell him to steal some for you or go and dig some ditches. Look, I have to get on the plane now. I love you for taking such wonderful care of her. This visit means a great deal to me, more than you know." She took Mary Lily's hands but the woman would not meet her eye. "We are glad you came to see us," she said, but Anna could barely hear the words. Then Olivia was there and the plane was ready to leave and they said their goodbyes and Anna boarded the plane and flew back to North Carolina.

*   *   *

It was raining in North Carolina and all along the Eastern Seaboard. A dark soaking rain that filled the rivers and turned the highways into danger zones. Anna drove home from the airport with the windshield wipers beating time to the radio. She was thinking as hard as she could. It was the modern world, surely there was a way for Olivia to know more than one world, a way for her to visit this older world and partake of some of it. Surely there was room for one little sixteen-year-old girl. Anna remembered the way Olivia had pulled herself up into the saddle, the lift of her neck, the strange quiet energy, the unanswered questions, the veiled threats, to do what? To write to Jessie? That wasn't veiled, she had said it in the car. Anna stopped at a lonely all-night Convenient Store and put a quarter in a telephone and called her brother.

"I went to see her."

"I was sure you would. Well, tell me what happened. What is she like?"

"She is ours, Daniel. I would bet my life on that. And she's very pretty and she's powerful, strangely powerful. You'll be surprised, I think."

"What did you tell her?"

"I told the aunt I'd send them money and I told them we'd send her to college and she said she was going to write to Jessie. She's mad at you for not coming to see her."

"Goddamn you, Anna. I don't believe you did this to me."

"I did what I had to do. It's your turn now. She might write to her, Daniel. She really might."

"When are you coming down here?"

"As soon as I get the house packed up. I want you to stop being angry with me about this. I want you to face this."

"Well, Sister, that won't be the first thing you want that you might not get. Where are you? Are you at home?"

"No. I'm at a filling station and it's raining. I'll talk to you again tomorrow. Can I call you at the office in the morning?"

"No, I'm leaving town and don't say anything to Jessie, Anna. Leave Jessie alone. I mean that."

"All right. I won't say anything to Jessie. But someone had better tell her soon."

"Goodbye, Sister." He hung up and Anna replaced the receiver and stood by the telephone watching the rain fall upon the earth. I don't think I'm getting anywhere, she decided. All these years and I think I just get dumber and dumber and dumber and dumber.

The next week Anna packed the rest of her things and left the mountains. Loaded it all on a moving van and moved home to Charlotte. In a week she was being sucked down into the vortex of the Hand-Manning-McGruder world as if she had never left. Both of her unlisted phone numbers were in her mother's address book and were being given out right and left to her cousins as far away as Louisiana and to any librarians or English teachers who thought they could make Anna's life more interesting. Also, both brothers, one of her sisters, and ten nieces and nephews with their combined excesses and miraculous escapes and occasional purposeful moves were walking in and out of her brain all day. The Hand family of Charlotte, North Carolina. The Hand eyes and the McGruder nose and pale skin and dark tragic red hair, left behind by the Irish Catholic strain. Also, light blonds and dark blonds and extra-wild freckled strawberry blonds. Pigment, Anna decided. We need some pigment to water this stuff down. She thought of Olivia. Well, the genes were definitely not being watered down in that beautiful girl in Oklahoma. The most amazing thing was that she had found Anna all by herself. Had recognized her family through Anna's books.

"This is my name," she had said to her aunt Mary Lily,

bringing home a book of Anna's essays she had found in the school library. She had already discussed the possibility of kinship with her English teacher. "Look, Aunt Mary Lily. This is my name and these pictures look like me and you said this is where my father came from. From Charlotte, North Carolina. Here, where this lady comes from."

"You don't want to go into that." Her aunt was terrified. She knew that Olivia was on the right track. She hung her head. Twisted her hands together. "Leave it alone," she said. "You have his name. You must not bother him aside from that."

"I want to see him. I want to talk to him and see him."

"Not yet. Wait until you are sixteen years old and I will ask him to come and visit you." Her aunt waited, frightened by the talk, and Olivia withdrew.

"Should I fix a meat pie for dinner again?" Mary Lily said. "Out of the venison Andrew brought for us? Would you like that, my little angel?"

"It would be nice," Olivia said. "It would be very nice. I am sorry if I bothered you."

"When you are sixteen years old. Then we will see."

But Olivia could not wait and when she had read all of Anna's books she asked her teacher what to do and the teacher said to write Anna in care of her publisher. The letter was forwarded and arrived on a cold day in New York City. Anna went down the elevator and opened her mailbox and took out the letters and threw half of them away and then stood leaning against a wall and opened the beautiful little blue envelope from Oklahoma. She was amazed at what she was reading. How strange, she thought, to live in the world and know its wildness and fecundity and till be surprised by birth and death, fertility and growth, the dark power of sex, life insisting upon itself, repeating and creating, breaking off and ending. All these still have the power to surprise and frighten us. So Anna stood leaning by the mailboxes and was surprised and enchanted by what she read on the pale blue stationery with yellow roses on the corner and on the envelope beside the stamp.

Dear Miss Hand,

I am your niece, Olivia Hand. I am the daughter of your brother, Daniel. My mother was named Summer Wagoner and they were married in 1967 in California. I have the marriage license. I never knew my mother so I would like to know my father and his family. I have read all your books and I think they are wonderful. I am enclosing a photograph of myself. I am five feet four inches tall and weigh 110. I have reddish blonde hair. I am writing for our school newspaper. Here are some pieces of writing I have done. Please write back to me.

Olivia de Havilland Hand

Now Anna was back in Charlotte and one of the main reasons she was there was to help resolve this business of Olivia.

7

‿⟋⟍ LATE FALL, nineteen hundred and eighty-four. Charlotte, North Carolina. Anna sat in a circle of books. Outside, night was falling on the lake. A lone duck sailed on a line of red light. A waltz was playing on the stereo. Anna was reading a book about quantum mechanics. The wonderful zaniness of that world intrigued her, made the world of books seem safe and almost orderly. Light and particle, she was thinking. Division and grace and ten live nieces and nephews walking in and out of my mind all day. What could compete with the randomness and wonder of that?

Her youngest niece came tearing in the door. Jessie, Daniel's adored child, Olivia's half sister. She was wearing enough Giorgio to fill an auditorium. The Giorgio preceded her into the room. The Giorgio drowned out "The Blue Danube Waltz." Anna walked over and turned the stereo down. "What's that perfume?" she asked. "What are you wearing?"

"Is it too much? You think it's too much?" She was taller than Anna, but with the same wide face, the same high cheekbones, the same pale skin.

"It's a little too much. You have to be careful with that stuff. What's up? What's going on?"

"I got the job." She moved back. She lowered her eyes. She shimmered and trembled and was wonderful and was sixteen. "The Blue Danube" rose to a crescendo and she did a little dance with her hands.

"How wonderful," Anna said. "Anyone would want you. I told you that. When do you start?"

"On Monday. Listen, the manager took me in his office. He said he thought I was twenty-one when I walked in the door."

Anna closed her eyes, then shook it off. "What about your music? You won't have time for lessons."

"It can wait. I have to have some money that I don't have to ask Dad for. I want this job, Aunt Anna. I can't wait to start. I get four dollars an hour and eight dollars on Sunday and maybe after Christmas they'll keep me on. If I'm good at it."

"You'll be good. Come over here and sit by me. Let me smell your Giorgio." Jessie came and sat on the arm of the sofa. Anna ran her hand down the soft white wonder of the child's arm. Such skin, she thought, so fine and new. Like velvet. Once a man I was leaving told me I could go if I would leave my skin behind. I was so young I didn't even know that I was wonderful, didn't even know that I was soft. I didn't know a thing. Does Jessie know a thing? I wonder if she knows how much I love her. "The bridge is love," the poet said. "The only survival, the only meaning."

"I just love you to death," Anna said. "Will you play for me? The things you've been composing. I love to hear them. Please play them for me." Jessie took her aunt's hands and held them, pleased to be reminded of her music. She was wearing a thin gold bracelet with a gold acorn for a clasp. Her wrists were perfect, the skin on her hands was perfect, the fingers so long and light, a musician's hands. "I'll come play for you later," she said. "As

soon as I get my homework done. We got a letter from
DeDe. Did I tell you that?"

"What did she say?"

"She got her real estate license. So she can work in the
afternoons and paint in the morning. She's going to bring
her boyfriend with her at Thanksgiving. They're going to
stay with us because Grandmother won't let them sleep
together at her house and neither will Aunt Helen."

"Well, some of you can stay here if you need to.
There's room here." Anna sighed. There went Thanksgiving.

"I've got to go," Jessie said. "I just wanted to see you."
She stood up, shimmered again. "Come and see us
sometime. You never go anywhere, do you?"

"Not much, not anymore." Anna stood up beside her,
took her arm, went with her to the door. "I'm glad about
your job. I'm proud of you." She stood in the door
watching as the child got into her car and drove off, still
waving. Then she went back into the house and locked
the door and took the telephone off the hook. I need to
write awhile, she decided, a perfectly valid thing to do in
a universe of particles and sixteen-year-old gene carriers.
If someday they read my books what will they think of
me? Will they remember how I seemed to them this year
and wonder who the other persons were? The invisible
organization of energy, all flowing in and out of one
another, and mind, what part does thought play? What
are we transmitting? I asked a physicist that question once
and he wrote me back and said, We transmit information.
I was dazzled by the simplicity of that answer and hated
myself all day for being stupid. But I am not a scientist.
I am a writer and can only do what I know how to do.

If I could tell one more story, and tell it absolutely
straight, tell exactly how it was and how it seemed and
what the people said and did and seemed to think. How
they loved and hated and plotted and pleaded and demanded. How they were never satisfied. All is yearning,

the Buddha said, but Arthur told me not to put the Buddha into everything I write. But I have to get it right, like Jessie's music that she makes up. She doesn't even call it composing, God bless her dazzling humility about that. Music is the most mysterious thing of all, and Jessie is going to work in a department store instead. Well, talent doesn't have to be plowed like a field. She's happy, she knows who she is. And if the knowledge of Olivia harms her it will be my fault. But it can't harm her. She needs the truth, needs to welcome it and learn to always welcome it. Still, Charlotte, North Carolina, what a hard town to be honest in. Calm down, Anna. Settle down.

Anna worked for a while in a desultory manner, finishing the copyediting for a magazine article about a canoe trip. Then she plugged back in the phone and called Daniel. "Did she come home yet?"

"No."

"I thought she was going to do her homework."

"She stopped at a friend's. The Larkin girl."

"Are they smoking dope, Daniel? I want you to watch her very carefully these next few years. These damn drugs are everywhere now. I don't think you know what you're up against."

"I'm doing everything I can."

"Is she passing?"

"No. But we got a tutor."

"Tell her I called. Tell her to call me when she comes in."

"I'll tell her."

"Daniel?"

"What else do you need, Sister Anna?"

"I know none of this is my business."

"You're right, it isn't."

"What do you hear from Sheila? Is she satisfied to let you do whatever you like with Jessie? Are you paying her off, or what?"

"She's over there in London doing coke with queers and pretending to make television shows. And yes, I'm paying her off and the more coke she snorts the more she can't get hold of my daughter and fuck her up and turn her into a queer, so does that satisfy you, Anna, or would you like to stick your nose into that too while you're at it?"

"You'll be glad I went to see Olivia. Someday you will thank me for it."

"Well, keep out of my problems with Jessie. She's the jewel in my crown, Anna. She's the only thing I've got and I'm going to keep her and raise her my way. She's doing just fine and she isn't taking dope and I like her. I like her just the way she is."

"I like her too. I think she's wonderful. But I wish she had more time for her music."

"She doesn't need some goddamn queer musicians fucking with her, Anna. She needs to learn to read."

"She can read."

"Barely. Enough to get by. If you want to do something for Jessie, get her to read something." He paused, "But not your books. She isn't ready for that yet." The line went quiet. Finally, after what seemed a long time, Daniel spoke again.

"How's your article coming along?"

"What article?"

"The one about the rivers that Daddy was helping you with."

"Oh, it's all right. I guess I'll finish it today."

"Finish your work, Sister. Don't worry about us. We're okay."

"That's good advice. I'll try." She hung up the phone and went back to work in earnest. Taped up the ends of her fingers with adhesive tape and typed happily along for an hour. The phone started ringing in the middle of the best paragraph. Maybe I won't forget the end, she told herself and answered the phone. It was Putty, the

wife of Anna's oldest brother, James. She was calling to
see if Anna wanted to go with her to visit her son who
was locked up in the chemical dependency ward of the
Baptist hospital.

"I know it would mean so much to him if you would
come," Putty said. "He was asking about you last week."

"When are you going?"

"For lunch tomorrow. We can have lunch with the
inmates. I thought it might give you some ideas for your
writing."

"I bet it will. Okay, come pick me up. What time?"

"About eleven thirty. Oh, I'm so glad you can go."

"I'll see you then. I have to go now, Putty. I'm working."

"Call your mother when you get time. She was worrying about you."

"Okay. See you tomorrow then." Anna hung up.
Then she started giggling. It was so funny. It was hilar-
ious. Day after day they called each other continuously.
No wonder none of them ever got anything done.
Maybe there's nothing that needs doing, Anna decided.
Maybe it's better to sit it out. Maybe they're right and
I'm wrong. Maybe all we're supposed to do is eat and
sleep and talk on the phone and give each other advice
and shore each other up. But I'm not normal anyway.
I'm with the ones that crawled through caves carrying
scaffolding to paint the caves. Crawling through open-
ings so narrow no modern man could squeeze through
one, carrying oil lamps and pigments and scaffolding,
for God's sake. I'm in that group whether I like it or not
and can't do this other normal thing. So I might as well
go on and finish the piece if I can remember the other
half of that goddamn paragraph.

At nine the next morning Putty called Anna back to
say she was going to pick up James's girlfriend, Shelby,
and take her along to visit him. Then Shelby decided to

take her little niece, Treena, and then Treena's brother, Andrew, decided to come along. By the time they arrived at the hospital they looked like a flying circus. Anna wearing old slacks and a sweater, her hair tied back with a gold barrette. Putty dressed up in a wool dress. James's girlfriend, Shelby, in a jumper and blouse and the little children in Superman and Supergirl shirts with capes.

"I don't think we ought to take these children in here," Anna said.

"It's just a hospital," Putty answered. "Besides, it might cheer James up to see the outside world."

"Let me stay downstairs with the little children . . ."

"It's all right, Anna. They know me here. James is on the board. Oh, hello there. Nice to see you again." They had passed through the doors and into the reception room. A drugged-looking boy was lounging on a black sofa. A woman in a nightgown came walking by. A girl waited with her parents. The two small children stopped to examine a jar of plastic-covered mints. A phone rang down a hall. Then an old Junior League buddy of Putty's appeared from a door marked DIRECTOR. She was wearing a black business suit and a white blouse with a ruffle. A large cameo was pinned to her lapel. She embraced Putty and spoke to the children and then to Anna. "I like your books," she said. "But I haven't read the last one."

"That's okay," Anna said. "I guess you're pretty busy around here."

"It's coming along." The woman twisted her hands together. "It's getting better. We're into the possible around here, knowing it's possible."

"That's good," Anna replied. "That's a good idea."

The director took them on an elevator to James's floor. He was waiting by the elevator door, looking frightened and unsure. An inmate, a sick boy, having been forced to admit he was not a god. The Hand men were raised to believe they were gods, expected to behave as if they were, expected to get it up and keep it up every day of their lives no matter what happened or who it inconvenienced or how much alcohol they had to consume to fuel it. Now, in this generation, it was coming to a stop. Here, on this ward of the chemical dependency unit of the Baptist hospital, one of them was having to admit that he was human. It broke Anna's heart. She was put off by James's vulnerability, his sadness, his need. She didn't know how to act when a man was vulnerable or in need. She watched him being kind to his girlfriend and his girlfriend's niece and nephew. She watched him being thoughtful to his mother and she kept wanting to find a reason to run away.

"I'm no good at this," she said, and James looked at her and laughed and she saw the spark, the thing she recognized in men, and felt better.

"Jesus," she added. "It's very heavy in here. James, this is really an ordeal, isn't it?"

"No," he said. "It's better than what I was doing. It's hard, if that's what you mean. It's the hardest thing I've ever done." Anna went to him and held him in her arms and was comforted. After lunch James's girl stayed to go to a group therapy session with him and Putty and Anna took the small children home.

"Is this what they will do for recreation?" Anna asked, when they were in the car. "The youth of America accompanying each other to AA meetings and group therapy sessions. It's the wildest thing yet, Putty. It's bizarre."

"James is an alcoholic," the little girl named Treena said from the back seat.

"Yeah, but now he's going to get well," her brother added.

"Don't go writing about this," Putty said. "For God's sake, Anna, don't go putting this in some stories."

౭ 8 ౭

౭ IT WAS CHRISTMAS EVE. "The season adulterers hate," Anna said. She sat upon her couch looking out on the lake. Six pots of paperwhite narcissus were on a table by the door. She looked out past the beautiful fragrant flowers to the dark blue water of the lake and the white clouds low on the horizon and the sun about to go down on her forty-second Christmas Eve. The pots of narcissus were Anna's Christmas tree. Six pots of paperwhite narcissus and a music box in the shape of a cathedral. She wound it up for the fifth time. It played "O, Come All Ye Faithful." Anna was wearing a bathrobe. Her hair was half-wet. She didn't want to get dressed. She didn't want to go out to communion with her mother as she had promised. She didn't want to go to dinner. She didn't want to go out to Niall's and watch people drink. She didn't want to do a goddamn thing but ride this goddamn Christmas out to its logical conclusion. She didn't want anything to eat or anything to drink or any presents. She just wanted to sit there and let her hair dry in the air and listen to her music box and watch the sunset on the lake.

"Me and Emily Dickinson," she said out loud. "Pining

over married men. What a lot of bullshit. The conscious mind is the size of a screw on the doorframe of the house of the unconscious. What did this to me?" She got up and went into the kitchen and phoned her cousin LeLe. It was five in North Carolina. It was two on the West Coast. "LeLe," she said, when her cousin answered. "It's me. It's Anna. Listen, I thought of the answer to why we love them. It's because they're babies and women are programmed to love silly, selfish egocentric maniacs. The wilder they are the better we like them. The more they drink the more we want to take care of them. And they know it. Down deep they know we don't want them to be good. We want them ready to kill at a moment's notice. Civilization is too new to be useful yet. How are you?"

"Horrible. How are you?"

"Terrible. I told Mother I'd take her to church."

"Oh, shit."

"Well, I'm not going to, so she will pout."

"You want to go to Europe in the spring? I have to go on an assignment in March. Come along."

"I might. It's that old daddy, LeLe. Those old daddies. That's who we love."

"You think so?"

"Sure it is. How are your folks?"

"Just like always. They argue all evening. Over the television set if nothing else turns up. I haven't been home in a while. So they're mad about that."

"How's the rugby player?"

"Are you kidding?"

"What else is going on?"

"Nothing I can talk about on the phone."

"Well, Merry Christmas anyway. I'll think about Europe. I'll let you know."

"I hope you get laid before the day is over. In honor of the Immaculate Conception."

"Is that all we think about?"

"Yes. How many times are you going to ask me that?"

"As long as you give me answers I admire. The problem with me is that I'm too particular. It has to be just so, I have to be in love."

"Write a book about it."

"I'm trying to. It's very very funny when you write it down."

"Write about me. I've had an interesting life. I don't know why you never write about me."

"I will write about the rugby player. How about that?"

"I wish you would. Well, listen, have a Merry Christmas. Go on and take her to the church, Anna. You haven't got anything better to do."

"Goodbye, LeLe."

"Think Europe over. For the spring."

Anna hung up the phone and went upstairs and started getting dressed for church. I could write about the time I asked Philip to marry me, she thought. Sitting by the ocean the first time we went to Maine. God, it was cold that day. I was having a hard time getting up the courage to ask him. I wasn't sure I wanted to keep house for a man. Then he said no. My God, it never occurred to me he would say no. If I loved someone I would always marry them and live with them no matter what I had to do or whom I had to hurt. Well, I have paid the price for being the way I am. Collected my karma. Body blows.

I can't even go through New York City on my way to Europe without suffering it. He has ruined it for me forever. On the day I left there I went down to Central Park and rode that wonderful old carousel for hours. I must have ridden it a dozen times. Riding that goddamn carousel and crying. What a spoiled-rotten brat. Wearing a cashmere sweater that cost six hundred dollars and riding that goddamn carousel and crying. Romantic love is so pitiful. I should have been a shrink. If I had it to do over again I'd be a shrink. It's all the mother-child relationship. I'll just go take my real mother to church while she's still alive and worry about the clones later. People are really something. We have the ability at any moment to work and play and sing and love each other and believe each other's craziness and take each other to goddamn Christmas Eve communion and instead we just feel sorry for ourselves. I am alive and I feel all right. At any moment that could end. I must get this goddamn makeup on my face and put on my best dress and go and be happy with them. Eat their food, drink their goddamn eggnog, love them, love them, love them.

৯৩ 9 ৩৩

৯৩ ANNA HAD A RECURRENT DREAM that winter. She woke before dawn one morning and got out of bed and wrote it down.

My dream in winter. I dreamed last night that I was back in New Orleans with a beautiful strong young lover. He wore a plaid shirt and a knit tie. He wore beautiful dark brown slacks and shoes of the finest leather. He was laughing and we rode the streetcar down to the Katz and Bestoff drugstore past Tulane, across the street from the Catholic nunnery and near the Methodist church where the preacher is from China and the signs are in Chinese and the people all look happy going in. I met one of the nuns once, at a pottery class. She wanted to build a kiln for the other sisters. I might have been a nun but I loved men too much.

My dream. In my dream the beautiful young man and I are leaning down off the streetcar. We get off at the corner. The streets are full of happy people, all bundled up in the sort of gorgeous winter clothes people wear in New York City. It must have been close to Mardi Gras. We swung our bodies down from the streetcar and walked across the street. We met my ex-husband there. He asked us to help him search for the lost children. They are Helen's children, all grown up and taking dope and drinking and being angry, lost and dying of ambitions they have no idea how to fulfill. No idea where to begin in the face of so much madness.

My ex-husband had a scroll from a lawyer's office. It had come out of the computer where they keep tabs on all of us. Helen's children get a rating of 10 to 15 percent out of a possible one hundred, he said. I looked around me. I was stunned by the rudeness of him saying that, spoiling all our pleasure in the day. Don't worry about it, the young man said. Let's go find them. Let's make them better than they are. I didn't ask how. I just followed him across the street and through the crowd of college girls gathered in front of the Chinese Methodist church and we began to walk toward the park. We were holding hands and my ex-husband was with us now and I had forgiven him. He was only trying to help.

"Help us find our children," we kept saying. "We are looking for a girl in a green sweatshirt. We are looking for a boy in running shoes. We are looking for a fat little girl named Stacy. Have you seen DeDe? Have you seen James or Stacy or DeDe? If you could give us a minute of your time."

"We can pay you money," Anna's husband kept saying. "Would you be willing to take a check?"

Anna looked up from what she had written. Across the lake the tops of the houses were powdered with snow. The coldest day of the year. She took the papers from the typewriter and put them on the pile of

things she didn't know what to do with yet. Then she
went into her bedroom and dressed in warm slacks
and a dark red sweater and boots and gloves and a hat
and walked out into the beautiful cold morning. I
have this day, she said to herself. Who knows how
many more. Drink to the bird, the poet said. Well, Mr.
Flood, since you insist, I will. She tramped down the
outside stairs making bootprints on the rungs and
turned her face up to the still falling snow. She
tramped across the parking lot and started up the hill.
As she passed the gates to the development she began
to drag her feet, making tracks as she had done when
she was a child. Then she walked to the store and
bought a paper carton of chocolate milk and a package of small white sugar-covered doughnuts and ate
that lovely stuff for her breakfast.

She spent that afternoon writing letters. She wrote to
Olivia and then she wrote to Adam.

Dear Adam,
   The winter is long, and I miss you. Maybe I made all
the wrong choices last year but remember that night we
swore never to regret a thing? Maybe I swore and you
did not. Your letter made me sad.

   Later: Daddy is selling me my inheritance. Is that
wild? He is making me buy these goddamn gold coins
from him, these Krugerrands and Canadian Gold Leaf
things. This is true. This is not some southern story in a
book. He nags me and nags me and nags me and gives
me junk to read about the collapse of the financial struc-
ture of the world and then he starts over again in this
very reasonable voice about the crash of 1929 and the
stock market and he is so convincing. One of Daniel's
business associates said he was the single most convincing human being he had ever *met in his life*. Anyway, he

just wore me down and finally I said, well, then sell me some. If I have to have some goddamn gold coins that much, you get them for me. I thought he would give me some, of course. But instead we have instigated this thing where he sells me these coins that eventually would belong to me anyway. He comes and gets me in the early morning and we drive by the back roads in his old diesel Mercedes out to the county to this bank he likes out there, a little country bank, and we wait in the parking area until the bank opens. Then we go in and get the coins out of a safe deposit box. They are wrapped up in thick butcher's paper with rubber bands around them. We unwrap them and count them several times. However many he is selling me on any given day. Then we wrap them back up and put the rubber bands back around them. This takes dozens of rubber bands. Then we put them in small white cardboard boxes and mark them with the date and the amount. 18 Krugerrands, 15 Canadian Gold Leaf. Dad to Anna, September 13, 1985. Or some such label. He writes it out very carefully in his beautiful old script. His hands are so beautiful and freckled and strong. I want to kiss his hands when I look at them. I love him so much and can never tell him so. I think he knows it now. It is very cozy going with him to get the coins. Anyway, then we put more rubber bands around the boxes and put the boxes in his briefcase and then we walk out of the bank nodding to people he knows. There goes old Mr. Hand with some of his coins, I guess they are saying. It scares me to death that someone will try to rob him. They did steal a safe full of the damn things several years ago. Out of his office, Daniel told me about it. Daddy never would tell anyone how much he lost. Of course they weren't insured. Anyway, we get into the old white diesel car and drive the back roads through the county back into Charlotte. I'm supposed to call the insurance people and insure them but I never do. I think I'll dig a hole and put them in the

ground. It is the funniest thing I have ever done in my
life and takes up a lot of time. It was right for me to
come home at this time. I needed to ride in his old white
car and let him tell me what to do.

I hope your studies are going well. Everything is always hard to do. I love you, but not the way you want me
to. Not enough. And I am too old to be your wife.

Love,
Anna

She sealed the letter in an envelope and addressed it
and then addressed the one to Olivia and pulled on her
old gray jacket and walked down to the corner to mail
the letters in a box with a late pickup. She saw the
Episcopal bishop of North Carolina riding by in a Volvo
station wagon talking on a car phone as he drove and
she took that for a sign that all was reasonably well with
the world on this particular winter day.

ல 10 ல

ல WHEN OLIVIA GOT HOME from school the following Friday, the letter from Anna was waiting for her, propped up on the table with the salt and pepper shakers. Also, a package from a bookstore in Charlotte. She read the envelope a dozen times before she opened it. My aunt Anna loves me, she was thinking. Someday she'll call me up and take me on a trip with her, one of her trips to give a speech. I wish she could have heard my debate speech in Tulsa. She would have loved hearing it. If she got sick I could go on for her. This is Ms. Hand's niece, Olivia, they will say. She travels with her aunt and if her aunt gets a cold or is very tired she will read to you instead. Yes, she is named for the actress Olivia de Havilland, but there is no relation. No, she can not be in a movie at this time as she is in college in Austin getting her degrees in law and aviation. Thank you. She is getting her degree in anthropology. She is studying to be a writer, she is a writer.

Carrying the letter and the package Olivia went through her bedroom and out onto the small unused patio. It was cold on the patio but protected by the walls of the house and Olivia often sat out there to read, even on cold days. She kicked the gathered leaves into a corner and pulled an old dilapidated yard chair around to face the sun. She dusted off the chair, then lowered herself into it, as though she were already in the fabulous drawing rooms of the places she would travel to with Anna.

Well, go on and open the letter, she told herself. It will be good news. All her letters are good. She has seen me and she likes me. She likes me and she writes to me and sends me presents. She said she wanted to borrow life from me. Well, she can have it. I have plenty of it if she needs it.

The letter was still unread. I can hold it to the count of one hundred without opening it, Olivia decided. But why should I? The sun came out from behind a cloud. It cast the shadows of the walnut trees across the yard and onto the patio and the walls of the house. Olivia took that for a sign and opened Anna's letter.

Dear Olivia,

I am so proud of you. The best debater in the whole state of Oklahoma. Tomorrow, the world. I wish I was there to tell you how proud I am of you. Write me more about the play. What play? What part? I used to act when I was young but I wasn't much good at it. I always wanted to rewrite my lines.

Listen, Olivia, please don't be bothered by your father, or by not coming here to visit. He isn't strong enough to love you and besides, this goddamn family is more trouble than it's worth.

None of it has anything to do with you and the wonderful life you are creating for yourself. Don't worry about college yet. You are going to have scholarships everywhere. Love and kisses from your very very very proud,

Aunt Anna

I am sending a book you might like to read.

Olivia unwrapped the package. It was a book called *West with the Night*. A photograph of a woman in an aviator's helmet was on the cover. Olivia caressed the book with both hands. The sun beat down on the patio and the chair. She opened the book and began to read. When her grandmother called her to dinner an hour later, she was still reading.

"Your dinner is ready. You must come in now." Her grandmother stood in the doorway, her dark eyes watching the child as if she were the sun itself.

"This book is by a woman who flew an airplane across the Atlantic Ocean all by herself. A long time ago before they even had radios."

"You could do it," the old woman answered. "If they showed you how."

"I could. I know I could."

"You will fly like an eagle. But not if you freeze to death. And not unless you fill your belly when it calls to you."

"I'm coming in." Olivia closed the book and put her arm around her grandmother's shoulder and went with her into the house. The world was opening out before her. There was no telling what might happen next.

Six hundred miles away, Anna decided to try again. She got into her car and drove over to her brother Daniel's house and got out and went inside and told him he should go and see the girl.

"I am not going to do that, Anna. I'm tired of hearing about it. I told you not to go and you went and now I have to worry myself to death about her calling Jessie. Don't start this again with me."

"You cannot do this to your own flesh and blood. You might ruin her life. It's a strange little lost world out there in Tahlequah, Oklahoma. There are grown men who look at her like they could eat her up. I dreamed she was raped by one of them the other night. I didn't tell you everything I saw out there." She waited, watched him square his shoulders, take it in. Then he took her arm and pulled her into the den and shut the door. He poured himself a glass of scotch and offered one to her.

"Okay, tell me."

"She doesn't have anyone to protect her, Daniel. She's really pretty amazing, self-protective, but she borrows horses from the grooms at a farm near where she lives. She goes out with some high school rodeo star. It might be all right. Maybe that's her world and she should stay in it. But she is ours. She belongs to us. We can't leave her there. There isn't a man to protect her. Her grandfather is old. There should be a man."

"How old is she?"

"She's sixteen. She's two months older than Jessie. I've told you that a dozen times. You know that. If you won't go get her I have to do something about it. At least go out there and be seen with her. Let them know there will be someone to answer to if anything happens."

"Are you doing a number on me, Anna?" He waited, drank his drink, looked at her. She moved closer, returned his look. Maybe I am, she thought. Maybe this is the meanest thing I've ever done to any of them.

"If it were Jessie you would be worried sick. If you go and see it you will want to bring her here."

"Did you send them money?"

"Yes, and I promised to take care of the college, when that happens. Please go and see about it, Daniel. Please do this for me."

"I'll think it over. I'm thinking about it, Anna." He poured another drink, a water glass full, and began to sip it. He was a powerful man, a ranked doubles player in the state, and an all-around athlete. He had never had to be afraid of another man in his life. Anna watched the old Hand madness and energy rising with the blood alcohol level. She even had sense enough to keep her mouth shut while it happened.

"So tell me about these grooms she borrows horses from."

"It's nothing really. Just that she has to be nice to them to have a horse to ride. When she's older one of them might try to collect. She's self-protective. I don't mean she's a victim. She just won the state debating contest, but I told you that."

"Yeah, she wrote to me. She sent it out of the paper. If I go out there and see her, I'll want to keep her. You know that, Anna. I couldn't see my own kid and then leave her out in Oklahoma. If I go out there, I'll get her and I'll keep her."

"You wouldn't have to. You could think of what is best for her. You can help without going crazy."

"You're letting it drive you crazy. You're nuts on the subject. So what did you dream?" He leaned back on his desk, looking right at her.

"I dreamed that she was coming down from the stage and there was no one there to congratulate her, no one to help her celebrate when she won the contest and then those men were there and took her off in a car. I dreamed it last week."

Daniel sipped his drink. He turned his head to the side, toward the door to the yard where the sound of Jessie playing tennis with her friends came in like a melody. A boy's voice, and then another's and then Jessie's lilting bossy insistence, then laughter. "You want a drink or not?" Daniel said. "Come on, Sister, have a drink with me. It's Saturday."

"Sure," she said. "Fix me one." He mixed her a scotch and water and carrying their drinks they went out through the French doors onto the balcony and stood leaning on the railing watching Jessie, wrapped up in a pale lilac sweatsuit, playing tennis with her friends.

"You worry too much," Daniel said. "I never knew anyone to worry the way you do. Don't you ever have any fun anymore?"

"I can't help it," she answered. "I'm a type A. I have to worry. The amazing thing is the years when I had fun and didn't worry. There must have been some years but lately I'm having trouble remembering which ones they were. Jessie's going to freeze to death playing tennis in this weather."

"No, she isn't. I used to play in January when I was really serious about it."

"And we always went swimming in March. Phelan always says that. He says, we always went swimming in March. Anybody that was too pussy to go in March couldn't run with us."

"What are Phelan and Niall up to? Is it true they're going to buy a plane together? That'll be the end of that friendship."

"Maybe they're going to smuggle Mexicans or something. They don't like being broke."

"Are they broke?"

"They bought six tickets to the NCAA finals. They can't be very broke." Anna laughed, then finished her drink. "I'm going inside," she said. "It's only February. I don't have to go swimming for another month."

"I'll think it over," Daniel said. "About Olivia."

"You said her name. Well, I'll be damned." She took her brother's arm, stroked his sleeve, wondered how in the world her baby brother had grown so tall, become so big, become a man. "Nice shot," Jessie called out from the court. "Love, fifteen."

That night Daniel called Olivia and asked her to come and spend the weekend in two weeks' time. Then he called Anna and told her he had done it.

"Are you satisfied?" he said. He was standing in his kitchen holding a glass of scotch in his hand. He was trying not to think of anything bad. He was trying to remember when the world had seemed easy to live in and if you wanted something you just did it or got it or demanded it. Before he had to run this goddamn business and compromise all day.

"Are you? That's the important thing. She's us, Daniel. It has to be done. Oh, God, I'm so glad you did it."

"But not to meet Mother and Daddy. It's only to be with me and Jessie and you."

"Sufficient. I love you."

"We'll see what happens." He went upstairs and found Jessie and told her everything he was doing and Anna's part in it and when and where and why it was going to matter to her. Then he drank another scotch and water and settled down to watch "Dallas" on television. He thought of Olivia's mother and how stoned they had been the day he met her and how young he had been and she had been and how jealous and proud he had been of her with her black hair to her waist and her wide shoulders and her haughtiness and her goddamn pride.

☙ **11** ❧

☙ HAZARDOUS MEETINGS THAT BRIDGE A CONTINENT. Anna was reading a note stuck with masking tape to her refrigerator. STOP LOOKING FOR AN EXTERNAL LOVE BECAUSE IF YOU COULD FIND IT, YOU WOULD WANT TO CONTROL IT, AND IF YOU COULD CONTROL IT, YOU WOULDN'T WANT IT ANYMORE. THERE IS A DIFFERENCE BETWEEN AN OBSESSION AND A LOVE AFFAIR. I wonder if that's true, she thought. The doorbell was ringing. It was ringing and ringing. Anna walked through the house and opened the front door. A dreary March day, cold gray rain. And there on the doorstep was Jessie, looking frantic. Tall as a tree and beautiful and sixteen years old and frantic.

"Can I borrow a sweater?" she said. "I don't have anything to wear."

"Of course you have something to wear. Come on in. What's really bothering you?" But Anna knew the answer to that. Still, maybe she *didn't* have anything to wear. Maybe there was nothing that could make a sixteen-year-old girl look the way she thought she needed to look to go to school in Charlotte, North Carolina, in the year of our insanity, nineteen hundred and eighty-five. "Come on in. Eat breakfast with me."

"I can't. I have to go to school. I'm sorry I bothered you."

"You didn't bother me. But you can't borrow my clothes anymore either. I promised your father. It's a bad habit to get into."

"I'm going to sing in the choir tonight. Will you come to hear us?"

"Of course. What time? I'd love it."

"At seven thirty."

"I'll be there. Listen, Jessie, people don't like you because of the clothes you wear. If they do, they aren't the people you need anyway. That's one of the reasons why you can't borrow my clothes."

"What's the other reason?" Jessie sat down on the end of the sofa and pulled her knees up.

"Because you don't remember to bring them back and because I promised your father. So what's going on with you and your dad?"

"My sister's coming. You know all about it, don't you?"

"Yes."

"Why didn't anyone tell me?"

"Your father didn't believe it and I didn't think it was my place. I wanted to tell you. I wanted to tell everyone the minute I found out. I don't like secrets. I think they do more harm than good."

"You saw her?"

"Yes. She's very pretty. She looks like you."

"Like me?"

"Quite a bit like you."

"What are we going to tell people around here, when she shows up looking like me and my own age?"

"The truth. There's no secret that your dad was married before he married your mom."

"But we're the same age."

"I guess you're like children in a harem then, aren't

you? A new twist in the family myth. Perhaps a coup."

Jessie looked away. "What a thing to say. Aunt Anna, you're terrible."

"Then why are you smiling? Why are you trying not to laugh?" Jessie looked up. She giggled, then put her head down into her hands and laughed some more.

"There could be nine or ten of us, I guess. I told Dad it was okay with me if she comes to see us. I just don't want to have to introduce her to my friends. Not yet. Not till I get used to this."

"Are you going to tell them?"

"I told MerryLee and Karen. And Connie."

"That's all." Now it was Anna's turn to laugh. "I'll tell you what," she said. "You can't borrow anything of mine, but you can have that blue cotton sweater if you really want it and if you'll keep it clean and not let it end up on the floor." Jessie threw her arms around Anna and kissed her. "Because," Anna went on, "and only because you look so beautiful in it that I don't want it anymore." Jessie jumped up and ran upstairs to Anna's room and came down in a few minutes wearing the sweater. She really did look absolutely marvelous in the sweater. "I bought that in London when my luggage was lost in Munich," Anna said. "It's perfect. And so are you. I'm glad you came by. Now get on out of here before you're late to school."

"She's coming the weekend after this one."

"I know. Your dad told me. It will be okay, honey. It will work out."

"Are you coming to hear me sing?"

"Yes. I wouldn't miss it."

"Okay. I'll see you tonight, then. Thanks for the sweater. It's the most gorgeous thing I've ever had." She kissed Anna on the cheek, then turned and flew out the door and got into her car. Jesus, Anna thought. She closed the door and went back to her kitchen, Daniel and his children. The unbelievable one who was coming soon and this one, this perfect perfection of a girl, with an ear for music so sublime it made the perfection of her looks seem insignificant. A perfect ear and a perfect body and a perfect face and she can't even read a book. Anna shook her head. Well, she doesn't need to read books. Gilding the lily. What was I thinking about when the doorbell rang? What was I going to do?

She picked up the phone and called the man she loved or was obsessed by. "Meet me in Atlanta for the weekend."

"I can't. You know I can't do that."

"Why did you do this to me?"

"I did it to myself as well. How are you, apart from all that?"

"I'm terrible. No, I'm okay. I'm working. And my niece is coming soon, the one I went to see. He finally asked her."

"That's good news. I know you're glad of that."

"I don't know if I am or not, now that it's happened. The other one is worried, but I think it will be all right."

"Why do we make such mountains out of everything? We're only human, Anna. We aren't perfected yet."

"I love you. I miss you. I miss you so much."

"So do I. It's all right, though. It's better this way. You were right about that."

"Goodbye. I'm tired of talking to you."

"Okay. Goodbye." She hung up the phone and went upstairs to her workroom and tried to find something she wanted to write. She walked around the room reading things that were pinned to the wall, picking up pieces of paper off the floor, waiting for something to happen, hoping to catch fire. *"The trajectory is indeterminate,"* she read. *"Light presses upon matter and changes it."* "Reality is neither spiritual nor material but rather the invisible organization of energy."

Why do I make everyone so unhappy? she was thinking. Why did I tell Daniel he's afraid? Of course he's afraid to see her. I would be too if she were mine. He got Jessie away from that bitch, Sheila, but that's still shaky. If Jessie stops liking what's going on, she might go to London and live with Sheila. Who do I think I am? What business is it of mine to move back here and start telling all of them that everything they do is wrong? It's no good to tell people the truth all the time. Leave them alone. Let them go on with their dreaming. I'm going out this afternoon and buy Jessie a useless birthday present to make up for those magazines I gave her for Christmas. It was just like me to send a *National Geographic* subscription to a child who doesn't even like to read. That's exactly like me.

It was the next day before Anna found time to go to the store. Just as she was leaving the apartment her sister Helen came driving up in an Oldsmobile. She parked carefully inside the lines and got out and locked the door to the car and came walking up on Anna's porch. All this time she had refused to look at Anna. "What's wrong?" Anna said. "You look like someone died."

"Why did you tell Jessie that she was born in a harem?" Helen stopped on the edge of the porch. She was wearing a little navy blue Chanel suit with Chanel jewelry and a Chanel bag. "Jessie went straight to Mother and Mother is so upset she won't even call you about it. I don't believe you did that, Anna. As hard as we are all trying to bring up these children."

"Come on in. Where'd you get that suit? Jesus, is that a Chanel?"

"Yes, it's a Chanel. I have to keep up appearances around here, Anna. I can't go around all day in sweat pants."

"Like some people you know. Come on in. The suit's great. I might borrow it the next time I go to New York.

I think I rented the mountain house, by the way. To a doctor from Chapel Hill."

"Don't change the subject, Anna." Anna held open the front door and Helen walked through the living room, trying to ignore the fact that the packing boxes were still piled all over the floor and the sofa cushions stacked on a chair.

"I'm going to finish moving in as soon as I have time. I keep forgetting about this room."

"I could lend you a maid. Mother has Victoria and she has a free day."

"Sit down." They were in the library. Anna settled Helen on the sofa and watched as she put her Chanel bag carefully on the coffee table and crossed her legs just so.

"What are you smiling at?"

"At how wonderful you are. My own little sister. My pretty little Helen."

"Why did you tell a sixteen-year-old child that she was born in a harem? It upset her very much, Anna. She went straight to Mother."

"And Mother bought her three new blouses to make up for the trauma and forgot all about the fact that she is failing half her subjects at school. Right? I did not tell her she was born in a harem, Helen. I was just trying to put this situation into some kind of historical perspective. This is the human race we are dealing with here. We are not perfected yet. We don't add up like numbers. We are passionate and idea-driven creatures and the higher the intelligence the slower the rate of maturation. Oh, well, that's beside the point." Anna was standing. She sank down into a chair near Helen. "Honey, you can't go crazy because Daniel has another child. It's good. It's a good thing. Jessie is an only child. It's good for her. Think where we would be if we didn't have each other. What about when Momma and Daddy die. Jessie needs Olivia the way —"

"Olivia!"

"That's her name and you will like her when you meet her."

"I don't want to meet her. We have enough trouble without you starting all this, Anna. James is in the hospital and DeDe's up there living with that man and I really wish you wouldn't do this to us right now."

"Let's go shopping. I need to go out and buy some presents. I was just going when you came."

"Well, I won't keep you." Helen stood up. Picked up her shiny navy blue Chanel bag. The chains on the bag matched the chain around her neck, a fat thick chain with Coco Chanel's initials on it.

"Have you changed your name to Coco then?" Anna was sorry as soon as she said it. "I mean, I heard you wanted a nickname."

"What? What are you talking about now?"

"I wish you wouldn't leave."

"I'm leaving."

"I'll call you for lunch soon. I need to ask you a favor." Anna walked her sister to the door, then walked her out to the car. Then put her into the car. Then watched her drive away. Wrens were sitting in the branches of the ginkgo trees beside the path that led down to the artificial lake. Anna watched them for a while. It was a brilliant day and she walked down to the water's edge and watched the ducks for a while and forgot what she had been on her way to do. She kept seeing Helen getting out of the Oldsmobile in her finery and it was so wonderful and endearing and like the ducks and the cool blue of the day and only Anna herself was a stranger to all that wonder and glamour.

Six hundred miles away Olivia was thinking about her father. She thought her father would be like her grandfather when she met him. She thought she would go for long walks with him as her aunt and grandfather did, out across the hills at sunset. She imagined herself arm in arm with her father in whatever sort of hills or fields he inhabited in the faraway state of North Carolina. She had looked North Carolina up in the encyclopedia at her school. It said there were rolling hills and pastures near Charlotte. They would walk there, and, perhaps, she would find a horse and show him how she could ride. A sister would be there too. The one he was protecting from the truth. Still, a sister might be nice. A sister might be good if you could make friends with her. But most important was the father. To walk the hills and tell him the secrets of her heart and ask his advice about her future. Olivia stood beside her bed, looking out the small paned window at the bare yard and the apple tree her grandfather had planted for her when she was four. Yes, it would only be ten days now and she would go on the plane; and take off and land and walk down a runway and her father would be standing there and would take her hand and then her life would be complete and not always weighted with the loss of a piece. As if her life were a picture puzzle on a table and a piece was gone.

Her grandmother came into the room. "Bobby Tree is here," she said. "He wishes to speak with you. Do not look that way when a friend calls on you."

"Tell him I'll be out in a minute. Go on, tell him to wait a minute." Olivia put down the book that she was holding. Pretended to be straightening her desk. Her grandmother waited. "Go on, tell him I'll be right there."

"Is this what the coming of those people does?"

"All right. I'll tell him myself." Olivia went out into the living room. He was sitting on the sofa talking to her grandfather. Wearing a plaid shirt and ironed jeans, with his hair combed and his boots polished. A fine air was about him, like a horse anyone would want to own. He stood up and spoke to her. "I've been missing you. You never come by the stables anymore. I've been wondering where you were."

"Why didn't you call me, then?"

"I just thought I'd come on over. You want to go ride around town with me? We could get a hamburger or just ride around. If they would let you." He turned to her grandfather. "Can I take her into town?"

"I'll go," Olivia said. "Let me get a jacket."

They walked out together into the darkening night. Small cirrus clouds drifted across the moon. The constellations were appearing. Always if she walked out on such a night Olivia was astounded that the stars were there. Bobby Tree took her arm, helped her into the car. She felt the soft flannel of his sleeve against her wrist. The smell of pine trees was everywhere. The last time she had gone out with him they had gone to Sam's room at the stables and lain down upon a bed but in the end she wouldn't take her clothes off or allow him to take off his and she had been angry with him ever since that night and would not talk to him on the phone.

"What are you thinking about?" he asked her now.

"I won't end up like my mother. I won't live in a trailer and follow a rodie around."

"Nobody's asking you to."

"So why did you come out?"

"I thought you might be lonely and want someone to talk to. I never see you since I finished school. You want to go to a movie?"

"I might."

"Is your dad coming out here to see you?"

"No, I'm going there to visit them before too long. To North Carolina where they live."

"You want to go look at the river? It's at flood stage. You ought to see how high it is. I heard it was going to flood part of Arkansas tonight."

"Okay. Let's go look." He turned the car off the main road and started toward the river. He reached out a hand and Olivia took it and moved over closer to the driver's seat. "All right," he said. "All right then."

Anna stood in the middle of her workroom thinking terrible convoluted thoughts. So he's letting her come up here. But that doesn't mean he's going to love her. God, she may have a terrible time. Jessie might get jealous and throw a fit. Anything could happen. Why did I get involved in this? Goddammit, it's because Philip won't meet me in Atlanta. No, it's honest. Goddammit, they are my genes. I care what happens to them. We have to help this girl. Have to see that she has what she needs.

Anna pulled a piece of white cotton bond out of a package, stuck it in her typewriter and started typing a letter. She was typing standing up.

Dear Daniel,
    I wish I would stop STICKING MY NOSE IN YOUR BUSINESS. Replicating DNA, that's what's causing all the trouble. They're calling the shots, making me crazy, my empty troubled womb.
    I keep wanting to make everyone be like me, sober, hardworking, driven, nervous, lonely.

Anna sat down. She felt terrible. She felt like she was catching a cold. She sneezed and wrapped her arms about herself. She was wearing a pair of washed-out lavender sweat pants from a gymnasium on Fifth Avenue in New York City. On top she had a dark soccer shirt with red and yellow stripes, a Christmas present from her cousin, LeLe. Above her head floated a single Ping-Pong ball, a gift from Captain Kangaroo. Wherever Anna lived that Ping-Pong ball hung from the ceiling of her workroom. She look at it now, floating in a little piece of light. She looked out the window. The rain was letting up. Maybe it would be a nice day after all.

The phone was ringing. Anna answered it, leaning back in her chair, blowing her nose as she answered the phone. "Hello."

"Anna, it's me. I've changed my mind about Atlanta. How soon can you get away?"

"Ten minutes from now. I think I'm catching a cold. Do you care?"

"No. Look, I can leave this afternoon at four. I got someone to take my calls. I can get to Atlanta by seven. Can you do that? Can you meet me there?"

"What's your flight number?"

"Eleven thirty-two. Are you all right to fly?"

"I'll probably be well as soon as I hang up this phone."

"Call me back and tell me what time your flight arrives. If I'm not here, tell my service. Look, I love you."

"I know you do."

So Anna closed the door to the house and carrying one small fold-up suitcase, and wearing a beautiful charcoal black Valentino dress and a Ferragamo scarf and camel-colored high-heeled shoes she boarded a plane for Atlanta. When she got there he was waiting and they went upstairs to the airport hotel and went inside and took off all their clothes and lay down upon a bed and began to make love to each other.

It is on this moment of balance I must end: the strange moment when spirituality rejects ethics, when happiness springs from the absence of hope, when the mind finds its justification in the body.

"What are you thinking?" he said later.

"I am thinking of Camus. That's what you get for fucking someone who reads too much."

"Do you want to go out to dinner?"

"No, I want to lie here and feel your foot with my foot and look at you. Call room service. Order something."

"Are you happy, Anna? I mean, in general, with the

world as it is, can you find a way to live in it? Because I can't lately. It isn't only missing you. It may be the time of year. I don't know what it is. Lately when things go wrong at the hospital. I've got a six-year-old kid with lymphoma, a friend's child. I was the one to discover it. So they asked me to stay in on the treatment. I should have done something else for a living. They told me that. They knew it in Boston. They told me a long time ago. Never mind. Why do you look that way?"

"I couldn't have borne that. Any kind of disease or disability. No wonder I wasn't a mother. If anything went wrong I couldn't bear it. I can't bear to cut my finger. If something disabling happened to me I'd kill myself. I know I would."

"Nothing will." He pulled her into his arms. It was dark in the room. The heating system hummed. The building creaked. Overhead the airplanes crisscrossed the sky.

"How can I bear to be this happy?" Anna said. "Listen, I'm no good at happiness either. I wish you'd leave right now."

"No, you don't," he said, and began to make love to her some more.

In the morning they moved to a better hotel in downtown Atlanta with a waterfall and shops where Anna bought pale pink underwear from Belgium and chocolates from Sweden and candles. She bought six beautiful white candles and lit them in the room and made love to him by candlelight.

"This will make me write a love story," she said.

"Go ahead. As long as I'm not in it."

"You'll be in it. You will be a Chinese graduate student who meets a girl at dawn on a bridge. Would you like that?"

"Will she make love to him?"

"If he wants her to. He will be very careful about

engaging his affections for someone who seems so far
away. She will be a beautiful Western girl and he will
think she is inaccessible."

"Will you write about the child with lymphoma?"

"No, it would make me too sad. I only write stories
with happy endings. What time is it?"

"Six o'clock. We don't have to leave until morning.
Don't think about it now."

"Let's go to a movie."

"We could."

They went out to a shopping mall and saw a Chinese film called *The Yellow Earth.* It was about a beautiful Chinese girl who falls in love with a brave man
and loses him. In the end the girl drowns herself in a
river.

"Why is this making me so happy?" Anna asked.

"Why did your cold go away?"

"Very mysterious. Inside this mystery is another
mystery. Also, you would never have seen this divine
movie without me. Think how marvelous it would be
to live with me. Always something wonderful going
on. Me thinking up wonderful things for you to do."

"You would be terrible to live with."

"I know. I am. I would be."

"We'd be terrible together. At each other's throats in
a week's time." He stopped and took her arm and pulled
her near him. They were in the middle of the pink
marble vestibule of the mall. People walking all around
them. "No, that's not so. We would be wonderful together. We would work."

"Oh, shit, Philip. Don't start that."

When they got home they made love again and this
time it was worse than before, more wonderful and
terrible than anything had ever been for him or for her.
" 'Death is beaten by praying Indians, by distant

cows . . . by hazardous meetings that bridge a continent.' "

"Who wrote that?"

" 'One could never die. Never die. Never die while
crying. My lover, my dear one . . .' James Dickey . . . It
was in an anthology I taught out of once. On the opposite
page was a poem about a man trying to make up with his
wife. It was a funny poem. The Dickey poem isn't funny."
She rolled away from him and sat up on one elbow. The
lamp on a bedside table cast pink shadows on her arm and
face. She looked very beautiful and he imagined how she
must have been when she was young. A luscious woman,
high cheekbones, wide eyes, small nose. A once-in-
a-lifetime woman and he could not keep her, even if he
was free. No one would ever get to keep her and Philip
knew that as well as he knew his own name.

"The other poem starts off with this couple riding in
a taxi through New York City and the man says, 'Come
back . . . forget that figment of your imagination, the
blonde . . . We will have a celebration to end all celebra-
tions. We will invite the undertaker who lives beneath us
and a couple of the boys from the office, . . . and Stein-
berg, who is off the wagon, by the way, and that insane
woman who lives upstairs, and a few reporters, if anything should break.' " She went on, not giving him time
to laugh. "It's a better poem than the Dickey poem. The
strange sexual tensions of the married state, so high-
strung and so funny, dear and funny. I wish we could be
married so we could have a fight and make up in a taxi."
She rolled back beside him and they held each other for
a while without speaking.

"Shit," he said. "What in the name of God did we do
this to each other for?"

In the morning they were very polite and both of
them pretended to be in a hurry to go home. They
dressed and went downstairs to the dining room to eat

breakfast. The hotel dining room was surrounded by a series of fake waterfalls. The very heart of nineteen eighty-five, Anna thought. After a long silence she remembered something that cheered her up.

"The passing within range of two powerful and mutually exclusive fantasy systems. Is that what has happened here? Or maybe my chemistry did a fix on your sperm and I have been inoculated with your DNA. In short, why do I love you?"

"I don't know. I tried all year to figure it out. I walked out one morning and stood by the East River and thought I understood it once, I tried to call you, I did call. At that time I thought we should do as you wished and just leave it all and go away and live somewhere. Anywhere, for however long we could make it last. I could practice anywhere."

"I know. You told me that. You called me."

"We would take the baggage of our lives with us, Anna." He was very intense, the freckles standing out on his face, a beautiful and haughty man. "So I talked myself out of that. But I have never regretted falling in love with you. We deserve our passions." She was listening as hard as she could, trying to find solace somewhere, anywhere, in any word, any idea.

"It's because we are growing older," she said finally. "It's tacky to mention it but the body ages and you and I both know damn well the great passions are behind us. This is my last, my very last. Goddammit, Philip, I give up. Let's get out of here." She stood up. "I'll go get my bags. Have a porter up for them if you will." She felt like herself, felt like Anna. She walked out through the dining room full of breakfast eaters, past newspaper readers reading all sorts of useless articles, poorly written about things that had no bearing on their lives. Her disdain and haughtiness caught up with her. She had been accused all her life of thinking she was above other people. Maybe I am, Anna thought now. I may be in this hotel playing out the end of a love affair with a married man who won't marry me but at least I'm not reading the *Atlanta Journal* at eight o'clock in the morning.

"I won't tell you I won't see you anymore," she said when she left him. "I'll never do that again. I have to come to the city sometime soon. In a month or so. I'll see you then." She raised her eyes. "I changed my mind. I will be your mistress, or whatever you will have me for. This is okay. Some love, some grief. I love you."

"I love you back. When will you be coming to New York?"

"This summer. As soon as I finish this book."

"I'll see you then. Call me when you know what day."

༭ 12 ཙ཰

ༀ Then Olivia was coming. Anna had barely unpacked her suitcase and opened her mail when it was
Saturday again and Jessie and Daniel asked her to go
with them to pick up Olivia at the airport.

"Oh, no. You need to go alone."

"But we might not know who she is. You're the one
who knows her." Jessie paused, then threw herself
across the room and into Anna's arms. Daniel stood in
the doorway.

"Are you okay?" Anna asked.

"Go with us, Sister. We need you to go."

They drove to the airport in the old convertible
Jessie used for transportation to school, all three of
them crowded into the front seat. Playing the radio.
Not talking. Be quiet, Anna kept telling herself.
It's only one more thing happening. Jessie's hands
were clenched into fists. Daniel was driving very
fast out Harris Boulevard to the Billy Graham Park-
way. They parked the car and ran into the airport
and were twenty minutes early and there was more
waiting.

"She looks like Jessie," Anna said. "She looks like me. She looks like you."

"I know that," he said. "You told me that already."

Then Olivia was there. They crowded around her. It seemed to Anna that the whole airport must be encircling them and everyone in the whole town of Charlotte, North Carolina. Daniel was being hearty and solemn and Jessie was being very formal and Anna was too busy worrying to register anything more interesting than fear. Only Olivia seemed to know what she was doing there. "I was scared to death to get off that plane," she said. "It's the hardest thing I ever had to do."

"Was it a bad ride?" Daniel put in. "Sometimes that flight from Nashville can get hairy. It looks like clear skies but you can't see far from here."

"It was all right," Olivia said. "I meant I was afraid to see how you looked."

"How do we look?" Jessie asked. She took her father's arm.

"Nice," Olivia answered. "Just fine, I guess."

"Listen," Anna said, for she had finally found some words. "This is basically an adventure, of the first order, of the first magnitude. You don't get moments like this very often. Let's soak it up. Don't diffuse it." The others all looked at her.

"I'm glad I'm here," Olivia said. "I'm glad to be here." She moved closer to her father and searched his face, then touched his arm, just the very slightest touch of her hand upon his rolled-up shirt sleeve. No one said a word. Then Jessie took Olivia's hand from her father's sleeve and pulled her away from him. "Let's go get your luggage," she said. "I know you want to get out of this filthy airport. You can't even breathe for all the diesel in the air." She pulled Olivia along with her. They moved out in front of Anna and Daniel.

* * *

Daniel reached in his shirt pocket for a cigarette and lit it. He offered one to Anna but she shook her head. "I quit," she said. "What do you think of her?"

"She's nice. A very nice girl. I think I'll take them down to the farm for the weekend," he added. "I don't want Mom and Dad in on this yet. She can see the old place. She'll like that."

"Do you want me to go?"

"Hell, yes. You damn well better go. You're the one who started this."

"I may have produced this segment but it started when you fucked their mothers seventeen years ago. I'm glad you did. My God, what riches, what beautiful girls."

"Anna, don't talk like that in front of them. I mean, just cut that out for now."

"Okay, whatever you want. People don't fuck. People spring up and get delivered by American Airlines. The world is a piece of cake."

"What do you need to go out to the country?"

"We can stop by my place and I'll get some things. Come on, let's go follow them."

They went by Anna's and got her things and then they drove fifteen miles out into the country to a farm-house the first Hand in Mecklenburg County had built for his bride in 1767. It was kept up by a black family on the adjoining property and the Hands used the place for a summer house and hunting camp. The Manning family had land that adjoined it and there was an old burial ground where the two families still buried their dead. A knoll under oak trees at the top of a ridge. The girls had been quiet on the ride to the farm. They sat in the back seat without looking at each other and Anna pointed out landmarks to Olivia. "We could stop at the cemetery and show her the graves of her ancestors," she said when they were almost to the house. "You want to do that?"

"Why not," Daniel said, and turned off the road onto the dirt lane leading up between the ancient trees.

"Why are we doing this?" Jessie said. "This is so morbid. Why are we going up there?"

"I would like to see it," Olivia said. "I'll see anything you want to show me." Daniel stopped beside the gate to the cemetery and they got out and walked past the ruins of the chapel and on past the abandoned gardens until they could read the names on the tombstones. James McNiall Hand and Lydia Anne Walker and Celestine Garth and the McLaurins and Purcells and Martins and Clarks. Augustus Garth, Augusta Light, Alice Armene Light, Alicia Augustus Hand, Charles Poteet Hand, James Alexander Hand, Anna Elizabeth Hand, Anna de Bardeleban Hand, Colonel James Alexander Hand, Junior, He Served His Country and His God.

"Here are your great-grandparents," Daniel was saying. "They say that she was Welsh."

And that's where Francis and I fucked one night when we were young and hot, Anna thought. Right there on that sunken grave and back there is where he is buried and here, by this grand old lady, is where Phelan and I hid a box of gold medallions and silver dollars and a handful of silver certificates which used to be called dollars. I wonder which one of us will get broke enough to have to dig them up. She walked over to the grave and examined the place beside it with her foot but the grass had not been disturbed for a long time. Phelan wouldn't steal my golden treasure, Anna thought, and laughed to herself. I wonder if Jessie and Olivia would have liked me in my wilder days. Well, they will never see my wildness and if I'm lucky I won't have to witness theirs.

Olivia had wandered back to the very edge of the graves. Daniel had followed her. Jessie was sitting on the foundation of the ruined chapel looking out at the road.

"This isn't working out very well," Anna said, coming

up behind her. "What do you think is going wrong?"

"She doesn't look like me. I don't look a thing like that. You said she looks like me."

"You don't like the way she looks? That's it?"

"I didn't say that. She looks okay. But I don't look like that. She isn't even as tall as I am."

"She isn't as beautiful as you are either, but she's nice to look at too. I'd be glad to have her for a sister."

"You always say things like that, but you don't have to do them. You do anything you want to do." Jessie turned around, gave Anna a black look. "What does she want here anyway? What does she want with us?"

Anna sighed. "She wants her father, Jessie. Everyone deserves to have their parents acknowledge their presence in the world. There's enough of your daddy. A girl has to know about her father, that's so primal. I don't know. You never had to share him. I was glad to share my parents, glad they had something to think about besides me. You never did this before, I know that."

"And you and Granddaddy hate each other. I never heard you be nice to each other a single time. You leave Grandmother's the minute he comes in. Everyone says you aren't even in his will." Jessie stood up, faced Anna. The wind played a song in the trees above the graves. When did I hear that last? Anna thought. Who were we burying to that old sound?

"I'm trying to change that with my father," she said. "That's one reason I came home to live. To make my peace with him."

"How long do we have to stay here?" Jessie said. "Go tell them to hurry up." They were coming down the path, Daniel was talking, Olivia was looking up at him, hanging on his every word. She had her hand back on his sleeve. Jessie turned away and walked off in the direction of the road.

*   *   *

"I'm starving," Daniel said, when they were all back in the car. "Let's get over to the house and fix something to eat. How about it, Jessie, you want to help me feed this long-lost sister of yours?"

"I don't know how anybody can eat after we spent the morning at a graveyard. I'm going to be cremated when I die. I wouldn't let anybody bury me in the ground in some old concrete box."

"All right," Daniel said."Remember that, Anna, if Jessie dies she wants to be incinerated. Write that down."

"It isn't funny," Jessie said.

"A lot of people get cremated in Tahlequah," Olivia said. "It's the thing to do in a lot of places now."

"We could go riding if we could catch the horses," Jessie said. "They haven't been ridden in ages. You want to catch them and all go riding?" She turned to Olivia. It was the first remark she had addressed to her in thirty minutes. "Aunt Anna said you knew how to ride. We only have eastern saddles. Can you ride them?"

"I can ride anything." Olivia lifted her shoulders. "My great-grandfather was the president of the Cherokee Nation. He is in the history of my people. There is a painting of him in a museum in Tulsa." Her voice grew softer as she said it. Jessie looked at her sister now, really looked at her, saw a whole history outside her ability to imagine, then she looked away. She leaned up into the front seat and touched her father on the shoulder.

They caught the Appaloosas, Shane and Cyprian, and an old gelding that had belonged to Daniel when he was a boy and Jessie's little dark-maned mare. When they had saddled the horses Daniel asked Olivia which one she would like to ride.

"I'll take the big Appy," she said.

"Cyprian," Daniel added. He offered her a leg up and she swung herself into the saddle and leaned down and spoke into the horse's ear and he was still and stayed that way while the others mounted. "Let's ride to the pond," Jessie said. "It's four miles across the pastures. It's nice." She was on the mare. Daniel was on the other Appaloosa and Anna was riding the gelding, a horse so old that they had all forgotten his age. He nuzzled her boot, remembering the sugar lumps she had fed him down through the years.

It was a warm day for March, sunny and clear with only a small breeze. Daniel led the way out of the barnyard and up to the crest of the hill. A fenced pasture stretched out before them. In the distance was the small lake they called the Pond. There was a dam at one end and a levee.

"This is the kind of day when Phelan would have made us all go swimming," Anna said. "I haven't been swimming in March in years. I guess that means it's all over, doesn't it? 'The days run away like wild horses over the hill.' " She giggled, reached down and patted the old gelding, whose name was Aberdeen. "This old sweetie is named Aberdeen," she said to Olivia. "Because Daddy liked it there the only time Mother ever got him to leave the country."

"Will Cyprian jump?" Olivia asked. "Has anyone ever jumped him?"

"I don't know," Daniel answered. "Jessie, would you jump Cyprian?"

"I think he'll jump," Olivia said. "He feels like a jumper." She pulled out in front of them and began to ride toward the fence. She tossed her hair over her shoulders and was gone. Daniel rose up in his stirrups and laughed out loud. "Catch her, Jess," he yelled. "Let's see you ride." But there would be no catching Olivia. She was across the pasture and over the fence and gone. By the time they had her in sight again she was swimming Cyprian across the Pond. He struggled up the bank on the far side and she lay her body down across his neck and spoke to him and he was still. She sat on the saddle soaking wet and shivering and waited for them to come around by the Pond's edge.

"I had to do that," she said, when they reached her. "I'm sorry that I'm wet."

When they got back to the house Olivia changed into dry clothes and Daniel took her off to see the buildings and barns from when the place had been a working farm. Anna went into the kitchen to make dinner. Jessie sat in the living room reading old magazines, curled up on the sofa with a dark expression on her face. Finally, she came into the kitchen and began to search the pantry for a Coke.

"What a rude thing to do," she began. "She could have killed Cyprian. He's too old to be ridden like that."

"She just wanted to show off for your father. You do it."

"I do not. I don't ever do stuff like that."

"Let's show a little humanity around here, Jessie. She's not going to take your father's love away from you. She's an addition to this setup, not a problem. Of course, if you perceive it as a problem, it will be one. If you perceive it as an interesting thing that could enrich your life, it will be that too. But not for free. Nothing is free."

"Oh, my God, are you going to start lecturing me?"

"No, but hear me out. That's what's wrong with old Charlotte, Jessie. When this country was settled, it was created by adventurous people who thrived on challenge. Who wanted new things to happen and new ways of being, a new government even. But now it's all settled down and nothing new happens and it's as bad as the old world the settlers turned their backs on and left behind. Except for New Orleans and maybe Williamsburg and, oh well, never mind. Look, be kind to her, okay? You might need her someday."

"I doubt it. Are there any Cokes around here? Did you bring any?"

"In the trunk of the car. I haven't had time to get all the stuff out. Bring the rest of the groceries in, will you?" Anna put down the tomato she was peeling, wiped her hands, and pulled Jessie to her. "No one will ever take your place with me or with your dad or with any of us. Do you get that? Jessie, look at me. Do you believe that?"

"Yes. I guess so. I just don't see why she had to come here." She bit her lip, looked up, saw Anna's smile, began to laugh. You can always make Jessie laugh, Anna thought. Nothing *will* ever replace that divine little spark. "She is pretty, isn't she?" Jessie said. "I was thinking I would like Karen to see her. In a way she does sort of look like me. She really looks like you, though. Like you and Grandmother." She laughed out loud, taking a cookie from a sack Anna had opened onto a plate. "Dad's harem children. It's making him really nervous to have her here. I can tell."

"Get the groceries out of the car," Anna said. "And you can help fix this supper."

Things were better at dinner. Jessie ate four buttered rolls and began to tell Olivia about her friends. "At night everyone goes to the parking lot at Southpark Mall and people sit on their cars. Dad never lets me go. He never lets me go anywhere."

"That's not true," he said. "You have lots of freedom."

"To go to school or glee club." She waved a buttered roll in the air. "I'm free to go to boring boring boring school five days a week."

"I let you go to Southpark last week. With your buddy Hanna."

"They're having a band there tonight. To raise money for the Special Olympics. We could go there if Dad would let me. I'm not just saying that to get to go." She looked at him. Daniel filled Anna's wineglass and then his own. He waited. Jessie went on. "I could show her where people go at night. We'd be back in a couple of hours. I'll just drive her over there and come right back."

"Then go on," he said. He took a twenty-dollar bill out of his billfold and handed it to Jessie. Then he handed one to Olivia. "You can give this to the band or you can blow it on makeup." He laughed out loud. The air had cleared, had begun to clear.

When the girls had left Daniel opened another bottle of wine. Anna did the dishes, knowing the skin would peel off her fingers for a week from the detergent; she scrubbed the pots and dried them to a shine and put them all away.

"She can ride a goddamn horse," Daniel said. "Goddamn, she can ride. I'd like to see her in a show, with a real horse."

"I think she's more rodeo material. Daniel, be careful about Jessie. Don't let her get jealous."

"You're the one that thought this up, Anna. You're the one that thought she had to know her sister. Well, I like the little girl. I'm glad she came here."

"You should talk to them about money. Tell them about their inheritances and how much you will send Olivia and keep it all aboveboard and out in the open."

"What are you talking about now?"

"If I was Jessie I'd be afraid that Olivia would cut into my inheritance. The real fear is loss of your attention but it could manifest as worrying about money. Just have a talk with them."

"Anna, have a drink. Okay. You worry too much. I never saw anybody worry about things the way you do."

The girls returned in a few hours and bathed in the old-fashioned bathtub and rolled up their hair and went off to bed.

"I liked your friends," Olivia said. "The boy in the

jeep with that other boy is really good-looking. I think he likes you."

"He goes to Washington and Lee. I don't know what he was doing hanging around with those kids. I guess he got home for the weekend."

"What's his name?"

"William Lane. His folks live near my grandmother. He thinks he's a big shot."

"Boys are different here." Olivia watched Jessie's face. It was hard to tell what she was thinking. Hard to decide what she liked. Hard to know what to say.

"I've been thinking all afternoon about the way you ride. Where'd you learn to ride like that? I guess you've been doing it all your life, haven't you? I mean, I have too, but only on weekends, not all the time. Half the time I had to be with my mother. We were in Washington one year. I almost failed a year of school because of that."

"Everyone rides where I come from. People go to rodeos and horse fairs. It's poor country, Jessie. Not like this. There isn't much to do."

"You live out in the country?"

"On the edge of town. It's not a farm. It's just a house."

"What does it look like?"

"Just a house. It's small but we have enough room. My grandparents are there. I told you that."

"Do they bother you? Grandmother would drive me crazy if she lived with us. She's so particular about things."

"The moon's full," Olivia sat up on an elbow. The girls were in twin beds, in a small rectangular room, with moonlight coming in the windows through the old white lace curtains. "I love the moon," Olivia continued. "My Cherokee name is Tree. But it should be Moongirl. I have a friend whose name is Moongirl, but I don't see her now."

"Is it funny being here?"

"Yes. I thought he would want to talk with me. I guess he doesn't talk much."

"Not to me. He talks to his friends. When they get drunk. Or to his girlfriends. He has about eighty girlfriends."

"Oh."

"He likes you a lot. I can tell."

"Well, I guess I was expecting too much." They were quiet then, the moonlight pouring in over the white linen covers on their beds. Cloth that had come from Virginia with their great-grandmother, loomed by a great-great-aunt from flax grown in her yard and harvested and dried and spun.

"I like you too," Jessie continued, "and I'm glad you're here. I never saw anyone ride a horse like that in my life. Aunt Anna's eyes were a mile wide."

"She's nice. But she's sad somehow. I mean, there is something sad about her. Then she changes and is so funny."

"Dad said she used to be different. He says she has changed a lot."

"I'm going to sleep now."

"Olivia."

"Yes."

"He likes you. Dad likes you."

"I hope so. I hope that's true." The girls lay back on their beds and Olivia closed her eyes and tried to think of her home, of the yellow prairies and blue skies and her friends. But all she saw was her father's face and she dreamed all night that when she touched it, it came off in her hands, a ceremonial mask.

Anna went to bed also and Daniel rolled out a sofa bed in the den. By eleven o'clock they had turned out all the lights and gone to sleep. Our dreams will mingle in this house tonight, Anna was thinking as she curled around her pillow. We will be changed by this encounter. None of our lives will ever be the same. Life is so fucking wonderful and fecund. One night, maybe in Momma's house, and then this child is here, galloping over the hills and into the water. Jesus Christ, I'm sorry if it bothers Jessie but I'm glad I lived to see that. Oh, there are so many of them, oh, thank God for them. Sleep, Anna, leave it for now.

On Sunday morning the girls got up early and saddled the horses and went off on a trail ride.

"I think Jessie's starting to like her," Daniel said. "What do you think?"

"I think she's fascinated. You can always count on that, along with excitement. Yes, I think Jessie likes her; whether it inconveniences her to have a sister is another matter."

"It's a long goddamn weekend, I'll tell you that much."

"You need to spend some time with her alone," Anna said. "You should give her a chance to get to know you. When is her plane leaving?"

"At five."

"Take her to the airport alone. Leave Jessie with me at my apartment and take her to the airport. She might want to talk to you alone."

"She'll have plenty of time for that. We'll have her up again." He reached up in the cabinet and took down a bottle of whiskey and fixed himself a drink. Anna knew better than to press him. She took a book from the dusty shelf and went into a bedroom and pretended to read until the girls returned.

After lunch they packed up and left and drove back into Charlotte. Daniel let Anna off at her apartment. She went inside and took off all her clothes except her underpants and sat down in the exact center of a rose Karastan carpet and began to do yoga postures. She moved in and out of the ancient postures, cutting herself off, cutting herself out of the system. Breathe, she told herself. Only breathe. Breathe and move. After a while she fell asleep on the rug. When she woke it was night and the moon was shining in the windows. She moved into a sitting posture and thought about the moonlight and the distance to the moon, about the long years of her life and the wonder of men and women and of all existence, about DNA and RNA and protein molecules and replication and Olivia swimming Cyprian across the freezing pond and Jessie pouting on the couch, priceless and perfect in her jealousy and rage.

Anna turned half a circle into the moonlight, thinking of a night long ago when she and Phelan and Helen and LeLe Arnold and Dudley Manning and five or six other people whose names and faces she had forgotten had gone in three cars out to an abandoned borrow pit to swim on the Ides of March. Phelan had just discovered Julius Caesar. Niall was a little boy that year, eleven or twelve. He had begged to come and threatened to tell on them if they left him behind, so Niall was there, with his scout knife in a scabbard tied around his waist and wearing his famous Australian bush hat.

They had sneaked out and gone to the borrow pit at two o'clock in the morning, the very darkest part of night, and one by one had gone into the water. "Buddhist monks go swimming in the snow," Phelan had kept on saying. "You can will yourself not to freeze."

Later that summer, when it was warmer, they had parties at the borrow pit and drank beer and the moonlight lay upon the dangerous deep water and Anna had always been the one who stayed in the water the longest. Never anything, she decided now, not even love, could equal the soft cold smell and feel and touch of that water. There was no world to contend with then, only night and excitement and water, night and the moon and danger.

We were so terribly alive, she thought. How did I get so far away from that and from my brothers and my sisters?

She got up and went to her typewriter and began to write.

Dear Jessie, dear Olivia,
There are two hands on each body. If the right hand gets hurt, the left hand takes over.
There are supposed to be many children in a family. They may drive you nuts but they are your brothers and sisters. Tomorrow I'm going to take Helen out to lunch. She's my sister. If I need a sister I know her phone number. If she needs me, she knows mine.

Love,
Anna

In the morning Anna went over to Helen's house and waited while Helen made phone calls to the plumber and the roofer and the gardener and the high school principal and the Junior League Thrift Shop. Anna sat in her sister's kitchen and listened with great interest, real interest. She watched Helen move around her house in her sexy pink kimono making phone calls and putting things away and talking and getting dressed. She thought about what it must be like to make love to Helen, what did Helen do to men? What did she say?

"Did you ever suck a man's dick, Helen?" Helen was putting on a dress, the dress was halfway over Helen's head. The answer was muffled. "Of course." The dress came sliding down. Helen looked in the mirror and adjusted it. "But I don't do it unless he eats my pussy and I mean good and as long as I want him to. He knows the rules." She added a scarf to the dress. "How many have you sucked, Anna?"

"Tell me the rules." Anna got up from the bed. She

was amazed. Helen went to the dressing room mirror and worked on her hair. "Jesus, I never had rules."

"Well, why would you?" Helen was finished dressing now. She picked up her pocketbook and clutched it, good old matronly clutching style. "You never had them for anything else. Well, come on and tell me about Olivia. I know she came here. Momma and Daddy know it too. Everyone in town knows about it and about Daniel going out to Summerwood to hide it. He's too silly to live. I give up on him about half the time."

"I'll tell you about it. But that isn't why I want to have lunch. That's a secret. Come on, let's go."

Half an hour later they were settled at a table overlooking the golf course at the country club. Helen was sipping a whiskey sour. Anna was drinking a martini. The story of Olivia's visit had been told and questioned and retold. Now Anna took her sister's hand.

"This is a request, honey. I don't want it to bother you in any way. It's just a legality really, but important to me. I want to ask you a favor."

"Shoot."

"I want you to be my literary executor. To share it with a poet, an old friend in Boston. You see, Joel died, my agent, I told you when it happened, and there hasn't been anyone to replace her. I've been derelict in not doing something about it. Mike couldn't do it alone. If anything should happen to me, someone has to take care of my papers. It's for the children, the money goes to them, so it has to be done right. Will you do it?" Anna lifted her hand, sat back.

"Well, yes, if you want me to. I'd be honored, flattered, I mean." Helen looked down, sipped her drink. "Yes, I will do that if you want me to. But don't die." She giggled. "I won't do it if you die."

"I won't die," Anna said. "I'll always be here." The waiter appeared to take their order and they moved

closer to each other and drank their drinks and then
had another one and had wine with lunch and went
home very drunk and very silly. The next day Anna had
her lawyer rewrite her will and signed it in the presence
of witnesses and a copy was sent around to Helen, who
hid it in her desk. For some reason she felt like it should
be a secret.

"Dad wasn't nice to her." Jessie was watching Anna
dress. Sitting on Anna's bed with her legs wrapped up in
a silk blanket cover, her shoes were off, she was wearing
Anna's sable jacket on top of a blue sweat shirt that said
Esprit in pale yellow letters. "Can I have this coat when
you're tired of it?"

"Yes, you can. I shouldn't have bought that silly thing.
Every time I see a nature film on television I'm sorry I
bought it.

"They're going to die anyway."

"That's one way to look at it. So what's this about your
dad being mean to Olivia?" Anna finished her makeup
and began to look in her closet for something to wear.
She was taking Jessie to the bookstore to find a book for
a book report she had to write.

"He didn't even kiss her goodbye. She was trying to
kiss him and he just held her away from him. I told him
about it. I told him if my mother had run off to London
with me he might be acting like that to me. I might go
up there and visit her this summer."

"To Oklahoma?"

"Yeah."

"Do you think she had a good time? Was she glad she
came?"

"I guess so. I got your letter by the way. It was nice. So
you should have seen Connie when I told her about it
today. She said she'd give anything to have a life as
exciting as mine."

Anna watched Jessie's reflection in the mirror. She

snuggled her chin down into the fur. Her flawless skin and her soft light hair lay against the dark fur. Her lips assumed a wonderful thick pout. Anna had been tired all day, had been in bed all afternoon getting up the energy to get dressed to take Jessie to the store. Now she drew energy from the child, she remembered her own skin and hair at sixteen, the burning energy of her blood. How do we bear to be that powerful? Anna thought. To be sixteen.

"Let's go get your book," she said. "And then let's go buy some clothes. Let's buy something sensational and wear it home from the store."

"Oh, Aunt Anna, you're really nuts, you know it. I'm so glad you're here."

৩১৩ 13 ৫৬৯

ৡৣ DURING APRIL Anna was not feeling well. She was sleeping late in the mornings. She kept getting tired. She shook it off, drank pots of coffee, felt worse. One morning she felt so bad she went down to the drugstore and walked up and down the aisles looking for something to make her feel better. She picked up a package of over-the-counter diet pills, read the claims, remembering Dexedrine and Ritalin in the days when people took drugs for fun.

She took the package of diet pills to the checkout stand. "Do these things work?" she asked the boy behind the counter.

"To lose weight?"

"No, to get you in a better mood."

"I wouldn't take them if I was you," he answered. "My sister takes them. She says they make her feel like shit. I mean, terrible."

"I guess I better not buy them then."

"Whatever you like." He wasn't annoyed. It was a slow morning anyway.

"I'll take them," she said. "Ring them up."

*   *   *

She walked out of the drugstore and threw the package into a trash container. Then she got into the car and drove back home and poured herself a drink. It was ten thirty in the morning.

This is just depression, she told herself. My lifetime of mania has finally caught up with me and now it's time to be depressed. She sipped the drink, walked over to her desk, and began to sort through piles of mail. There was an anthology from Ireland containing one of her poems and a letter from LeLe Arnold and a card from Adam. In the middle of the stack of mail was the latest box of gold coins her father had sold her. She picked it up, shook her head. It made her feel better just to hold the box. That glorious old man, she thought. My God, I love him. Every man I ever loved is just a replay of those emotions. I remember every word he's ever said to me. Indelible, never to be erased. Not to mention all those goddamn handwritten letters of advice that have followed me around the world. Those goddamn yellow legal pads. Every time I ever saw one I thought a piece of advice was going to jump out and grab me by the throat. Whatever goes on between that old man and me is the real thing.

She sat down in a chair, feeling woozy and disoriented. The gin was not helping. The gin was making it worse. I think I'll go bury these coins out at the cemetery where Phelan and I buried those medallions and silver dollars. I can't keep a hundred and fifty thousand dollars' worth of gold coins lying around an apartment. I'll do it. I'll bury them today. That ought to cheer me up.

She got up, poured another glass of gin and drank it, put the package of coins in a canvas bag, and began to collect the other boxes from where she had hidden them around the apartment. One was in a pottery urn from Greece. One was in an old cosmetic kit. The rest were in a drawer with her nightgowns where she had put them hoping to remember to take them to the bank. She packed up all the coins and drove over to the hardware store and bought a shovel and started driving toward the country. I'll make a geometric design, she decided. I will make a parallelogram. I always liked parallelograms. They were always my favorite geometric figure.

By three that afternoon the coins were in the ground. When she had patted the last piece of earth down on the last box of coins Anna sat on a tombstone and drew a diagram of where they were. Then she translated the diagram into complicated mathematical formulas. Then she made a fake list of dates and amounts. Then she got up and walked around paying her respects to her grandparents and great-grandparents. Then she walked back to the more recent graves and stood by the grave of Francis Gautier. "I would have stopped by when we were here with Olivia," she said. "But I didn't want to make those young girls sad. I'm sorry the water has left your protein molecules, Francis, but I'm not mad at you for dying anymore. I don't think I'm mad at anybody. I might be. Otherwise why do I feel so terrible all the time. I was drinking in the morning, Frank. Can you believe that? Well, what the hell. I love you and now I'm going swimming."

She walked back to the car. She drove down a dirt road and across a pasture and through a gate and came to a stop beside the Pond. She got out of the car and took off most of her clothes. She took off everything but a pair of cotton underpants and white silk T-shirt. She walked over to the Pond's edge and waded in. She waded out until the water was waist deep. It was just cold enough to be exciting. Remembering excitement is better than no excitement at all,

Anna decided. But goddamn the bottom of this pond is filthy.

When the children were small Mr. Hand had kept sand poured for a beach but it was all gone now and the bottom was full of leaves and mulch. Anna walked out farther until she could stretch out in the soft muddy water. She floated for a minute, then began to swim. She swam out to the dam, gingerly at first, then with more abandon. When she reached the dam she pulled herself up onto it, scaring a pair of mud turtles from a log. Something's wrong with me, she told the Pond and the turtles and sky. Why don't I do something about it? Why don't I care?

She slid back down into the water, feeling better than she had felt in days. It's the end of April, she thought. I'm a month late. We have turned into pussies, Phelan. We have turned into pussies in our sleep.

That was April. In May and June and July Anna worked on a new book, keeping the phone off the hook, working very carefully, agonizing over details, more serious than she had been in years about her work. It was a strange tangled manuscript, written in several voices. It was called *Winter* and it was about Jessie's mother. Sheila, Anna would say to herself as she worked. Our Richard. The winter of our discontent. When I finish this I could write the history of Olivia, a girl named Tree whose mother was named Summer.

"What's going on with Olivia?" she asked Daniel whenever she saw him. "When are you going there to visit?"

"Before too long," he would answer. "When I can take time from work."

By August Anna was feeling better. She felt better for many weeks. She went to New York and got drunk with her editor and told him about the book. "It better not really be her mother," he said. "Is it really her mother, Anna?"

"No, only my perceptions. Do you know the line from *The Tempest,* 'Come, Spirit, it is time to deal with Caliban'? That's the theme of it. I want to explore evil and Sheila MacNiece is evil. She's the closest thing to evil I have ever known. I want to sort it out, try to understand it."

"Has anyone seen it?"

"No, it's in a suitcase. It's the kind of manuscript that needs to be kept in a suitcase."

"Are you seeing Philip? Do you want to bring him out to dinner?"

"Yes. No. Do you want to see the book?"

"Whenever you want to show it to me. Whenever you are ready."

She stayed in New York for several weeks, seeing Philip, buying clothes, feeling good in the clear fall weather. She even started making plans to go to London to do research for the book.

"I will make it up," she told her editor. "I will make up every word of it."

"You better," he answered.

In October she went home and canceled the plans to go to London. She had begun to sleep in the daytime again.

"What's going on with Anna?" Mrs. Hand asked Helen.

"How would I know? I'd be the last to know."

"I don't like the way she looks. She looks tired. She's too thin."

"I begged her to go to Brian and get a checkup or vitamins or something, but you know Anna, Mother. She doesn't do anything unless she thinks it up."

"I would go over there and see about her but she always acts like I'm in her way."

"You are in her way. Everyone's in her way. She just stays over there like a hermit."

"What did I ever do to raise someone to be a hermit. Just tell me that. To raise someone who doesn't have time for other people."

"It's all right," Helen said. "Maybe it's just a stage she's going through."

෴ 14 ෴

෴ NOVEMBER, NINETEEN EIGHTY-FIVE. It's getting worse. The cuts don't heal. Every time I scratch my leg it takes forever to get well. I've got to take some vitamins or something. No, this is stress. This is some sort of stress and all I need to do is some yoga and get a new lover. Or an old lover. I should call Adam at Vanderbilt and have him come down for the weekend. I should do that. But it isn't right to make him love me. Why did I go and fall in love with Philip? Why is it taking so long to get over it? I almost fainted the other day and my hair is getting thin, it is, I'm not imagining things. I am imagining every bit of this. It's all imagination. The whole thing. Reality is our conception, all of it, Philip, Adam, and even the memory of Francis, I dreamed he came to me and wept for the loneliness of my life. I dreamed he begged me to forgive him for dying. Hit, hit, hit. Where is that from? Never mind, I'll go back to New York and see Philip and be happy for a few days. I'm happy now. Go to sleep. I'm my mother's child. She is right around the corner, loving me. And Daniel and Jessie and Olivia and James and Niall and Louise the runaway and Helen, God bless her little bourgeois heart, and so many. LeLe and Phelan and Crystal and that crazy little girl of hers, Crystal Anne, my God. I had not known life had undone so many. Sleep, Anna, close your eyes and sleep. Stop thinking.

A week later she found the first lump. She was walking across her bedroom wearing a slip. She was thinking about something that had crossed her mind in the shower, or in a dream, or in the middle of the night. She stopped and touched her breast with her hand and it was there. Very large, larger than she had dreamed such a thing might be. As large as a marble, as a golden taw. I knew this last night, she thought. I knew it yesterday. I have known it for a long time. Even I can't ignore this goddamn lump.

She walked across the dressing room and picked up her clothes from a wooden bench beneath a painting and put them on without looking in the mirror. Without glancing one time in the mirror she finished dressing and went downstairs and got in the car and drove to Brian's office. A nurse took blood from her arm and she lay down on the table and Brian found three more. Two on one side and two on the other.

"If it were cancer, how long would I have?"

"Maybe forever. There are lots of things to do."

"Like be a cripple, an invalid, have my breasts cut off, have my hair fall out. Go to the hospital all the time, have people feel sorry for me."

"Anna."

"I won't do it, Brian. I don't have children. How soon can you know?"

"We can do the biopsy in the morning."

"Not here. Not in this hospital. It will be all over town."

"Where else?"

"I don't know. Lexington maybe."

"You can go there if you like. Anna, this is crazy. I can keep it confidential."

"All right. What time tomorrow?"

"Is eight all right with you?"

"It's fine. Don't tell anyone. Don't tell a soul."

Two days later he told her the results. It was very bad. It had to be stopped at once. It had to be stopped with all the ammunition he could muster. She agreed to let him treat her. Then she left by the side door and walked down the stone steps to the parking lot. The leaves on the oak trees were golden and orange and dark red. Like the heart of fire, she thought. Our brains are not programmed for infinity. Death and infinity. I am glad I have spent my life thinking of these things. It will come in handy now. Ought to come in handy. Don't think, Anna. Just drive the car.

Anna pulled a pair of beige slacks off a hanger and a soft white blouse and put them on and added a tweed jacket and ran a comb through her hair. Live the moment, she told herself. There is nothing to fear. Nothing in the world to fear. Matter is neither created nor destroyed. All I'm going to do is shut down a system.

In the downstairs hall she added a yellow scarf to her outfit. An artist must remind the world of yellow, she was thinking. Remember that terrible writers' conference on the West Coast and the poet who always wore a red scarf and took his children everywhere. There were wild flowers on the bluffs that summer, huge wild flowers as big as my hand. And all the women stayed inside and worried about getting published. I went to the poet's dances and ate the wild berries we picked and walked at dawn and one morning I came upon four young people sleeping on the grass at the very edge of a precipice, asleep on thin, gray blankets, all wet with the dew. I have lived my life. I have not forgotten to be alive. I was glad to be here.

She picked up her bag and the small suitcase containing the manuscript called *Winter* and turned off the lights and went down the stairs and out to the car and drove to the airport the long way across the lake, where once she had driven a motorboat fifty miles an hour from one end to the other from the simple joy of being alive. She looked out across the water, remembering the spray coming in around the windshield of the old Boston Whaler and how she had had the lake to herself that day, so early in the morning on a summer day and she was celebrating because she was going to marry a poet and get the hell out of North Carolina forever and ever, amen. A new world where she would be happy all the time. And I would have been, Anna thought. If he hadn't died I would have been happy. Now I'll see him I suppose. Wherever I'm going Frank will be there too. Don't start that. Do it with courage. See Philip one last time, then do it. Let him be there when I call. He won't know. If I get sick I can take the pills Brian gave me. He will touch my breasts. He will know. I can get around that. Somehow.

Anna crossed the lake and turned off past the Little People's Company, a kindergarten where one of her nieces was spending an IQ of 140 teaching three-year-olds to swing. Blaming herself for her mother's weakness and her father's winesoaked nights and mistresses.

Wasted intelligence is nothing, Anna told herself as she passed her niece's school. You should have been lucky enough to spend your days with children. Maybe Aleece will go back to school in a few years. I left the money for them, all those crazy nieces and nephews. Poor Helen, having to administer all that. Don't think of Helen. Don't think of Helen with the papers. My God. Still, it might get her through middle age. Who

knows, she and Mike might like each other. Let go,
Anna, leave the world. It's okay. They won't even miss
you in a year or two. You have a day, two days, three
days if he'll go up there with you. This last little piece
of time, like a ball of the densest material in the universe, like uranium, dense, thick and round. It will
burst apart and sail out across the stars when you have
used it up.

She hurried into the airport and checked her bags
and walked down a ramp to the plane and sat back and
ordered a Bloody Mary.

He said yes. He came and got her off the plane and
drove her up the coast to Biddeford. He knew something was wrong, but he thought it was a man. He
thought it was another man he was up against.

Saturday morning was snow-covered and cold and
clear. Philip stepped out onto the porch of the rented
cottage and watched the wind bending the trees on the
bluff across the way. The wind sailed up and down the
screens on the windows. It howled across the water and
tore past the neighboring hotel and disappeared over
the hills in a sea of flattened grass.

Philip's hands were thrust deep into his pockets. He
was wearing wool slacks and a blue sweater his wife had
bought him in Scotland. He was thinking about Anna,
the alarming pallor of her skin. It read like disease. It
smelled like disease.

"I love thee," she said, coming to stand behind him in
the doorframe. "Thee and thy cashmere sweaters. Come
back here." He turned and took her into his arms and
began to waltz her back down the hall. He lifted her
body from the floor as she hummed "The Blue Danube
Waltz." He waltzed her all the way down the hall and
into the parlor with the fire and around the soft rugs
and onto a sofa. She was worn on top of him like a badge

when he stopped. "How do you remember all the notes?" he asked.

"I'm a musician. You always forget that. You've never even heard me play."

"And I've never read the books."

"That's a lie. You have read them all a dozen times. You read them before you met me."

"What makes you think so?"

"Arthur told me so. We got drunk together the last time I was in New York and I got it out of him."

"He would never tell on me."

"I got it out of him in the bar of the Warwick Hotel on Sixth Avenue. Last August."

"Why didn't you call me? Why didn't you tell me you were there?"

"I wasn't there. I stopped off for one day to be on some television show and talk to Arthur and he came and got me and we got drunk in the Warwick Bar and he said, did I still see you, and I said no, and he said, well, he didn't either, and then he said, well, that's the price you pay for getting involved with a fan. Then I didn't say anything, and he said you adored my books. Or your wife adored my books. Did you make that coffee or not?" She was lying across him with her legs spread out over his legs and her hands across his cheeks and a very long time seemed to go by while no one said anything. "This is the time of times," she said finally. "This is an eternity if we let it be." He moved her body until she was sitting across his lap.

"No, it isn't. It's a long weekend in Maine in dangerous and dramatic weather. God, you have me talking like you do. Look at me, Anna. Look at me." She looked at him. She raised her face to his, feeling the beginning of the pain in her arms and chest but only the beginning, nothing that would show.

"I'm looking."

"You must marry me. Or, more correctly, I must

marry you. We must be married. You were right about
that. All these months that have gone on without you
and every day I thought about you. No, wait, don't turn
away. I've already told her. I told her when I left yesterday. I told her that I loved you and was going to ask
you to marry me. She took it pretty well. She took it
okay." Now it was his turn to look away. "She said she
was relieved."

"No, no, no," Anna said. She kissed him. Then kissed
him again. "That's a big fat lie you made up to get me to
cook breakfast and it isn't going to work. Make the
coffee. Cook the eggs. Fuck me, my slave."

"Will you? Will you marry me?"

"I might. And then I might not. Show me why I
should want to."

She meant to wait until Monday to do it. Until after he
had left, but on Sunday morning he brought up the
subject of her health and he wasn't satisfied with her
answers so she went on and did it Sunday morning
instead. She left him at ten o'clock on Sunday morning
saying she was going to drive to the store for marmalade.

"Goodbye," she said at the door. "Wait, come here, I
want to tell you goodbye." She put her arms around him
and held him for a long time. They had made love not
thirty minutes before, but now she held him and would
not let go.

"Why are you going out in this weather?"

"Because I want some marmalade. You're the one
who says I'm thin. Well, I'll fatten up." She was saying
this but it wasn't what he was hearing and Anna never
lied. "Goodbye," she said again. "Goodbye."

"Anna." She turned him loose, then walked away,
then stopped and buttoned her jacket, then walked back
into the foyer and hugged him again. Then she ran
down the steps and got into the car and drove away. He

would be playing this scene in his mind over and over for years, and then only occasionally, and then only when he heard the sea or saw one of her books somewhere or walked into a dark room or attended a funeral. After enough years it was only another memory.

One last thing remained to be done. Anna stopped at an oyster bar that wasn't open yet. An old man was sweeping the steps and he smiled at her out of old blue eyes and agreed to let her use the phone. Anna thanked him three times for letting her come in. Then she put a quarter in the pay phone and called Adam. He was asleep when the phone rang, in a room near the Vanderbilt campus. He was alone and asleep and the ringing of the phone was wrong and bad and he knew that across all those miles and answered it without the sleep showing in his voice.

"Where are you, Anna? Where have you been?"

"It doesn't matter. It's all right. Listen, Adam, I love you. I want you to know that. I love you and I care about you and I'm proud of you. What a fine man you are."

"What's this about? Why haven't you answered my letters? Anna, where are you?"

"I'm in Maine. I called to say goodbye." She paused, bit her lip. "Adam, I called to tell you goodbye."

"Why don't you come to Nashville and live with me instead? I think you sound terrible. I haven't liked anything since you went back to that goddamn Charlotte and I'll tell you something else. I'm lonesome, Anna. I miss you."

"You need a girl your own age to have children with. Don't think of me. Adam, listen to me."

"Dammit, where are you, Anna?" There was something in her voice, something terrible and compelling, and he listened.

"I love you. I called to tell you goodbye. To thank you

for the days and nights we had. Oh, this is terrible. I shouldn't do this."

"If you won't live with me, it is. Wait a minute. I want to get a cigarette."

"Adam."

"Yes."

"I love you. Take care of yourself." She hung up. She was ashamed of herself for calling him. Shame will be a nice final emotion, she decided. That's a good one. Remember when Francis told me that when we died the world would still owe us plenty so not to worry about any happiness we could steal. I remember that. And I knew it was true. It is true, goddammit.

She thanked the old man again and walked out past the dirty bar stools and then through the dirty foyer and down the dirty wooden steps and the ocean lay before her, gray and stormy and real. Cold and real. It was possible to turn back but she didn't want to. The alternative was a bed in a hospital and knives and terror. One big terror or a lot of little terrors. Death was going to win, either way. Poor Helen, Anna thought. She'll never figure this one out. Time will heal the others, except for Adam. He may be stuck with me. I hope not. Oh, God, I hope he gets some joy. What a joyous light-hearted lover, with his tool belt and his grace. So graceful. I bet LeLe would like him. I should have left him LeLe's address. Now, get in the car and go on. It's getting late.

It was getting late. It was eleven o'clock in the morning. By eleven thirty she was gone. She left the car beside the pier with the letters on the seat. By two o'clock the police had opened them and called Philip. Then they came to get him and took him to the pier. He waited until four to call Anna's sister Helen. Then he had a drink with the police chaplain and called Anna's editor. Then he called his wife.

* * *

He threw the blue sweater away. He threw away everything he was wearing, piece by piece. Over a period of months he identified every article of clothing he had been wearing on that Sunday morning and he got rid of them. He punished them as if they were bad children or as if the germs of Anna's madness could hide in clothes and germinate and grow.

Not madness, he decided finally. Mortality. It is mortality that maddens us. That goddamn child in Saint Vincent's. His pain. Anna. Me. We have a right to anger. We have a right to thrash out against it and take it into our hands. She could have told me. I might have helped her. I might have done what? Being here, and then gone forever, and we are supposed to rationalize that, justify it, forgive, I wish I had been born in an older world and could blame it on the gods.

⁖ II ⁘

Elegy and Psalm

ᔕᑫᓫ 15 ᓂᔕ

ᔕᑫᓫ NIALL AND DANIEL went with Helen to tell their parents. Daniel picked up Niall and they picked up Helen and she rode in the middle of the front seat of Daniel's Jaguar and they all talked at once, then they were quiet. "I knew she was sick," Daniel said. "She was acting so bad, being such a bitch to everyone. Something was wrong."

"She told you you were drinking because it was true. But she shouldn't have done this like this. I will never forgive her." This from Niall.

"No," Helen said. "She was sick with cancer. It's okay. She had a right to her death." Phelan will be here, she was thinking. He will come as soon as he hears.

"Then she should have called them and told them she was going to, or written a note. God, I can't believe it. If it gets on the news or something before we get there."

"We're almost there. It's only a block." Daniel speeded up, passing the Hands' next-door neighbor out for a walk with her Seeing-Eye dog, then almost knocking over the garbage cans as he turned the car into his parents' long uphill driveway. They got out and walked into the house. Mrs. Hand was in the kitchen making a cake. She had on a yellow silk dress and beautiful little high-heeled shoes. She was so soft, so sweet, so gentle. She turned as they came in.

"Anna is gone, Momma," Helen said. She went to her mother and took her into her arms, encircled her mother with her arms. Daniel moved in, close, with Niall behind him. "Anna has been in an accident."

"Gone," their mother said. "Gone. What do you mean, Helen?" She pulled out of Helen's embrace, leaned into the kitchen counter to escape Helen's arms. They were in a narrow part of the kitchen, the four of them crowded into a space between three doors. "Where has Anna gone?"

"She was in an accident," Niall said. "We think she might be dead."

"She is dead," Daniel said. "She is gone."

"How?" Mrs. Hand said. "How is that? What are you saying, Daniel? What do you mean, Helen?"

"She was sick." Helen looked at her brothers. They had always taken the blame for each other, all of them had always taken the blame for everything any of them did, as if any one of them could have done anything that happened and the villain of the moment was only the one who got there first to act it out. Helen felt guilty now, terrible and guilty, and Niall felt especially guilty because he had just been saying terrible things about Anna to his wife. Daniel took over. "She killed herself, Momma, because she had the worst kind of cancer you can get. She is gone."

"Not Anna," Mrs. Hand said. "Anna wouldn't do that. Anna wouldn't deny God. How could she kill herself?"

"She was sick, Momma," Helen said. "Come on, let's go lie down on your bed. We have to tell Daddy. Where is Daddy?"

"Daddy's here. He's in the back. He might be reading. Not Anna, Helen. She just got home." Then Mrs. Hand was in Daniel's arms and he was leading her through the house to her bedroom and Niall followed them and reached out a hand and touched his mother's back.

They found their father in the bedroom reading a book and they sat around him on the bed and told him and his eyes sought out his wife's and he put the book away and began to cry. At that his children began to cry also and the wake of Anna Elizabeth Hand, which would last six days and end in a silly pointless memorial service in a church she hadn't entered for years, began.

The first night lasted until dawn. Mr. Hand finished weeping and washed his face and hands and sat in a chair by the fireplace allowing people to embrace him. Mrs. Hand sat across from him on a sofa by the telephone, answering the phone and telling the story over and over again. People began to appear. Children and grandchildren, friends, men and women who had worked for Mr. Hand, people who had known Anna when she was a child. "I knew it all along," her mother kept saying. "It was in her face."

At some point in the evening Helen remembered Olivia. She took Daniel into the kitchen. Mrs. Hand's maid, Victoria, was there, with her sister, preparing food, asparagus casserole and a roast. Victoria was weeping as she cooked. Helen envied her that. Helen squeezed the hand Victoria offered her and took the extravagant sympathy that accompanied it. Victoria's sorrow was twofold, empathy for Mrs. Hand and regret that she had taken advantage of Anna's poor eyesight and inattention to detail to never really clean the corners in the apartment when she helped out over there. They will all see it now, she was thinking. When they go over there to sort out her things.

"I'll help you with Anna's apartment," Victoria said. "If you need help with that, let me know."

"I will," Helen said. She took a piece of asparagus in

her fingers as she pulled Daniel past the ovens and the breakfast table into the pantry.

"You need to call that child in Oklahoma and tell her," Helen said. "Before she hears it on the news."

"Oh, God, I hadn't thought of that. I don't think we should do that."

"Of course you should. She adored Anna."

"All right, I'll do it later. I'm glad you remembered. What will I say to her?"

"Tell her the truth. There aren't going to be any secrets about this, Daniel." He was quiet and Helen went on. "Eat something. Get some food. We've got to stay here tonight. We all have to sleep here. Send for some things if you need them."

"I'm all right. Daddy has everything I need."

"It couldn't be true. How could this be true?" Helen put her arms around her brother and they held each other, surrounded by the cake pans and Waring blenders and breadboxes and flower vases of their childhood. They could have opened the breadbox at any moment in their lives and found soda crackers and graham crackers and vanilla wafers and whole wheat bread and dry cereal. A big black breadbox that had come from a river house on the Catawba River they had gone to every summer when they were young. Helen opened the top. Everything was there. She took a handful of vanilla wafers and held them out to her brother. They ate the cookies in silence, then Helen started again.

"You need to call her right away."

"Goddammit, Helen, don't start in again."

"Well, it has to be done soon. I'll call her if you want me to."

"I'll call her. I said I'd call her. When I get time."

"She'll hear about it on the news."

"You've told me that. All right, I'll call her now. What should I say?"

"Just call her up and tell her. Perhaps you should ask

her to come to the service. No, I don't suppose that's necessary."

"I'll decide if it's necessary. Jesus, Helen, you're worse than Anna. Stop sticking your nose into my goddamn business, please. I've got a funeral to run." He stared down at the top of her head. Her soft little permanent wave was not holding up very well this week. She had missed her appointment at the beauty parlor when news came that she had to go to Boston. She pushed the curls up around her temples.

"I look like hell. I know that. Well, do you want me to call her then? Someone has to do it, Daniel. We can't let that child read about this in a newspaper." He gave up. He was not going to overpower Helen tonight in this pantry.

"Okay. I'll call her. I'll call her as soon as I can. You go take care of Mother. Don't leave them alone in there to greet people." Helen left and Daniel stopped in the kitchen and fixed himself a drink, three jiggers of scotch and four cubes of ice and no water, and, carrying it, he went into the library to make the call. When he picked up the phone Phelan Manning was on the line. He was on his way to Charlotte with his nephew, King Mallison, Junior. He talked to Daniel for about ten minutes and as soon as Phelan hung up, James Junior called from the hospital. Finally Daniel went into the kitchen and fixed a second drink and walked out the back door and around through the yard to his mother and father's part of the house, a bedroom and guest room joined by a bathroom. The guest room was an octagonal-shaped room with many windows, which looked out on a rose garden. When the Hand children were small the room was used as a sick bay. Any child who was sick was put to bed in there so that Mrs. Hand could hear them if they cried.

Daniel sat down on the bed to make the call. The bed was covered by a yellow and blue chintz bedspread that matched the trim on the wallpaper. Daniel sat with his hand on the telephone looking back and forth from the bedspread to the bedside lamps, which were cast in the shapes of shepherdesses holding crooks. Once, right after the room was decorated, Daniel had spent two days there recuperating from having his wisdom teeth extracted. He had been eighteen years old, on his way to the university in two weeks' time. It was the very heart of August, the hottest part of summer, and Mrs. Hand had come in and out of the room bringing fans and ice packs and glasses of cool weak tea, which he sipped through bendable straws. In the night he had heard his mother and father talking about him in the adjoining room.

"It had to happen now," his mother was saying. "Why did this have to happen now?"

"It's only his wisdom teeth," his father answered. "Daniel's got worse problems than having his wisdom teeth pulled the week before he goes off to school."

"He's too young. We should have held him back. It's your fault he started so young. He was too immature and he should never have gone that soon."

"Oh, for God's sake, Annie, would you let me get some sleep. Come here, I want to hold you." Daniel had put the pillow over his head so he would not hear the rest. He sat on the bed now and ran his hand across the chintz bedspread. It had been the height of style when his mother folded it across a chair during his recovery to keep him from bleeding on it as he healed. I have to call that little girl, he thought. That goddamn Helen's going to drive me crazy if I don't, so, what the hell.

The line was busy to Olivia's house in Oklahoma. Daniel tried the call several times but the line kept being busy. He gave up. Then he went into the living room and found Jessie and told her he had been trying to call her sister.

"Do you think she will come here, to be here?" Jessie asked.

"Oh, I don't think that would be a good idea."

"Why not? Why wouldn't it? She might feel left out."

"Don't worry about it, Jess. Just leave all that to me. I thought you were going to get your clothes. Phelan's coming. He's bringing his nephew from New Orleans. They were on their way to go hunting so he's got this kid with him. Do you remember King Mallison from New Orleans?"

"Why couldn't she come if she felt she wanted to?"

"Jessie, take your car and go on out and get your clothes. Bring me a shirt if you think about it."

"What kind?"

"White oxford cloth, a dress shirt. Anything, go on." He left her then and went to see about the guests and she got in her car and drove out to their house.

Olivia was waiting for her aunt Mary Lily to have a prescription filled. She had left her homework and gone with her aunt to a store on the edge of Tahlequah because it wasn't good for women to be out alone at night in that part of town. Her aunt was standing in a long line of customers at the Economy druggist's window. I wish we didn't have to use food stamps for everything, Olivia thought. When I get older, we won't have them. We will pay for things with cash because I am going to make enough money for everything. I am going to be a pilot if I have to or whatever I have to do. A newspaper editor might make a lot of money. I know I can do it. I don't have any doubts about it. I will never turn in a food stamp or a welfare check or take charity from anyone, even my father. I am a Hand and we don't take coupons. She turned to the magazine rack, picked up a *USA Today* and there was Anna's picture, on the front page. "Noted Author Dies by Drowning." She read the story quickly, then walked over to where her aunt was standing. "My aunt's dead," she said. "It can't be true. How could she die?" She leaned into her aunt Mary Lily's soft black coat.

There was a letter in the mail to Olivia from Anna but Olivia wouldn't get it for many days. *Dear Olivia,* the letter began.

I am only writing three letters before I do this thing. This is the last one. It is to say I love you and beg you to forgive me and to understand. I can't bear pain, can't be in the power of other people, even in a hospital. It is a fault of character and has limited me in many ways. I write that but I am not sure I believe it. Live a long and happy life. Create if you can and always wonder and always laugh. Don't be afraid to love or to cry. Love Jessie and care for her. Don't tell her I wrote to you or, if you do, say this letter is for her too. It is. I'm in a hurry now. Everything is so good and goes too fast. It has given me great joy to know you were in the world. Thank you for finding me. There is a provision in my will to help with your education. Someone will contact you about it later. Forgive me. Love and love and love —

Aunt Anna

"I have to go there," Olivia was saying now. "I have to go to Charlotte to be with my father and my sister. I have to go to her funeral."

"Yes," Mary Lily agreed. "It would be right. What should we do?"

"Is there money in the bank now?"

"Yes."

"Then we must go home and call the airport in Tulsa and see when they have a plane."

"Now?"

"Yes, now. Go on, get the prescription for Grandfather. Then we must leave." Mary Lily turned back to the line and explained the problem and the other customers allowed her to be waited on next and when she had collected the prescription she and Olivia left and drove as fast as they dared to their house. Olivia made a reservation on a plane, then tried to call her father's home. The phone rang for a long time. At last Jessie answered it.

"I want to come there," Olivia said. "I read about it. It can't be true."

"Dad called you. He tried and tried to call but the line kept being busy."

"I have an airplane ticket. To come tonight. Can I come there, Jessie? Is that all right?"

"Come on," she said. "I'll meet your plane. When does it get in?"

"At five thirty in the morning. Will it keep you from getting to school?"

"School doesn't matter. I can't go now anyway. Oh, God, you wouldn't believe what's going on. They can't even have a funeral. It's so terrible. It's terrible. Everyone is crying and standing around. Granddaddy had to go to bed. He never goes to bed. No one ever saw him cry unless he wanted something he couldn't have. And listen, she knew she had it and she told our friend Brian, he's a doctor, that she would go into the hospital and instead she went off to be with this man she loves and then she did it. It's unbelievable." Jessie paused for breath. "Listen, they found cyanide in her car. We think she got it out of our cousin James's darkroom. He used it for making blueprints. Or else she bought it at a camera store. James is getting out on leave from the hospital tonight to check to see if any of his is missing. He thinks it might all be his fault. He was crying like crazy when I talked to him. He's as bad as Granddaddy. Listen, we don't know what will happen to Grandmother. She's acting like it's some kind of wedding. She keeps saying, 'I don't know how we'll have a wedding if we can't find Anna.'

The police have been there four times. And these reporters."

"Are you sure you can meet me? I could get a taxicab. I have plenty of money."

"No, I'll be there. Dad's at Grandmother's. Don't tell him you're coming. I'll come get you. What's the number of the flight? Listen, I was such a disappointment to her. I think I may have made her sick. I wouldn't go to my piano lessons. She got me lessons with this wonderful teacher she knows and I didn't go half the time. Listen, don't bring many things. You can wear my clothes."

"It's Delta flight four forty-six. It gets there at five thirty in the morning."

"I'll be there." Jessie hung up the phone. It was dark in the living room. She turned on a lamp. Took one of her father's Camel cigarettes out of the package and lit it. She sat in the dark, smoking, squeezing a few tears out of the sides of her eyes. I'd better take a bath and change clothes and get some makeup on, she decided. I may have to be up all night.

Olivia's family hovered around as she packed a few things in a suitcase and brushed her teeth and combed her hair and tied it back with a long blue scarf. She took off the dress she was wearing and put on her best school clothes. Her navy blue skirt and a long-sleeved white blouse and a navy blazer. Her grandfather had polished her shoes while she was packing. He held them out to her now. Olivia pulled navy blue knee-socks onto her legs and then sat on the edge of the bed and laced the brown shoes. She stood up and kissed each of her grandparents goodbye, very seriously and slowly. Her grandmother reached in her pocket and took out a ten-dollar bill and put it into her hand.

"You should have told your father," her aunt said, as

she was taking her to the airport. "He should know that you are doing this."

"It's all right," Olivia answered. "It's how Jessie does things. She's probably told him by now." She giggled. "She's probably told ten or eleven people by now."

The plane was almost empty from Tulsa to Dallas. A drunk man from Jackson, Mississippi, kept trying to talk to Olivia. She had very obviously been crying. "What's wrong, little girl?" he kept asking, but the stewardess interrupted him and took a seat beside Olivia. "You're going to a funeral?"

"My aunt died. She was a writer."

"Oh, I read all the time. What's her name?"

"Anna Hand."

"I know that name. Sure, I think I've heard about her books. Look, let me make you some hot chocolate and you let the seat back and try to sleep."

"I can't sleep."

"You can try." The stewardess brought pillows and a thin blanket and tucked the girl in. "I'll get you some chocolate." When she returned, carrying a cup of instant hot chocolate, Olivia was asleep. The stewardess sat down across from her and drank the chocolate herself. She was thinking about her own aunt, who had married a Seventh-Day Adventist and run off to Texas with him, leaving her three cousins to be raised by their grandparents. Nobody had even cared when she died.

Olivia was dreaming of water. She dreamed Anna was swimming in the water wearing the shirt she had worn the day she came to visit. The first time she had seen her, walking down off the ramp of the airplane in a soft blue shirt, bigger and sweeter looking than her pictures, with her hair pulled back in a chignon, very simple and open, so easy to love. "Let's go get lunch," her aunt had said. "Let's go talk."

"I had so much to say to her," Olivia said in her

dream, then woke up and began to cry again. The stewardess put the cup of chocolate down and sat beside her and held her hand. "You ought to be glad you had an aunt to love," she said. "My aunt was such a bitch her own children didn't care when she died." By the time the airplane got to Dallas the stewardess and Olivia had exchanged addresses and phone numbers and become fast friends.

Jessie put some clothes in a suitcase and drove back over to her grandmother's house. Her cousin James had just arrived and she started to tell him that Olivia was coming, then changed her mind. James knew about the marijuana she got at the beach and she was afraid he might tell on her and she'd be locked up too.

She wandered into the dining room where people were fixing drinks and started to tell her father but he was talking to a man named Mr. Alsop who always asked her embarrassing questions so she gave that up.

She watched her aunt Helen moving around the crowd and started to tell her, then changed her mind. Aunt Helen might start going crazy and take charge of going to the airport.

Jessie went into the den and sat down beside her grandmother and let her grandmother pet her. She'll be glad when Olivia is here, Jessie decided. It will give her something to think about except Aunt Anna swallowing cyanide. Only the week before Jessie had come by her grandmother's one afternoon after school and shown her grandmother a picture of Olivia.

"I'm sick of everyone pretending like they can't tell you this," she had said. "Even Aunt Anna won't tell you because Daddy told her not to."

"I know about it," her grandmother had said. "Helen filled me in. Helen tells me everything whether I want to know it or not. I say, Helen, don't tell me so much. Please spare me the details." Mrs. Hand adored her youngest grandchild. She adored Jessie for being beautiful. She adored beauty in any form and the children and grandchildren who possessed it could have anything they liked from her. The others could have anything they liked because she felt sorry for them for not being beautiful. "What does she look like?" she had said.

"Well, there's the photograph. Look at it."

"I can't tell anything from this."

"She looks like me. She looks like Aunt Anna."

"Her mother didn't look like us. I knew her mother, Jessie, don't forget that. That was one of the worst weeks of my life, when that happened. Her mother looked like a Spaniard."

"She's half Indian, Grandmother. Her mother was a full-blooded Cherokee Indian. It's something to be proud of. Her great-grandfather was the president of the Cherokee Nation. She's really nice. It doesn't matter who your mother is. Or your father. It's who you are." Jessie buttered a piece of homemade salt-rising bread and chewed it as she lectured. "You can't meet her if you're going to act like that. Why do you say she looked Spanish?"

"Because she did. Well, don't put so much butter on it, honey. It will make you fat."

"You ought to read the letters she writes to us. She's a very good writer and she makes A's. You ought to want to meet her." Jessie buttered another piece of bread, this time putting twice as much butter as before.

"Oh, my darling. Please spare me this. I've had enough for one lifetime. I just don't need any more. Bring your bread. Here, put that on a plate and let's go out to the garden and see the birds. A nest of redbirds are learning to fly. Oh, they are so precious. I could die when they can't make it. One of them was on the patio for hours last week. I had a terrible time making it fly."

"You can't stick your head in the sand about Olivia forever." Jessie added three chocolate chip cookies to the plate holding her bread and butter, grabbed a Coke out of the refrigerator, and followed her grandmother out to the patio. "You can't pretend she doesn't exist. Aunt Anna says the worst thing in the world are secrets. She says what you don't know can drive you crazy." Mrs. Hand led the way and Jessie followed her, eating and lecturing, dropping crumbs on the oriental rugs for Victoria to vacuum up in the morning.

Well, Grandmother doesn't even know what to think about me, Jessie decided, as she watched the wake from her vantage point in the hall doorway. That's because she and Granddaddy are old and don't want to learn anything new. They've had enough. They don't want anything else to happen and this terrible thing happens that is the most terrible thing anyone could imagine and I know it's going to make them feel better when they see Olivia. I will bring her to them and they will be glad. Jessie stood in the doorway, casting a cold eye on the wake, watching everyone, sure she was the only one who really understood anything, the only one who knew what people were really doing or why or what was really going on. I'll never be like them, she decided. I'll be in London with Momma having a career. I'll never get to the point where I spend my life saying things I don't mean to people like the Alsops. I don't know why they even came over here. I bet they never even read one of Aunt Anna's books. I can just imagine Mr. Alsop reading one of them. He'd probably go crazy or something if he picked one up. Jessie sniffed, and reminded herself that she should read the books herself as soon as she found time to do it.

She wandered into the kitchen and spoke to Victoria and made herself a sandwich and then went out into the yard to make sure there was a key in one of the cars. There was one in her grandmother's Oldsmobile. She took it out and put it in her pocket. She walked around the yard for a while. Then she got into the car and backed it down the driveway and parked it behind her old convertible. She looked at her watch, a new Seiko, a birthday present from her grandparents. She had only had the watch five days. Aunt Anna practically killed herself on my birthday, Jessie thought, and looked up at the stars. The stars were too much, too mysterious and far away. She went in the house and back to the guest room where she had put her suitcase. She took out a long handmade red vest Anna had sent her once from Peru. She tried it on. It was getting too tight in the shoulders. She took out a long pleated navy blue skirt and put that on. It was a skirt she wore to sing in the choir. She put on kneesocks and brown lace-up shoes and then she took it all off and laid it on the bed and put her old dress back on and went into the living room and told everyone goodnight. She set the alarm in the guest room for four o'clock.

She lay down on the bed. It was all so mysterious and scary. Death was so strange. It could happen to anyone at any moment. They could disappear, be snatched away, get cancer, have their appendix burst and die at school like Mary Harbison almost did. She pulled a knitted coverlet up over her legs. She reached over and got the princess phone and set it on her stomach and called her boyfriend and told him everything that was going on.

"What will you do when she gets here?"

"I don't know. I haven't thought about it."

"You better tell your dad."

"No."

"You want me to go with you?"

"No."

"My grandmother died last October. It was terrible. My mom's still not over it. She cries all the time and she's got all this stuff of my grandmother's to sort out. She had this one cedar chest with about four hundred rain scarves in it."

"You're kidding."

"No, I'm not. Listen, she had all these bridge clubs and they gave these rain scarves for prizes and she won all of them."

"So what will your mother do with them?"

"She doesn't know. That's the kind of thing she's dealing with all the time now."

"I hope I never get old."

"Me neither. It's too horrible. Look, are you going to school tomorrow?"

"Probably not. I'll be up all night."

"Let me know if you want to go to school. I could pick you up and meet your sister."

"I better go now. They might want to use the phone." Jessie hung up and lay with the phone on her rib cage. She was thinking about Olivia on an airplane. At any moment the plane might crash and her sister would die before they even really knew each other. Jessie squeezed out the first few tears, the rest of them came more easily.

The sun was barely beginning to light up the fields around Charlotte when Olivia's 747 landed at the deserted airport. Jessie was standing by the gate. The ticket agent opened the door and three passengers got off, then Olivia. She was wearing the long navy blue skirt and her blazer, carrying a small leather bag.

Jessie ran to her. "We're dressed alike," she said. "It's unbelievable. We are practically dressed exactly alike."

"We're on a wavelength," Olivia said. She put down the bag. She took Jessie's arm and they sat down on the plastic airport seats. They sat back and took each other in. Their eyes would meet, then they would look away. She looks great, Jessie was thinking. She looks so good. She looks so old.

She looks so soft, Olivia was thinking. Her skin looks

like a baby's skin. She's the prettiest girl I've ever seen in my life. If I could stay. If only they would let me stay.

"I've been crying all morning," Jessie said. "Sometimes about Aunt Anna and sometimes for you."

"Why would you cry over me?"

"Because Dad didn't love my mother either. They hate each other's guts. So why do I get to live with him and you don't? It isn't fair. I could turn into you or you to me."

"I like where I live, Jessie. I have a good life. It's okay."

"It's so hard to talk to him. I want him to sit on the floor and hold hands with us and really talk. I want it the way it should be. Not like when you were here."

"I want to meet my grandparents more than anything else. To tell them how sorry I am about Aunt Anna."

"They want to meet you too. I gave your picture to Grandmother. She's dying to see you. But she never does anything Dad tells her not to do. She's his slave because he looks like her father. If I have kids they aren't going to tell me what to do."

"What will they do if they can't find the body? If they can't have the funeral?"

"There's going to be a memorial service as soon as everyone's here. But not at Grandmomma's church. At the Episcopal cathedral because Aunt Anna was friends with the music director. Uncle Niall says the only thing that matters is the music and, well, because she took her own life and she didn't go to church anyway."

Olivia stroked Jessie's arm. She gentles like a burro, Olivia thought. Like a little jack. Jessie went on.

"My music teacher is going to play the organ. The one I wouldn't go to. And we think the doctor's coming, the married man she was in love with. Dad and Aunt Helen haven't told Grandmother he is married. Don't tell her. He keeps calling Grandmother on the phone and she keeps saying she knew Anna was dying, like this is a natural death and no one really took their own life."

"My aunt Mary Lily said it was all right to take your life to keep from being in terrible pain. I can't believe she said that, she's so devout."

"What do you think?" Jessie leaned back in the chair. The place was empty now. The ticket agent had left the booth and no one was within sight.

"I think it's very sad that she is gone. For me I thought I would know her for many years and maybe travel with her one day. I would like to travel, to see the world."

"Dad takes me to Switzerland. Maybe you could go with us. Oh, you can go. Next summer when we go you'll come too. I know you will. We see these people that live there, they have a bank and we go to their house on this lake, the most beautiful lake you've ever seen in your life. In Vevey. Will you go with us?"

"If he lets me. If he wants me to." Olivia removed her hand from Jessie's arm and straightened her back. Jessie began to cry again. "Oh, God, it's not fair for you never to go to Switzerland. I'm not going anyplace as long as I live unless you go with me."

"Let's go and see our grandmother," Olivia said. "If it's all right. When she's awake I would like to see her."

"She's awake. There are so many people in that house. You wouldn't believe who all is here. Some little kids, some cousins that live in Richmond, my cousin Kenny's little boys, are there. We got them this toy basketball goal and everyone sits around the living room watching them shoot baskets. Those little boys never got that much attention in their life. And Dad's there. We spent the night over there."

"Then let's go." Olivia stood up. She remembered something Anna had told her about her grandmother. She is a Christian of the old school, Anna had said. She thinks she is an extension of Christ. She has to do what Christ would do. She models herself on Jesus Christ."

Daniel had just put the coffee on and walked outside to see if the paper had come. He had noticed one of the cars was gone but so many people had been there the night before he supposed someone in the family had borrowed it to drive home. His mother's spaniels were jumping on the fence, begging to be let out of the back yard. He walked over to the fence. Then he saw the Oldsmobile driving up. He shook his head. His heart opened and closed and opened again. His breath caught in his throat from so much strangeness, the strangeness of women, of two beautiful seventeen-year-old daughters. He reached over the fence and patted the dogs. "Wait a minute," he said. "These girls are here."

He stuck his hands in his pockets. He stood in the yard and watched them come driving very slowly up the driveway. Jessie stopped the car beside him. She was wearing the look she wore that always preceded the remarks that began, Don't get mad until you hear what I have to tell you. Her face was almost clean. She had cried off so much makeup he could almost see her face. Beside her, Olivia stared at him out of big dark eyes. They rolled down the windows and waited.

"Well, get out," he said. "I bet neither one of you has had any breakfast."

Four people were on the flight from Nashville to Charlotte that same night. American Eagle flight two twenty-three left Nashville at eight forty-five carrying LeLe Arnold, Adam Halliday, Phelan Manning, and his nephew, King Mallison, Junior, of New Orleans, Louisiana. LeLe was on a continuation of a flight from L.A. Adam had finished a trigonometry exam and gone to the airport still carrying his books. He was trying to believe that Anna was dead, he kept hearing her voice.

"Goodbye. Adam, listen to me, no, listen to me, I called to tell you goodbye." Phelan had been in Maine with his nephew, about to go hunting with a party from Europe, including one of the French Rothschilds. It was costing Phelan ten thousand dollars to turn around and go to Charlotte to see if the Hands had found a body to bury. He leaned back in the seat, thinking of Anna's fine long legs, her mouth and breasts and hair. He was also thinking of King and what a good chance it would be to show him Charlotte at its quintessential most. Mourning and with all those men and women in the house at the same time. Crystal was spoiling him to death in that swamp. It was time for him to see what a feast there was waiting for a man. Phelan was almost asleep when he saw LeLe Arnold stand up and ask the stewardess a question. He had not known she was on the plane. "It's starting," he said to King. "This wake is about to begin."

King thought his uncle was talking about the stewardess. His uncle seemed to know half the stewardesses in the United States. Also, when his uncle said something was about to begin he usually meant something about women. "See that woman back there," Phelan went on. "That's your cousin, LeLe Arnold, from the West Coast, she's one of the Arnolds from down around Rosedale and Cleveland, Mississippi. She's the West Coast stringer for the *Philadelphia Inquirer*. You must have known her when you were little. She and your mother are old buddy buddies."

"Should we go back there and talk to her?"

"In a while. The stewardess just handed her blankets. She might be trying to sleep. We're all going to need plenty of sleep before this is over."

"I'm sorry we can't go to Germany and France," King said. Phelan had talked his mother and his school into letting him leave for a month on the promise that he would see the world. He was doing so badly in school that they had all been relieved to get him off their hands for a while. Now King had a lingering suspicion that as soon as the funeral was over in Charlotte he would be right back in Saint Martin's being bored to death by bored teachers. He shook his head, saw the Alps, lost to him because of some friend of his mother's dying.

"How could someone kill themself?" he said. "At least I'd get some good drugs if I had to do it. No, I'd shoot myself."

"Pretty women don't shoot themselves, son. They don't want anybody to see them dead. Anna wanted to get rid of herself, rid of her body. Hell, maybe she was mad at the cancer, well, she picked the right ocean, the North Atlantic will take a body off your hands. We'll go up there someday and look at the place." He put his hand on his nephew's arm. "Death isn't the enemy, King. Fear is."

"Mother said she might come up. If she can get Crystal Anne out of school. What a brat that kid is. Mother lets her do anything she wants to do. I hate to have her around a funeral. She'll embarrass everyone to death."

"Put your seat belt on." Phelan removed his hand from King's arm, tightened his own. The lights dimmed in the cabin and the plane began to taxi down the runway toward the east.

The plane hit an air pocket over a lake. LeLe woke up from a terrible dream. In the dream she was standing in a long stone room with her father and the rugby player she had been fucking on and off for three years. Her father was wearing a suit. His hands were folded. He stood shoulder to shoulder with the rugby player, they were catty-corner to each other. There were stone slabs everywhere. It was a morgue. Or a museum. LeLe had come there to receive an award, some silly award from the state of California. No one said a word in the dream. I have to get to Charlotte, LeLe was thinking. They have to go with me and take care of me. They have to forgive

Anna so I won't be alone. She sat up in the seat, shook the sleep from her head, reached up and turned on the air vent. Cold stale airplane air rushed down upon her face. She pushed on the light. The young man across the aisle was watching her. He was a good-looking man with a trigonometry book on the fold-out table. A troubled-looking man, a man with things on his mind.

"Where are you going?" LeLe asked.

"To Charlotte." He paused. Twisted his hands together on top of the book. "Someone died, someone I knew."

"You're Adam Halliday, aren't you? You got on in Nashville."

"Who are you? You're going there because of Anna? You are, aren't you? I started to ask a moment ago."

"I'm her cousin, LeLe. I just came in from San Francisco. I started at five this morning and missed a connection in Memphis. Jesus Christ, I hate airplanes. I hate the goddamn things."

"When did you talk to her? Look, come sit over here. I'll move this stuff." He moved to the window seat, stowed his book satchel underneath his feet, made a place for her. He was very graceful. Elegant. A graceful savage, Anna had told her once. "The best piece of ass I ever had and I'm not the only one. His old girls all say it too."

"Who told you?" LeLe began. "When did you find out?"

"She called me right before she did it. She called me about five minutes before she did it but she didn't tell me what it was about. She said goodbye. She just kept saying goodbye. Everything I said she just said goodbye. It was the strangest conversation I ever had in my life. I didn't know where the call was from and then she hung up. So I started calling around, looking for her. Dan called me back when they found out. Her brother Daniel. When Helen got back and told them. It was nice of him to call me. I know they didn't approve of her seeing me."

"He's a nice guy. They never have found her body. Maybe she isn't dead."

"She's dead. You should have heard her voice." He turned away. Looked out the window. "She said she'd do this. Every time she saw someone that was really compromised. She said Einstein didn't get fixed."

"What?"

"Einstein. You know how she liked that stuff. She said when he was old he wouldn't have an operation to remove a tumor."

"We're going to blame this on Albert Einstein?" LeLe shook her head, raised her hand and pushed the button to call the stewardess. "Let's get a drink," she said. "I need a drink of whiskey."

The stewardess appeared and took their order. A minute later Phelan came down the aisle and hugged LeLe and sat down on the arm of her abandoned aisle seat. The men were introduced. Adam extended his arm. The men shook hands, looked each other over.

"I've got King with me," Phelan said. "Crystal's boy. How long has it been since you've seen him?"

"A long time. Since before she married Manny. Where were you going?"

"Hunting. I was taking him to the Alps. Well, that's over. I guess I'll stay in Charlotte for a while. Take care of Grandmother, straighten out her affairs."

"He used to cheat her at Chinese checkers," LeLe said, turning to Adam. "That's how he made money to bet on the races."

"Oh, don't go telling that." Phelan laughed. He smiled at Adam. "That was one summer when I was fifteen. Jesus Christ, I guess I'll never live that down."

"He used to move the marbles when she got up to get him things to drink." LeLe touched Adam's arm, watched Phelan watch her do it.

"Grandmother's taking this hard," Phelan added. "She was crazy about Anna. She made all her old buddies buy the books. She wouldn't let them borrow hers. They had to send their chauffeurs down to the House of Books and buy them. I talked to her from the airport in Boston. You ought to go see her while you're here, LeLe. She loved Anna. Anna always went to see her when she was in town."

"Everyone loved Anna. I loved Anna."

"She was good to people," Adam said. "If she thought they were smart enough for her she'd do anything for them."

"She ignored the rest." Phelan drank his airplane wine. "Well, shit, she's gone. I never could imagine the life she led, going around to colleges, hanging out with professors. What did she talk to those guys about?"

"She called me right before she did it," Adam said. "She said she was calling to tell me goodbye. She kept saying goodbye. No matter what I said, she just said goodbye. I didn't know where the call was coming from. Then she hung up."

"Push the button, LeLe. Get that stewardess back here to sell us some more of this trashy wine."

The stewardess brought the wine. LeLe and Phelan began to talk about old times. Phelan told her about a Kleingunther gun factory he was opening in San Antonio and LeLe told him about interviewing George Bush and then Phelan told her about going to New Orleans to pick up King and LeLe told him about her house in Sausalito. "Sitting on a hill overlooking the bay," she said. "Falling off a landfill for two hundred grand of borrowed California money, what the fuck." She giggled, got softer and softer. She liked where she was, sitting between two good-looking men on a darkened airplane was her idea of the right place to be, no matter what the reason. She was very soft, very sexy, a very sexy

woman, sexy in a way that Anna had never allowed
herself to be. Adam watched her talking to Phelan. He
kept remembering once when Anna had returned from
a trip to the West Coast wearing a pair of LeLe's underpants. A very small lavender bikini with tiny violets em-
broidered on the crotch. "My cousin LeLe's," she had
said, letting her skirt fall to the floor, "I asked her if I
could borrow a pair of underpants and this is what she
hands me."

"Come here," Adam had said. "Let me see those little
flowers."

He watched LeLe now, wondering what she was wearing underneath the brown skirt. He sat up, began to talk
to Phelan about squirrel hunting. "Except for turkey
hunting it's the best," Phelan agreed. "Except for tur-
keys. Everybody in Mississippi's cultivating them now.
They'll give you a chase. They'll dump on you from the
trees. It's like hunting monkeys."

"Well, I hope you don't hunt monkeys. You don't
hunt monkeys, do you?" This from LeLe.

"This wine's okay," Adam said. "Once you start drinking it."

"It's what we have to drink on this airplane anyway,"
Phelan added.

"Wine is wine," LeLe said. "And monkeys are monkeys and death is death and Anna's dead."

She moved her arm close to Adam's body. She was
getting really tipsy, drinking on no sleep and no food.
She felt the warmth of his jacket, the warmth of his
chest. He was too cute to go to waste. If Anna wanted to
go and kill herself and leave this good-looking man
lying around the world unfucked, then to hell with it.
She would fuck him herself. And anything else she
wanted to do. Anything at all. "Fuck," she said. "Fuck
Anna jumping in the ocean without telling me."

"Well, I better go see about the boy," Phelan said.

"We'll find you when the plane lands. Do they know you're coming?"

"Helen knows. I called Helen. She's sending James Junior out. They let him out of the dope center for the funeral so they're trying to keep him busy."

"I thought he was through with that by now." Phelan stood up. "Did you hear the story about Daniel going out there to take him some shoes? Right after they cornered him and locked him up. Niall told me. James's wife sent Daniel out there with a pair of tennis shoes so James Junior could get some exercise. And this nurse started trying to take Daniel's history. 'How long have you had a drinking problem?' the nurse said.

" 'I'm just here to deliver these shoes,' Daniel said. 'I'm just here to deliver my nephew's tennis shoes.' Then he drops the shoes at the nurse's feet and runs out of the hospital. I can just picture him sprinting out of there. He used to run in high school, Adam. He was a great four-forty man."

James Junior was waiting by the gate. His girlfriend, Shelby, was with him and one of his old friends from his dope-running days. Olivia and Jessie were there too. They had come on a separate mission, to meet Anna's baby sister, Louise, who was coming from Washington at twelve thirty. She had been off shooting a National Geographic film in Scotland and had been hard to find.

"It's a documentary about bagpipes," Jessie said, giving LeLe a hug. "They are really weapons. It's against the law to take them into the House of Parliament. This is my sister, Olivia. By Dad's first wife. Olivia, this is our cousin, LeLe Arnold. She's a reporter."

"I'm LeLe," she said. She hugged the second child. Adam started to walk away, following King and James and Phelan. "Don't leave me," she said. "I want to go where you go."

"Sure," he said, and returned to her side. LeLe introduced him to Jessie and Olivia. They looked like Anna, especially the smaller one. He couldn't put his finger on it, but the resemblance was definitely there. He drew in his breath. Whatever desire he had begun to feel for LeLe was dissipating. Grief was returning. Real grief. He felt tears forming behind his eyes. The smaller girl kept watching him. Some of the tears began to fall.

James Junior stood beside Phelan at the baggage carousel. King stood on the other side. Traveling with Phelan was never a simple matter. People never stopped showing up, phones never stopped ringing, someone was always ordering drinks, going off, coming back, buying or selling or renting a car or a truck, betting on something, getting on or off an airplane, carrying guns. When Phelan tired of this he lay down and took a nap. A Phelan-Nap, his friends called this strange event. He took a nap and then he got up and things began happening again. If you could live without sleep you could make it traveling with Phelan. If not, you had better stay at home.

"What do you think of Jessie?" he asked King, using his low voice, the one he tracked with. King didn't answer, and, as if in answer to a summons, Jessie came over to where they were standing.

"This is my sister, Olivia," she said. "Dad's daughter by his first wife. This is Mr. Manning, our cousin," she added, turning to Olivia. "And this is King Mallison, he's from New Orleans." She turned her full attention on this boy, drew him in, collected him.

Olivia held out her hand, searched the grown man's face, then turned to the boy with red-gold hair. He was the most beautiful person, male or female, she had ever seen in her life. More beautiful than a movie star or a rock star or any picture. He was perfect. He took her hand. He smiled. Then he turned his attention back to Jessie.

Tennessee walking horses, Olivia was thinking. At the fair. She squared her shoulders, turned and talked to Adam.

"I don't live here," she said. "I live in Oklahoma."

"I know. Anna told me about you. She was always talking about you."

"Was she?" Olivia asked. "I wish I had been there. When you were with her."

"I've got to get these bags," King was saying. "We've got gun cases and a lot of bags. I better get them to the car."

"I'll help you," James said. He had just been talking to his therapist about how people in his family acted like they owned anyplace they were. Now they were here, doing it in real life, taking over everything in sight, except each other. They came up against it when they faced each other. The girl from Oklahoma's a strange one, he was thinking. I'd sure like to get in her pants. I bet she's been around. I'll bet she's got some things to show Jessie.

His girlfriend, Shelby, collected him before he could finish the thought. His old buddy, Ray, was standing against a wall by the public phones smoking a cigarette and trying to look cool. Ray's too wasted to be real, James thought. Ray's like an old song I'm tired of hearing. He walked over to the phone booth and told Ray to go on home alone. Ray had followed him out to the airport, waiting for something to happen. "Will I see you later, man?" Ray said. "You want to meet somewhere?"

"Not tonight," James answered. "I'll call you sometime tomorrow."

"That's cool," Ray said, and put out his cigarette on the floor. Phelan was watching them. James could feel Phelan's hunter eyes taking it all in.

"Well, I don't care if you think it's cool or not," James began, then backtracked and took Ray's hand. "Take care, man, take it easy."

"I'm history," Ray said, and moved like a whisper across the floor and out the glass doors.

"Come on," Phelan called out. "Come help us load these guns, James. I got some new thirty-eight-caliber rifles that will knock your eyes out."

Then Louise was there. She was the only passenger on a commuter flight from Washington and Raleigh-Durham. She came into the terminal wearing a green tweed suit and a very soft pale silk blouse. Very elegant, very thin, her high leather boots polished to perfection, her soft brown hair in a short pageboy, very smooth, very polished, very slick. The coldest and meanest and youngest of the Hand children. The most selfish, perhaps the most selfish person in the world, as Mrs. Hand was fond of telling her husband. "Louise is the most selfish person in the world. Did I make her that way, James? Am I responsible for her?"

"You raised her, didn't you?"

"Well, they aren't my genes. No one in my family has ever been selfish. No matter what else you might think about my family they aren't selfish people."

"And you think the Hands are? You think my people are selfish?"

"Your mother was a sweet woman."

"Louise is selfish because she's spoiled rotten. Just like Sheila MacNeice. She even looks like Sheila. Now make me some dinner please, Annie, and don't cry over spilt milk. Louise is what she is. At least she works for a living."

"I hate to think of anyone marrying her. She'd make a terrible wife."

"Annie." Then Mrs. Hand would leave the subject of Louise's selfishness and fix dinner for her husband and whoever else happened to be there or drop in.

"Did they find the body yet?" Louise asked, allowing Jessie to embrace her, trying not to look at Olivia. She had been warned on the phone that the Indian girl was there. The Indian princess, Daniel's souvenir of California.

"This is Olivia," Jessie said. "My sister. Dad's daughter by his first wife."

"Oh, well," Louise said. She had spotted Phelan by the baggage carousel. She had spotted the gun cases. She drew her mouth in. "I can't believe none of my brothers came to get me. Where is Daniel? Where is Niall?"

"They're at the house with Grandmomma and Granddaddy. It's terrible there, Aunt Louise. Everyone in town is there. The reporters call up Grandmother. And someone wrote this terrible thing in the paper about Aunt Anna setting a terrible example for young people and they should take her books out of the libraries and take back the award the governor gave her last year when she came home. The paper printed that and then it printed some letters that said the same thing. It just made things worse for Grandmother, and Uncle James and Granddaddy want to sue the *Charlotte Observer*."

"You need a haircut," Louise said. "I can't believe you did that to your hair." Now Louise saw LeLe. She handed her makeup kit to Jessie, who handed it to Olivia, who held it. I should have known better than to come, Louise was saying to herself. Taylor told me not to come. He told me I wasn't strong enough to do this yet but I had to come and here I am and I can't get away until morning. I left the greatest opportunity of my life to come here. I walked off in the middle of a shoot and came here to see this. This Indian girl and Phelan Manning and a bunch of elephant guns and the newspapers saying nasty things about Anna. Well, she deserved it. Imagine doing anything as crazy as killing herself. A terrible death in the ocean. She could have used pills or gone to India or somewhere where we don't know people.

Louise's eyes met Olivia's. Olivia held the cosmetic kit. It was made of crocodile hide. She thought Louise was the most unhappy-looking person she had ever met in her life. That's the Tennessee walker, she decided. Hobbled and crippled and about to fall apart. LeLe had seen Louise now and came over and put her arm around her.

"Did they find the body?" Louise said. "Did they find a body yet?"

"No."

"Then what are we going to bury? Why are we having this funeral?"

"It's isn't a funeral, honey." Phelan had joined them now. "It's a wake."

It lasted six days. Back at the house people were beginning to smoke. People that hadn't smoked in years were lighting up, bumming cigarettes from Daniel and Phelan, talking in hushed voices in small groups, moving out onto the patio and out into the yard, flicking cigarette ashes into watering cans and beside the birdbath, dropping cigarette ashes on the leaves from the ornamental cherry apple trees, leaving glasses on the picnic table and the old iron typing table painted with white enamel that had held Anna's first typewriter when she was fourteen. The table had been on the patio for so long that everyone had forgotten where it came from or what it was originally for. Once, in the past summer, the last summer, Anna had been sitting on the patio with her mother and had recognized it under its ten coats of white paint, had meant to say something about it, had meant to say, Momma, that's my old typing table isn't it? But her mother had been talking away about James and the dope recovery hospital and would not be interrupted. Anna had listened to her with great tenderness, thinking how strange it was in a world full of poorly, oh,

badly mothered people, to have had such a wonderful
mother, such a great beginning. A mother who would
deliver the latest in typewriters and typewriter tables
to the room of her oldest child just because the child's
teacher had said the child could write. So there it was,
Anna was thinking, right in the middle of my ruffled
room, a typewriter table and a little black Royal typewriter. Maybe she knew there would be no babies for
me. Maybe she knew I was going to need something
special to make up for that. Who knows what we
know, or in what sequence, all of us here on the
planet Earth, which Freeman Dyson says we might
have helped to make, might have dreamed up.

In this particular sequence, in this particular group
of homo sapiens, gathered at this particular house for
this particular reason, on this day in this place these
people were angry at the idea of their common and
particular mortality and to make up for it, as a sort of
limited South Charlotte zeitgeist, they smoked, bumming cigarettes from Daniel and James Junior and
Phelan.

"Jesus Christ," Daniel finally told Helen. "Go to the
store and get us some cigarettes. Get some cartons." He
handed her a fifty-dollar bill and his car keys.

"What are you going to do with her now that she's
here?" Helen said.

"Who? Oh, the little girl?"

"Olivia. Olivia. My God, it's just like Anna to start that
and then go kill herself and leave it to me to clean up."

"To you."

"Well, someone has to decide what to do with her."

"Helen, I've got a funeral to run. Please leave me
alone. The little girl's all right. She's with Jessie out at
the house. She's okay."

"Mother told me to find out what you plan to do about
her."

"Nothing. I'm not going to do anything about her. It's

okay. Go get the goddamn cigarettes, Helen, or if you won't, I'll do it myself."

"I'm going." Helen put the fifty-dollar bill down on the table. "Daniel?"

"Leave it alone, Sister. If you say another word about that little girl I'll break your goddamn neck. She's with Jessie and she's here and that's that. Go get the cigarettes!"

Helen walked down across the lawn and got into Daniel's car and put it into forward gear and began to drive. If he thinks he can move her down here and just confront everyone with this he is crazy. She's a nice little girl. I like her. She was doing just fine out there in Oklahoma where she lives, but she will never fit into Charlotte. Oh, my God, Anna is dead, goddamn you, Anna, for bringing all this horrible stuff on Momma and Daddy and bringing that girl right up in the middle of it. Who is supposed to pay to educate all of these children, do you think? Are you going to do it, selfishly dead as a doornail? Oh, my God, some fish is eating her right now, some shark. Helen drove madly down the street, barely missing a jogger. She slammed on the brakes, then pulled over to the side of the street and turned off the motor and began to cry. She cried for all the days of her life with Anna and all the things she and Anna had done. She cried for the time they went to see *The Song of the South* and the time they went to see *Bambi* and the time Anna screamed at a girl who slapped James at recess and the nights they slept together in Anna's four-poster bed, curled up like spoons. Helen inside so nothing could get her and Anna's arms curled around her and Anna's voice telling her stories about the fairies who come to get good children and take them away to the land of lost dolls. I can't make it, Helen thought. It's no good now. Anna being eaten by sharks, already eaten and digested and her voice gone forever. There will never be that sound again. I will never hear her speak.

And that girl is here and what in the name of God will we do with her? Momma is going to start liking her. And then what will we do? Oh, God, give me strength. Why have you forsaken me and why do Spencer and I have to be so mean to each other? No, he was nice last night. He was just as nice as he could be and is being so helpful to Daddy. I have to get back. DeDe is coming and Stacy, that little bitch, how did I bring such a child into the world? It's all messed up now. Everything I had such hopes for. Well, I've got to get those cigarettes before Daniel gets any madder.

She wiped her face on her sleeve and started the motor and drove to the 7-Eleven store and bought three cartons of cigarettes. Camel Filters and Pall Malls and Salem 100's and took them back to the house and dumped them all out in a cut-glass crystal bowl on the dining-room table.

LeLe and Adam checked into adjoining rooms at the Park Hotel. When the bellboy brought their bags, LeLe told him to unlock the door between the rooms. "I can't be alone now," she said. "I can't do this by myself."

"Neither can I," he answered. "Come on in. Stay with me." LeLe lay down upon the bed and watched him hang up his suit. "I hope this is all right to wear. It's the only suit I have."

"It doesn't matter."

"Yes it does. We have to do right by her. Not let her down."

"Then don't talk to reporters. Don't say you were her boyfriend."

"Oh, I wouldn't do that. I wasn't important to her, LeLe. I don't know what was but it wasn't me. She just liked to have me around when she wasn't writing."

"I don't believe that."

"Well you might as well because it's true."

"She wasn't that cold."

"Not at first. When I first knew her she was so excited about the world." He came and sat on the bed, still holding the coat hanger and his suit pants. "About the house, me, everything. Other people. Then, after she came back from New York, she was changed. Like the sharpness wasn't there. Maybe she was sick."

LeLe was quiet. It seemed impossible that he didn't know about Philip. Still, young men were so egotistical, maybe it had never occurred to him that there might be another man. Maybe he was waiting for her to tell him. Maybe he was pumping her. "Let me hang those up for you," she said.

"No, they're all right." He put the pants on a chair, then stretched out on the bed beside her. "What are we doing here?" he asked.

"I don't know but you can get closer if you want to."

"Could I ask you something?" he said. "Something very personal?"

"Sure, go ahead."

"What kind of underpants are you wearing? I mean, what color are they?"

Jessie and Olivia slept that night at Jessie and Daniel's house. "You can sleep in the bed with me if you want to," Jessie said. "Or you can take one of the guest rooms or whatever you want to do."

"I'll stay in here," Olivia said. "I'm not used to sleeping far away from other people. My grandmother always lets me sleep with her if I want to."

"Aunt Anna used to sleep with Grandmother when she'd come home to visit. One of Dad's girlfriends that's a psychologist thinks that's so weird. She was always talking about it. I can't stand her anyway. I guess she thought just because Aunt Anna was famous she wouldn't want to sleep with her mother."

"Then where would Granddaddy sleep?"

"In his room I guess. He has a room of his own. He has all his books about money in there. Are you going to call him Granddaddy?"

"He told me to."

"I just have to get used to it." Jessie was taking off her makeup with theatrical cold cream. A big black tin her mother had sent from London for Christmas. She smoothed great handfuls across her face, then rubbed it in. "What do you think of King?" she added.

"I think he's the most beautiful person I've ever seen in my life."

"Are you in love with him?" Jessie wiped the cream from her face with tissues, then began to scrub her face with a green felt washcloth. Olivia was sitting on the bed. She was tired now and she was beginning to feel disoriented and she didn't want to talk about King to Jessie. "No," she said. "I guess he's our cousin, isn't he?"

"He's so far away it doesn't matter. He's our sixth cousin or something. His grandfather was Dad's grandmother's first cousin. So, are you falling in love with him?"

"No, I just think he's beautiful. He's so strong looking. Like no one could knock him down. He looks like a great yearling. Oh, I shouldn't say that. People aren't horses. Don't tell him I said that."

"I'm going to tell him you're in love with him." Jessie had gotten up and come to stand by the bed. She dropped the towel on the floor and began to turn down the covers on her side. "Come on, get under."

"Don't tell him anything I say. I mean that. I don't want you to say I said anything about him. Promise me, Jessie."

"Okay, I'm sorry. Olivia, I'm going to make up a nickname for you. Just for you and me. I'm going to call you Sissy or Sandy or Scooty or something cute. You wait. I'll think of something."

"You swear you won't say anything to him, anything at all about me?"

"I swear. I swear to God. I could call you Sutter. That's what Aunt Helen used to call Aunt Anna. She called her Sutter because she couldn't say sister when she was little."

"I wouldn't want to be called Aunt Anna's name."

"Then I'll call you Sissy. Goodnight, Sissy, sweet dreams."

"You promise."

"I will never say a word to him about you."

"Goodnight. I like being here with you."

"I do too. I'm starting to love you. I guess you could say we are in training to be sisters."

In the night Jessie woke up and shook Olivia awake. "Starr," she said. "I am going to call you Starr. I always wanted to have a friend named Starr."

"Okay," Olivia said. "It's okay with me."

A few hours later Olivia woke up and slipped out of the bed and went into the guest room where she had left her things. She took a notebook out of her suitcase and began to write.

Starr to Sun, Starr to King
King of the Sun, King of the Moon,
Light of the day and the night,
What dark dream brought us here?
Is this wrong or right? Bad or Good?
Where the moon shines on you there the world ends for me.
I am so lonely, Mother, speak to me from your cold bed.
Father, Father, learn to look at me.

She folded the poem in half and put it in the pocket of her suitcase. She was ashamed to have written such a self-pitying poem and slept the rest of the night alone to punish herself for her cowardice.

* * *

Daniel came home at four and tiptoed down the hall and looked in on them. First on Jessie, sprawled out across her bed. Then at Olivia, curled up around a pillow in the guest room. She seemed so small, and, even in sleep, so serious. He covered her up and patted the covers with his hand. As he was walking out she opened her eyes and watched him leave. When he was gone she reached her hand up on the covers and felt the place where he had touched her.

On the fourth day of the wake news arrived that another body had been found near Biddeford and Philip was going up there to identify it. At six in the afternoon he called to say it was not Anna.

"We will have the service on Friday," Mrs. Hand told him. "The children want to have it. Don't come unless you really need to. You have work to do. There is nothing you can do to help out here."

"I need to come," he said. "I'll be there somehow."

Phelan and LeLe were alone in the Hands' library. Phelan got up and shut the door. Then he came back to the sofa. A fire was burning in the fireplace. He watched it for a while. "You need tell that kid about Philip," he said finally. "Someone needs to tell him who he is."

"Why?"

"Because he'll know. Because a man doesn't need to meet his girlfriend's lover at her memorial service at ten o'clock in the morning on a workday. He needs to get back to school. Maybe you could get him out of here before Friday."

"I doubt it."

"Maybe if you told him he would leave."

"You tell him."

"No, you do it."

"Why do I have to do it?"

"Because you're the one that's sleeping with him." He smiled at her, then he got up and poked at the fire.

"Okay," she said. "I'll tell him. I'll tell him Anna's doctor is coming. I'll say he used to be her boyfriend."

"You'll do great. You'll do it fine."

"I don't know, Phelan. I just don't know." It is Wednesday afternoon, LeLe was thinking. Then Thursday, then Friday, then we will all go home and I will go back to being lonely. Everything will be the same, except if I want to call up Anna on the phone I am one hundred percent and completely out of luck. LeLe began to cry. It was the first time she had cried all day. Phelan leaned over the fireplace, poking at the logs and crying too.

Friday morning was beautiful and clear. The trees of Charlotte were brilliant in the fall sunrise. Brown oaks and river birches and yellow walnuts and willows and elms. Silver maples turning the palest of golds and dark crimson maples at the corners of yards. Burgundy hawthorns and purple dogwood, carpets of purple and gold and dusty orange beneath the trees.

Her feet have walked across this yard, Mrs. Hand thought, and went back inside and lay back down upon the bed. It was the first time since Helen and Daniel and Niall had come with the news that she had really faced the knowledge that Anna was gone. She picked up a small gold case containing photographs of her parents and closed it and held it beneath her bosom on the bed. The sharp edges of the case cut into her skin. Outside the French doors the birds flew from the feeders to the oak trees and down onto the lawn and back again. I have to get up, she thought. I have to set an example. I have to find that child from Oklahoma. I have to take her into my bosom. I should have kept her here with us last night. Oh, Anna, my precious little baby girl. My own

little precious girl. My precious baby girl. I have to go
and find James. I have to see if James is awake.

She got up from the bed and walked barefooted into
the guest room and found him sitting up in bed reading
a book. He had been crying again. She walked over to
the other side of the bed and got in beside him and
cuddled down into his chest. There was nothing to say
and neither of them said a thing.

Phelan Manning's sister, Crystal, was staying at the
Hands' house for the duration of the wake. She was up
and dressed and in the living room with her three-
year-old daughter, Crystal Anne. She was trying to keep
Crystal Anne quiet. She had dressed the child in a
crushed brown velvet dress with a white lace collar and
white silk tights. Now she was trying to fit the child's feet
into a pair of white patent leather shoes that she hadn't
worn since summer. The shoes were too tight and Crystal Anne refused to put them on.

"Then wear your brown shoes," Crystal said. "No one
is going to be looking at your feet."

"Yes they will. Brown doesn't go with white."

"Yes it does. It looks just fine. You have a white collar
on your brown dress, don't you?"

Crystal Anne walked down the length of the living
room to a table at the end with a big gold mirror hanging above it. There was an arrangement of flowers on
the table. "I can't see," she said.

"Wait a minute." Crystal moved the flower arrangement to the floor. Then she pulled a chair up in front of
the table and Crystal Anne stood up on the chair and
inspected herself. "See," Crystal said. "Brown and
white."

"The brown shoes are lost. The brown shoes are
gone."

"No they aren't. Stay right there and I'll go get them
and you can see how they look." Crystal went back to the

room where they were staying to search for the shoes and Crystal Anne began to do a dance for her reflection. It was a dance based on her Barbie Pet Show set. "Oh, the girls were going to the show with their dogs. They were putting on their blusher for the show." The door opened and Crystal Anne's uncle Phelan came in with LeLe. "Crystal Anne," he said. "How wonderful you look in your dress." He scooped her up.

"My shoes are too little. I have to wear my brown ones."

Crystal came back in carrying the brown shoes. She kissed her brother and handed them to him. "Put these on her, please, while I talk to LeLe. Louise is ready. She's back there somewhere." The door opened and Adam entered.

"Has Annie gotten up yet?" LeLe asked.

"I haven't heard a sound."

"It's eight thirty. We have to leave soon."

"Go wake them up."

"Ask Louise to do it. Oh, never mind, I will." Crystal left the room. She met Mr. and Mrs. Hand coming down the hall. They were completely dressed, ready to leave for the church. "I'm sorry I didn't get up to make you breakfast," Mrs. Hand said. "I should have been up sooner."

"We were fine," Crystal said. "There was nothing to do." She embraced the older woman, held on to her. Then she embraced Mr. Hand. Light was pouring into the hall from the doors that opened into the bedrooms. I never thought I would live to see this day, Crystal was thinking. To begin to bury my friends. I didn't really think this day would come.

Then they went into the living room and everyone was there. Coming in all the doors at once, Daniel and Jessie and Olivia and Daniel's girlfriend, Jean Winters, and Helen and Spencer and DeDe and Kenny and Winifred and Lynley and Stacy and Kenny's wife and

James and Putty and Little Putty and James Junior and
Aleece and Niall and Louise. They all milled around the
living room and kitchen and den hugging each other
and getting sadder and sadder. Then they all began to
go out the doors and out into the yard and into the cars.

LeLe took Adam's hand, led him out the front door of
the house into the front yard. Seven huge old live oak
trees commanded the yard. Their dark shadows made a
network on the lawn. A taxi drove up at the end of the
oak-covered lawn. A man in a dark suit got out and paid
the taxi driver and began to walk toward the people
getting into cars. Helen disengaged herself from her
mother and walked down the yard to meet him. She
took his arm and led him toward her parents. LeLe
steered Adam toward a car holding Phelan and Louise
and King. She hadn't told Adam about Philip after all
and she wasn't going to. As soon as the service was over
she was going to drive him out to the Charlotte airport
and put him on a plane to take him back to Vanderbilt
University where he belonged. She wasn't going to
dump the knowledge of Anna's lover on Adam this day
or any other day and she had told Phelan so. "Who was
that?" Adam said.

"I don't know," LeLe said. "Some old friend of
Helen's."

The cars began to drive in the direction of the church.
James and Putty and James Junior were in the front seat
of James's Buick. "I want to talk to you later today,"
James Junior said. He was talking to his father. His
mother looked out the window. He had already talked
to her.

"Okay, shoot."

"I'm not going back to that place. I'll go to AA meetings every day if I have to but I won't go back to that
place."

"We'll see."

"I don't need to be there, Dad. I'm not going to do any more drugs. I won't go back. You can't make me."

"This is Phelan's doing."

"No, this is my own doing. I'm okay now. I'll go to AA. You can go with me if you don't believe it."

"Then what are you going to do?" His mother had decided to join the conversation. "It's too late to go back to school this semester."

"I'll get a job. Phelan said I could work for him while he's here. He's going to stay until January. He said I could be his gofer."

"His what?"

"His errand boy. He has a lot of things to do for his grandmother and the businesses she owns. She still owns that paper plant in Clover and he's going to be spending time over there so he said I could ride back and forth with him. Uncle Niall thinks it's a good idea."

"Niall has always worshipped Phelan." This from Putty.

"How do you know, Putty?" James Senior put in. "You don't know a damn thing about Phelan and Niall. We'll talk about it this afternoon," he added, to his son. "After we get through with the funeral. My sister is dead, son. I wish you would try to remember that for the next few hours. Grandmomma and Granddaddy and Aunt Helen and Uncle Niall and Daniel and all of us have lost our sister. We'll work on your problems when we get through with this morning. And, Putty, you just stay out of this. I don't need you in on this today. You're the one that had to go and spend fifteen thousand dollars locking the boy up."

"Well, I think you could say he has profited from it."

James Junior put his left hand on his father's arm and his right hand on his mother. "It's okay, everybody," he said. "Calm down. I'm sorry I brought it up. She's right, Dad. It was a good thing to do. I'm glad I went to the hospital and now I don't need to be there anymore. Let's all just calm down."

"My God," this from Little Putty in the back seat. "I'm going to throw myself out of this car if you all keep arguing."

"Me too," Aleece said. "I'm jumping out on the pavement."

The church stood on its sloping lawns. It was made of brick from the time of Thomas Jefferson. Brick painted white. Its bell tower rose into the clear blue sky. Behind the church a row of elms rode along the crest of a hill. Above the elms small white cirrus clouds moved slowly along the sky.

The minister stood in the doorway waiting to greet the family. The driveway was packed with cars. The church was full of the people from the cars. The Hand family filed their way into the sanctuary.

As they were being seated, a limousine pulled up to the front of the church and Mimmi Farrell staggered out of the back seat and into the church and down the center aisle to the pews reserved for the family. She was wearing black. Black, black, black. Long black veil, wide-brimmed black straw hat. It was a summer hat but Mimmi had been too drunk when she got dressed to know the difference. She had left her tobacco planter–dilettante painter–lawyer husband stretched out on a deck chair by an indoor pool and gone up to her room and dressed herself and called the driver. Somewhere in her drunken consciousness she remembered Helen calling to say that Anna was dead. It behooved her to put in an appearance at the service. If Sykes Farrell was too dissipated to do his duty to Charlotte, then it was a good thing he was married to a lady. She dressed and got into the limousine and snored all the way into town. As they pulled up to the church she took a big drink out of a container of gin and followed it with a breath mint. She moved into the cold perfumed air of the church and down the aisle as if following an ancient neural pathway in her brain. She was wearing dark glasses and she could barely see. She looked out from in between the top of the glasses and the brim of the hat. She spotted Phelan and Crystal and LeLe. She fell into the pew beside them and clutched Phelan's arm. "It can't be true. It cannot be true." Her voice was beautiful and audible. She had once been on the stage, had even starred for one glorious week in a Broadway play. "Oh, I just found out," she said in her loudest stage voice. "This is the beginning of the end. The universe is playing tricks on us. Oh, my God, the cost. My God, the cost."

Phelan cuddled her into his coat. The minister raised his hand. The organ began to play. Bach's Prelude and Fugue in C Major. The minister stepped into the place between the pulpit and the altar rail. Anna's friends began to cry. "Pray for the living," the minister began. "Pray for us all, most holy and loving Lord Jesus Christ. Pardon us and take us into your care in this time of our need."

The morning sun poured in the stained-glass windows. The smell of L'Air du Temps and Chanel Number Five and Jessie Hand's liberal extravagance of Giorgio mixed with the smell of lilies. Lilies and chrysanthemums and orchids, hair spray, cleaning fluid. An orthopedic surgeon from Asheville who had gone to school with Anna and Helen had to be helped from the church. He was extremely allergic to perfume and had once fainted in an operating room from a nurse's Jungle Gardenia. His wife helped him down the aisle and out into the air. The minister, a young man from Sewanee just beginning his career, thought the doctor had been overcome by grief.

Mimmi Farrell let out a loud cry. The minister went determinedly on.

" 'No man is an island, entire of itself; every man is a

piece of the continent, a part of the main; if a clod be washed away by the sea, Europe is the less, as well as if a promontory were . . . any man's death diminishes me, because I am involved in mankind; and therefore never send to know for whom the bell tolls; it tolls for thee.'

"So the great writer John Donne taught us and so the great American writer, Ernest Hemingway, quoted him as saying, and now I borrow from both these men to memorialize another writer. Our Anna, who lived among us and helped us to understand ourselves. We are doubly burdened when an artist dies. Still, as Donne said, a clod is as important as a promontory."

Mimmi Farrell moaned a great long moan. The minister continued.

"Anna was also a child and a sister and a friend. She will be missed and mourned at the human level. Her books were translated into many languages. People share our sadness all around the world. It is difficult to accept death in the modern world. We have made such strides in all directions. It seems as if we should be doing better." He was lost in his scribbled notes. Caught up in the spirit of the dead writers he had conjured.

Mimmi let out a louder cry. Phelan pressed her head into his chest. Mr. Hand took off his glasses and wiped them on his handkerchief. He was sitting with Jessie on one side and Olivia on the other. Then Mrs. Hand by Olivia, then the rest of their grandchildren spread out in two rows. Their sons- and daughters-in-law flanked the children on the sides. Mr. Hand returned his glasses to his nose, looked up and down the ranks of his progeny, counted his grandchildren and his daughters and his sons. But the first one was gone, the very first one, the one who had resembled his own mother, his very first little baby girl. Had died without progeny or issue. Anna. There was no casket, nowhere to look, no place to rest his eyes. He stared at the rose window above the altar. Olivia turned her face to his. He thought of Anna's cheeks, Anna's eyes, his mother's hair, his mother's eyes.

The minister had found his place, was off again. "I absolve Anna Elizabeth from her means of taking off. I am sure God absolves her also. But if he doesn't I am certain Anna would be satisfied to be absolved by us, by the ones that loved her. I am going to read a few passages from her work, pieces I found as I read over the books last night."

James Junior began to squirm. He had met the eye of Jesus in a stained-glass window of the Sermon on the Mount. It reminded him of a time when he and Ray Trimble got stoned with some devil worshippers at a rock concert in the park. I won't go bad, James Junior promised Jesus. I'm through with all that shit. If you will get me out of there and let me have Shelby I swear I'll never do dope again, not even grass. You can count on me. From now on you can count on me.

"Sit still," his mother whispered. "It can't last much longer."

"I cannot bear it," Mimmi called out. "If he reads her work I'm going to faint."

"Hold on," Phelan said. "Hold on, Mimmi. We're going to make it. Hold on to me."

Mimmi sobbed. The minister read on.

The reading ended. The congregation rose and sang "The Church's One Foundation." The minister stepped down to the communion rail. No one knew what to do next. It was the first memorial service for a suicide ever held in Grace Episcopal Cathedral and there wasn't any protocol. There was no choir to march out and nothing for the pallbearers to bear, so everyone just stood around and talked to each other. Finally Mr. Hand took charge and led his coterie of granddaughters up the

aisle. Mrs. Hand followed with Helen and Spencer and
Louise. Phelan took Mimmi out a side door to her car.
Crystal Manning Weiss marched out holding King's
arm. Crystal Anne went in the other direction and
climbed up on the organ loft to take off her shoes. King
marched back down the aisle and scooped her up and
carried her outside. "She's too young to go to a memorial service," he said to Jessie. Jessie and Olivia had
followed him to a spot on the lawn. "She's only a little
girl," Olivia said. "She was fine."

Crystal joined them and took the child off their hands.
Then Jessie and Olivia and King walked off together in
the direction of Phelan's grandmother's car.

"Where are they going?" Daniel asked. He was on the
sidewalk below the church. Phelan had joined him there.

"It's okay," Phelan said. "There're three of them."

"What difference does that make in this day and
age? Goddammit, Phelan, go ask him where they're
going."

"The one to worry about is King," Phelan said. He
took a package of unfiltered Camels out of his pocket and held it out to Daniel. "That pair of yours look
like they could take care of themselves in a riot in
Haiti."

Crystal walked their way carrying Crystal Anne. Daniel thought of a night at Hilton Head when he and
Crystal had been left alone. She was twenty-six and
just divorced from King's daddy. He was eighteen.
There had been a red tide and the water was full of
phosphorescence and they had gone out into the surf
and thrown their bathing suits away and she had
climbed up on his body and put her legs around his
waist. I can't remember if she let me put it in, Daniel
was thinking. I think I must have come a hundred
times that night but I can't remember if she ever let
me put it in. Did I put it in? he always wanted to ask
Crystal but he knew he never would. As old as he was

he could barely even talk to Crystal Manning in the daylight.

"Give me a ride back to your momma's," she said now. "Are you going there?"

"If we can go by my house first. I have to call Sheila. She's been calling all week from London. I'm trying to keep her from coming here." Crystal stood beside him, holding her beautiful little spoiled-rotten half-French, half-Jewish, half-shod child.

"She's lost one of her shoes," Daniel said. "You want me to go back in the church and look for it?"

In the afternoon people began to leave. Adam went back to Vanderbilt, carrying a card with three different telephone numbers for LeLe. Not that he would need to use them. She would call him nearly every night for the next six months.

Louise flew back to Scotland. She put on her new dark green Anne Klein original and Niall and James took her to the airport.

"Am I in the will?" she asked.

"No, it was all for the kids."

"All for your kids? That's it? She didn't leave me a thing?"

"Why would she, Louise? Daddy takes care of you. Remember, I sign the checks."

"She was my sister. Well, I want to see the will. Send me a copy and I'll have my lawyer read it. I don't believe she didn't leave me a single thing."

"I didn't write it, Sister. She had it done someplace else. Some friend of hers downtown. Helen is her literary executor."

"Helen. My God."

"I didn't write it."

"Well, I don't even care. It's all so embarrassing anyway. What are people who have the courage to fight cancer supposed to think when they read about something like this? It's just like Anna to think she's never supposed to suffer a minute in her life. I know a bunch of people that were cured of cancer."

"Not of what she had." Niall pulled into the airport passenger zone and turned off the motor. "I don't want to hear any more of that, Louise. James, you take her in." Niall got out and went around to the trunk and got out Louise's suitcase and put it on the sidewalk. Then he walked off in the direction of the rental car parking lot. Louise stalked into the airport with James behind her carrying her bag. While she waited for the ticket agent to check her bags she reached her hand up underneath her coat and felt her breasts for the seventh time that day. She thought she felt a lump beside a mole above her rib cage but no, it was only a little muscle or milk gland. Maybe it was a muscle. Maybe it was a milk gland.

Back at the house Victoria was getting drunk. She had had a drink out of a bottle of bourbon before she went to the service and now she was drinking the rest of it.

"My niece got throat cancer from smoking," she was saying to Helen. "And she wouldn't let them do the biopsy tests. She said, no way, José. So the lady doctor that was seeing her came over to her house and said, Eileen, you got cancer. You have got to have these tests. That knot is as big as a fist. This knot in her throat. In her glands of her throat. What you coming over to my house to tell me something like that? Eileen said. Come driving up on my property telling me I got throat cancer. I don't want to hear it. If I got cancer I'll get rid of it my own way. You not getting any more of my money down at the so-called free clinic where you have already put me into debt at the drugstore. No one going to give me a three-hundred-dollar test to tell me I got cancer. She ran that lady doctor out of there. Said you tell them at the clinic I got my own chemotherapy if I need any. I got all the painkillers that I need and rat poison if it come to that."

"Did she get the tests yet?" Helen asked.

"No, ma'am, and not going to. So I know what you all are going through with Anna killing herself instead of going to the hospital. It seems to be a run of that this year."

Stacy came into the kitchen and began to cut off pieces of the pound cake and eat them with her fingers. Little slivers at first, then larger pieces. Stacy was the baby of Helen's family. She was nineteen, the same age as James's Aleece.

"Get a plate and fork," Helen said. "Don't just nibble like that."

Stacy didn't acknowledge that she had heard her mother.

"Is this when you throw up?" Helen added. "When you finish the cake?"

Stacy took the piece of cake she was holding and wadded it up and threw it into the sink. "I'm going to our house. I don't think I'm helping Grandmother. She doesn't even know I'm here."

"Eat the cake if you want it, honey. Only put it on a plate and don't throw it up afterwards."

"Fuck you," Stacy said, and walked out of the kitchen.

"She's a sad girl," Victoria said. "Don't let it get to you, Helen."

"It does. It does get to me. Get me a glass of wine, will you, Victoria. I'm going in and see about Momma. A glass of white wine will do."

"Where you want it? In there?"

"Yes, bring two glasses. Bring it to Momma's room."

Helen left the kitchen and Victoria went into the pantry and took a drink out of her glass of bourbon, then found two Gibson glasses and rinsed them out and filled them with white wine and put them on a tray.

This is my life, Helen said to herself as she passed James Senior and Putty and James Junior on their way out the door. This is my portion of the world, my appointed place, and these are the ones I have to spend my life with and there is nothing I can do about James Junior or anything else. I could go and lock up all the toilets in the house and then I guess Stacy would throw up outside on the rosebushes or I could go crazy and have myself locked up or I could see about Momma and then go home and make Winifred and Lynley do their homework but they are twenty-one years old and if juniors in college do not do their homework there is nothing a mother can do. I am going to go and take care of Mother and sometime tonight I am going to get a bath and sit down and read a book. I would like to be in a beautiful clean room with the ocean outside and a good-looking man sitting at my feet reading Cervantes to me. I would like to be young again but not in this world. I would like to know what time it is. What time is it anyway? I feel like I forgot to do something. I know I was supposed to do something about Louise going to the airport but there is too much going on.

She opened the door to her mother's room and found her mother lying on her side on the bed holding onto the folded gilt frame that held the photographs of her parents. Her mother was almost asleep and Helen sat down on the bed beside her and held her hand while the birds of North Carolina flew from her mother's feeders to the trees and back again.

They want her to turn on the radio, Helen decided. They don't know where the music is today.

~ III ~

The Anna Papers

❧ 16 ❧

ANNA'S PAPERS, SORTED BY HER SISTER,
HELEN ABADIE, LITERARY EXECUTOR

WHY DID SHE make me the executor? I don't want this
job. I went over there this morning; drove over there in
the worst ground fog we've had all fall. I couldn't see
out the window of the car but I woke up thinking about
those papers and the other executor, the poet from
Boston, is coming any day now so I thought I'd better go
on and see if there is anything that will embarrass
Momma to death. If so, I would just put that away for
later. It didn't take long to find something. Right out on
a table on this little filing stand made of red plastic trays
stacked up on top of each other. In the second tray
there is the true story of something that pertains to
Phelan Manning. The Manning family are our closest
friends in the world. She hadn't even bothered to
change the names. Just wrote it down, but not in her
own voice, it was written in the one that Momma says
Anna borrowed from listening to me. I don't sound like
that. I have a degree in elementary education from
Hollins and I have never been this chatty and never

gossiped in my life. That's what writers do and why I wouldn't stoop to be one. They twist the truth around to make it sound like they want it to. Anyway, here is an example of what I have to deal with as her executor. First this preamble:

> Wages of sin, urges to ecstasy, manifestations of grace, some notes on time and space as evidenced in the life of an alpha male during his residence in Jackson, Mississippi, in the later part of the twentieth century. Pray for us sinners now and at the hour of our death, amen.

Then the story:

ANNA AND PHELAN GO TO THE COAST, A MYSTERY

Anna called Phelan at his office and suggested they go to the coast for the weekend. She called him because it was one of those perfect spring days that make the whole town start acting sixteen and because she had dreamed of making love to him and woke up with her body soft and warm and filled with tenderness. She had gone by his grandmother's house the day before to leave off some flowers, and a caribou Phelan had killed was hanging on the wall in his grandmother's pristine and carefully decorated solarium and it was so big and so goddamn funny and so silly that Anna had dreamed all night of making love to him.

"I dreamed I was fucking you," she told him on the phone.

"Was it good?"

"It was wonderful. Listen, let's go down to the coast for the weekend and make love. Let's see if we still know how to have fun."

"Do you mean that?"

"Of course. I wouldn't ask you if I didn't mean it. You want to go?"

"God, yes. Let me call you back. I'll have to change some things. When do you want to go?"

"Whenever you can."

"How about this afternoon?"

"All right." She was laughing. It was already starting to be fun. "Phelan?"

"Yes."

"I think I'll fall in love with you. Do you mind?"

"I'll call you back in a few minutes. Call and see if we can get reservations."

Imagine writing that!

At four that afternoon he picked her up at her apartment and they stuck a pitcher of martinis in the back seat of his car and started driving to the coast. The Emerald Beach Hotel and Racquet Club. Old headquarters on the Carolina coast. Hardly a bedroom in the huge hotel that had not fostered adultery after adultery, also, plenty of honeymoons and reconciliations between married couples.

"I haven't had an affair at the Emerald Beach since nineteen sixty-eight," Anna was saying. "I had an affair with one of the quarterbacks for the Chicago Bears. I think he was a quarterback. It was a lot of fun but I was calling people up by the second day to get them to come down. That's always a bad sign."

"That's a sign of whiskey," Phelan said. "Let's don't get drunk. Let's don't even drink the martinis. I've been wanting to fuck you for about twenty years, Anna. I don't want to drink with you. I want to make love to you. Come over here." She slid across the seat of the car and cuddled up against his arm.

"Tell me about Africa," she said. "Tell me about killing lions and tigers. Say a lion was killing all the children of a village and they called you and asked you to come and get rid of him."

"It's happened." He was getting his serious look.

"Oh, bullshit, Phelan. Don't start that stuff."

"It has. The last one I killed was maimed and had been killing everything that moved for twenty miles. It took a month to track and kill him."

"Then what?"

"Then we had a party."

"Do you fuck the black women over there?"

"No, I take my own women. Or I do without. It's pretty uncomfortable. You don't think about fucking much in the veldt. Intercourse assumes huge proportions under those circumstances. You don't go looking for it out there."

"Like going to the Emerald Beach?"

"Yes." He put his hand on her leg and began to move it up and down. "Goddamn, you're a fine piece of something, Anna. What a waste for you to live alone. Why don't you move in with me?"

"Maybe I will." She laughed again. "If I like the way you fuck me."

They drove along in silence then, the long hills of North Carolina rolling along beside them, the beautiful woods and fragrant fields and a thousand shades of green in the brilliant cloudless spring afternoon. Anna was forty-three years old and Phelan Manning was forty-two years old and yes, they still knew how to have fun.

As if Phelan Manning wasn't my boyfriend every day of our lives. As if it wasn't me who broke his heart. As if I wasn't the one who had enough sense not to marry him when Daddy told me not to. What in the world was he doing with Anna when they didn't even like each other? It might not be true. Maybe she just used their names because she was too lazy to make up fiction ones. Fictional or whatever they call it. But it sounds just like them. It sounds just like something they would do except for the part about going to bed with one another. I just guess Anna and Phelan never even heard about sexually transmitted diseases. I know they never heard about monogamy or fidelity or any of the other small inconveniences civilized people have to put up with. Well, here's the rest of the story —

Later, in a suite of rooms overlooking the Atlantic Ocean, they took off their clothes and lay down upon the bed and began to examine each other, muscles, bones, scars, stretch marks, tight and loose flesh, nails and skin and teeth.

"You are holding up remarkably remarkably remarkably well," Anna said. "Look at this muscle. This is a divine thing." She was examining the long muscle of his hip.

"When do we get to make love?"

"When I get through looking you over." She sat up in the bed, crosslegged and still wearing her bracelets and her earrings. Wearing a small pink undergarment that had been handmade in Paris, France, and had cost two hundred and fifty dollars and was about to become drenched in sweat and end up torn and lying on the floor in about one minute because Phelan Manning was just about to decide that he didn't give a damn if she was his best friend's sister or the sexiest cheerleader he had ever seen bouncing around a gym floor because now he wanted to fuck her and he was tired of playing games.

"Come here to me," he said. "Come to me." And she came.

It is a fault of some people that they can only desire what they cannot have. Anna Hand was one of those people. So was Phelan Manning. Three days later, after they had both had a wonderful time and fucked each other like teenagers and gone swimming in the pool and waded out into the Atlantic Ocean and sat for hours on the warm sand telling stories and walking along the beach and even gone out and bought a couple of joints and gotten stoned, just for good measure, just to be sure they left nothing undone. After all of that they were not falling in love and they packed up their bags and drove back to Charlotte, North Carolina, in a light rain. They didn't talk much now, just sat on the front seat of the car, holding hands and being sad as hell that they could not fall in love. "I love you," Anna said, when Phelan left her at her door.

"I love you too. Want to have lunch on Tuesday?"

"If I can. I'll call you." She leaned in the doorway and kissed him once again. "Damn," she said.

"Damn," he answered. "Damn, damn, damn."

ADDENDA: A BIOGRAPHY OF PHELAN MANNING
(by Anna Hand)

Phelan Phinnessy Manning, born 1943, in an army base in Indiana. (Terre Haute? Call old Mrs. Manning out at Summerwood and ask her.)
Raised in Jackson, Mississippi. Summers in Char-

lotte, North Carolina. Education, Columbia Military Academy, Columbia, Tennessee, Baylor Military Academy, Chattanooga, Tennessee. Sewannee, University of the South, Harvard (two years). Degree in engineering. Small manufacturing plants in Texas and Mississippi, duck decoy factory in Atlanta. Where did all of Phelan's money come from?

One sister, Crystal Manning Mallison Weiss, dancer, collector of wealthy husbands, famous southern beauty.

Parents, William Phinnessy Manning and Christine Manning. Father a businessman and sometime politician. Mother, a typical indulgent southern lady. Why are Crystal and Phelan so unusual? What did the union of Big Phinnessey and Christine create? Solve this problem. Why did Helen like Phelan so much? Was it wrong of Daddy to keep them apart? Why has Phelan never appealed to me?

This is me again (Helen). Most of the stuff makes sense. She had an orderly mind. Folders are dated by events but I can sort it out.

Except the mathematical equations. I don't know what they mean. I think it's about physics. There are some letters from some Englishman who is some kind of nuclear physicist and pages of these real small figures — like math problems. I'll show it to Phelan when he comes back. Or to a professor at the university if I get time. For now I've put it all back where I found it, in a folder marked *The Midas Syndrome*.

"Hang on to your chlorophyll," that was written on the top of one page. And "Let your right hand know what your left hand is doing." That was on the page dated *two months* before her death. There are seven pages of calculus and trigonometry problems. A drawing (like a maze) of Summerwood (notations of survey markers; pages from books at a courthouse somewhere). Could it be a treasure map? A joke? How long did she know she was sick? Did she know before Brian told her?

Anna and Daddy: Why did they fight all the time? This is killing him. A death blow. That she would die this way. A terrible treasonous death. *"She knew you loved her."* I keep telling him that, but it isn't true. Here's something she wrote about him: "He doesn't know how to love. He probes and pushes and demands and extracts and extracts and extracts and is never pleased or satisfied. He has harmed us all by being so powerful and demanding. Jealous. A jealous king. Everything he touched turned to gold." (This from a folder marked *Father,* 1969.) Here's a strange coincidence. Daddy is always saying, "Hang on to your gold."

WEDNESDAY AFTERNOON, NOVEMBER 3, 1985,
2:00 P.M.

I cleaned out the little cherry desk Mother gave her when she was sixteen. I have one just like it only mine has been refinished and looks new. Jack Benoit did it for me last year. I was going to give it to Stacy before she started throwing up for Jesus. I'm not trusting her with anything until she comes to her senses. She's driving me crazy trying to get part of Anna's money to give to that preacher who has her hypnotized.

Never mind Stacy for now. I'm Anna's executor and that's my main concern this year (for everyone's sake).

There is this little black ledger. About five inches by seven inches with figures of money and dates:

F.T.O.M.	$22,000.00	Feb. 20, 1984
F.T.O.M.	17,000.00	Apr. 11, 1985
F.T.O.M.	50,000.00	June 10, 1985
F.T.O.M.	54,000.00	July 22, 1985

It is almost $150,000.00. Some are marked K.R., others say C.G.L., others A.E. There is a drawing stuck in it, a parallelogram.

I think it might be something she has invested or maybe something for a book she's writing. I put it back in the desk and locked it.

TUESDAY: I AM GOING TO WRITE DOWN EVERYTHING I KNOW ABOUT ANNA.

Anna. What she looked like, what she wore, what she read, how she slept, her bed, her shoes, her gowns, her cosmetics, her fingernails, her feet and legs, her hair. Her way of turning her head and listening, her bells. All her life she would buy bells and wind chimes and set them out so the wind would never let her forget that we are spinning. She liked to hang strings of bells on doors or over the arms of chairs.

She was far away from us. Either far away or completely here and all the way into our heads, digging in and searching for secrets we didn't even have. Everyone in this family tells everything they know the minute they find it out. She was always planting ideas in our heads, giving us books, writing us letters with half the words underlined. Later, when she was older and the family fell apart, she left and went off to the mountains and wrote things that shocked and hurt us. Do people need to know that much? In the end she forgave us and came home.

Did we need forgiving for being ourselves? Where was I? I was going to tell you what she looked like. But I am thinking of how she would always disappear. I was two years younger, her baby sister. She was the oldest and I was second. She was always in the world for me, like Mother or Daddy. I can't believe that she is gone. Perhaps, if some heaven exists, but that's crazy to think like that.

I was always in her shadow and I didn't mind that, as long as she allowed me to stay there. But she would disappear, out to a corner of the lawn, hiding, or down the riverbank or up a tree. She would climb higher and higher, up a magnolia or pecan or crepe myrtle, knowing I'm afraid of heights. Once she propped a ladder against a pecan tree and when she was in the low branches kicked it down so I couldn't follow even if I wanted to. It was the tree our grandfather hung himself from when he got cancer. When (if?) Anna followed him to hell, when she turned her back on God, scared to death of pain or disfigurement, when she stepped off into the ocean off Biddeford, "into the trillion stars" as she wrote in the letter she left. On that night I remembered how of all the cousins only Anna would climb that tree, or play on the patio below it, or set her dolls on the wooden table or swing in the creaky web-covered swing. She said she could remember sitting on his lap and wore yellow all her life in memory of how he loved her in that color.

No wonder no man could ever satisfy or keep her. If she had been able to have children perhaps she would have been satisfied to stay with one of them. She was so restless, liked so much to be alone. Maybe she willed herself childless. God knows she hated to take care of people. Where is she now? Why did she leave us in that terrible way? I must keep asking these questions while these cold rainy days go by. Then Christmas, then Mardi Gras, then her birthday, then mine and then spring. I will be well by spring, this grieving will be over. I have enough to do without missing Anna. My girls are acting as crazy as loons. And my boys too. My God, I'm getting as critical as she was. Maybe she is haunting me. Maybe it's being over here all alone. As alone as Anna was when she went up to New England to die. But she wasn't alone. Philip was there. That poor man. He can't believe she didn't tell him. I can believe she didn't tell me. It is just like Anna to die without telling a single soul she was going to. How did she keep from telling?

But I was talking about her clothes. I was going to tell you how she dressed and what she wore.

When she was working she wore an old pair of gray wool slacks and a light brown cardigan sweater. She wore leather tennis shoes or high brown boots. She wore her hair straight and parted on the side. She only wore makeup when she went to town. She wore leather gloves that covered her wrists. You would have known she was somebody special if you saw her on the street. So self-possessed and careless. So cocky.

She owned thousands of dollars' worth of beautiful clothes she never wore. She would get into spells of buying them. Then she would give them away. She would give my girls armloads of things. Calvin Klein and Giorgio Armani and Valentino, Geoffrey Beene and Nipon and beautiful white blouses and sweaters of all kinds. Boots and shoes. Three fur coats and a leather raincoat from Paris and an old houndstooth jacket she had written her first book while wearing on winter nights in the house in the mountains. I bet she wore it to die. It would be the thing she would want to wear to die. Surely she didn't want to die. I have never known anyone who loved life as much as she did. Seemed to love it. I imagine she put on that jacket and maybe took a small bag, but if she did we never found it. It never showed up anywhere. Some hotelkeeper in Biddeford is still wondering what to do with it, I suppose. It's in a closet somewhere waiting to be claimed. She mailed letters from Boston but he didn't see her mail them. She must have fucked him one last time as much as she loved to fuck. Listen, this is too much. I don't have any business writing this stuff on her typewriter. I'm beginning to sound just like her. I'm going to the grocery store and get some food to feed my family. The girls are coming over and I'm not going to write any more of this just now. How do they know when to stop? The ones that do this for a living.

✂ 17 ✂

✂ SHE USED TO SAY, Helen, if anything ever happens
to me, be sure and go lock up my papers so Momma and
James won't burn everything up. Okay, Anna, I'd say, if
anything ever happens to you I won't let them burn
your papers up.

Her workroom, office, whatever you want to call it,
was only a spare bedroom in her house. The girls were
disappointed when they saw it. They had imagined it
more like something at a play, looking out upon a lake
or with a chaise lounge or a nice walnut desk.

Anyway, when they called me from Maine and told
me what had happened I went straight over there and
double-locked all the doors. The other executor is a poet
up in Boston. I called him and he told me just to lock
everything up and not to move anything until he got
here. His name is John Carmichael, an Irish name. She
called him Mike. He could be one of her old lovers. I
think he used to be in New Orleans, a long time ago. It
all seems like a long time ago.

The house was in perfect order. Not a thing out of
place. There was a note pinned up on the wall above the
typewriter. A quotation about infinity. It said science

can only give us glimpses of what is going on. "These concepts belong to a level of reality which is *above our heads.*" She had underlined those three words. Do you think that meant she had started to believe in God? It would make things a lot easier for Momma if she thought Anna had started to believe in God. I read a poll the other day and it said ninety-seven percent of the American people believe in heaven and think they are going there but they think only sixty percent of their friends will get in. It is unlikely Anna will get in if there is one. She didn't want in. She said the kind of people that will get in wouldn't amuse her. She said a lot of things I hope she didn't mean. Here's a list of the records she had out on the floor. The Köln concert by Keith Jarrett, Andreas Villenweider, Verdi and Puccini, Dire Straits, Bach, Tales from the Vienna Woods, Motown hits, Mozart, Pachelbel, Miles Davis, Coltrane, Loggins and Messina. She used to play music for my kids when they were small. She used to read them books. She read them the King Pellinore chapters out of *The Once and Future King* when they were so small they could not have understood what any of it meant but they would sit still and listen. She had a lovely deep voice, a haunting voice. Well, anyone would tell you that. I guess the married doctor knows it. I bet he feels like hell. He probably thinks he made her do it. I would if I was him. She might have wanted him to think that. There were darknesses in Anna. There was a part of her that was capable of anything. Which she proved to us all over and over, before we even got to this last terrible darkness. I forgive her. I swear I do. I completely understand and forgive her.

What she liked. She liked to read *The Bear* and *The Old Man and the Sea* and *The Bridge of San Luis Rey.* She hated *Finnegans Wake* and had reservations about Picasso. She liked Woody Allen and Fellini. She loved Tommy Tune. She saw a musical called *Nine* about ten times. She liked to be in love. She fell in love too easily, she fell in love too fast, she fell in love too terribly hard, for love to ever last. Every time I ever heard that song I thought of Anna.

But I meant to write down what I know about freedom. I came over here with the dishes not done and my teeth unflossed and the beds unmade to write about the way Anna felt about freedom. She thought about it all the time, talked about it, brooded upon ways it could be taken from her. She knew too much about our family to ever let down her guard a moment. Daddy is a communist where the family is concerned. From each according to his abilities to each according to his needs. So naturally Anna never got a cent or a car. Also, she was expected to show up at every college and school that any of our children or even cousins were going to. Show up and lecture and refuse to be paid. He made a deal with her that if she would do it for free or give the money back after the school paid her, then he would reimburse her. But he never did and Anna got really mad about it. She and Daddy would invent something to argue about. She never could get him to admit that she was more wonderful than the rest of us. That's what she wanted from him. Momma said that to me. I didn't say it first. So anyway, that was Anna and Daddy, and I guess some of those fictional fathers she created were more like him than he wanted to admit. He pretended the only reason she wrote books was to make money and he said anyone that read novels deserved whatever they got.

Wait a minute. I'm getting so lost. If you think all the time about things you get all tangled up. It's better to just march ahead with your life. I wish Daddy wasn't so very very sad about this loss. Our loss. She was gone most of her life. We didn't get to have enough of her. Up in the mountains, she didn't even ask us to come visit. She was always in mountains, the Appalachians, the Rockies, the Alps, especially when she was married to Francis. Well, they didn't get to Tibet. They planned to go to Tibet. No one in our family ever got to Tibet, except for Louise and she came home with the hives and was sick for months. The next year she went right back. Of course, Louise is as stubborn as a goat.

ဆ 18 ဆ

ဆ I FOUND THIS TODAY. I was going to throw it away but I thought I should wait and let Mike [John Carmichael] read it first. Imagine writing something like this down.

The time I picked up the Norwegian sea captain in the British Airways lounge in Los Angeles and flew across the ocean with him. I knew I was doing it. He was so gorgeous and so tan and looked so irritated and European. I had on that long pleated white skirt I wore all summer that summer. I was so thin and LeLe and I had been having such a good time in San Francisco, eating sushi and running in the hills and seeing movies. Then she backed out on going to Greece with me because the rugby player came back to town so I went alone. The travel agent was a woman from the Philippines and she sent me out to the airport in a white limo driven by a huge black man. It was all so goddamn silly from the very beginning. A woman we knew had died and LeLe and I were trying to shake off the haunting. So I was alone and there he was and he never took his eyes off me the whole time we were in the lounge. Finally I straddled the edge of the sofa he was sitting on and called Charlotte to talk to Mother. I told her I was on my way to Athens and when I got off the phone the sea captain said, Are you going to Athens? and I said yes, and he said, So am I, we'll be companions all the way.

He was traveling first class and came and found me in business class and asked if he could sit down. His English was so good and we used my Swedish and some French. It was very jolly and by the time it was dark outside we were eating together. He was drunk by then. I have never seen a man drink that much whiskey on an airplane. It amazes me when people drink and don't get drunk. I admire it as I do all power and excess.

So the plane was stopped in Munich because they had blown up the Athens airport and he picked up my bag and took me to a hotel and ordered dinner in German and then we stayed together for three days. I forgot to call the agent in Athens and they thought I was lost. Everyone was looking for me and all I was doing was lying in bed with Hakon listening to stories from the war. He was a child in Norway while I was a child in North Carolina and his father was a hero of the underground. Where is he now, that Hakon? He called me once or twice, later, but it never worked out for us to see each other. We were in different countries. Perhaps I should call him. Perhaps I should make a list of people to see and men to call and maybe fuck before I do this thing. But the pain might start. I am already beginning to look very bad. The fear is on my face. I think I smell of it. I don't know if I can see

Philip without him knowing. He will know. I don't want him to remember me with fear in my eyes, the smell of fear. What could I take? Cocaine? Dexedrine? Brian would give me a Dex or two if I absolutely begged. I have to touch him once more. I have to see him. Have to prove the world is not niggardly, that we can have something.

I would call Hakon. If Philip won't meet me I will fly to Norway or Greece or Spain and see him. If he's at his place in Spain I will definitely go. What a wonderful lover he was, so strong and funny and wild. It was like playing a wild powerful Nordic game. I thought, this is why LeLe likes the rugby player. To fuck power. A man who goes to sea. I have not missed much. Thank God for that. I was here. I was definitely here and all the time I was here I played.

The more I read these papers the less I understand her: What did she need from us? What did she want us to do? Why couldn't she love us as we were? Accept us for what we were? We weren't as smart as Anna, I'll admit that. We weren't as smart and we weren't as lucky and we didn't get to live alone and have all that time to ourselves. All those years alone? Nine, ten, however many it turned out to be. She said she would rather be alone than cook dinner for people. She was so selfish. The oldest child gets selfish. Marry an only child if you want an unselfish person. So she went away and then she came home and took the phone off the hook and disconnected the doorbell. Did she love us? I suppose so. We loved her. We needed her. We needed her to look up to and get bawled out by and looked down on when our children married people with no background or education. She was right about that. We have pretty much thrown it all away. I'm

crying again. Crying on her typewriter. Oh, my God. I
wish I hadn't even come over here this morning. I wish
I didn't even know Anna. When we were little I
would climb into bed with her and she would cuddle
me up like I was her little girl and tell me stories
about how we would grow up and fly airplanes high
up above the clouds and reach out the windows and
feed the flocks of geese or talk to the stars and she
said we would fly all the way to China and put on an
air show for the Chinese. I used to dream about it
after she would tell it to me. In the dream I'd be all
alone in an airplane and I wouldn't know how to fly it.
She asked too much of us. She wanted us to be like
her. She was the only one who ever had Mother to
herself. A psychiatrist told me that, when I went in to
find out why I never finish anything I start. I'm better
now. I say this stuff to myself about putting one foot
in front of the other one until I finish climbing up the
hill. I pretend like the hill is green and not very steep
and covered with beautiful white and gold and yellow
flowers. Sometimes I pretend there's this real good-
looking guy with black curly hair standing on the top.
With his hands stuck deep down in the pockets of his
trousers.

Daniel came over last night and he was drunk. In a
good mood for the first time in weeks. He's been having
a fit ever since that little girl got here from Oklahoma.
He wouldn't let her go home. She has missed almost two
weeks of school. "I need her," he kept telling everyone.
"Jess and I need her here." Daddy has been talking on
the phone five times a day to her aunt and the school
principal out in Oklahoma because Jessie and Daniel
were adamant about her staying. They even went over
and registered her in Jessie's school.

"What's happening now?" I said, when he showed
up on the front porch. I had been keeping out of it as

much as I could. I had enough to do with these papers driving me crazy. "Come on in," I added. "What's going on?"

"He took her home," Daniel says. "Daddy's driving her to Oklahoma. He and Jessie and Olivia got in that old car and took off for the Indian territory. Has he got balls or what? Goddamn, Helen, he's seventy-nine years old."

"Oh, my God. When did they leave? He can't drive to Oklahoma. My God, Daniel, how did you let this happen?"

"It's all right, Sister. Olivia's going to drive. She and Jessie will drive most of the way. He wants to go and so he went. You should have seen them driving off. Momma made them a lunch in a shoebox and they drove off with the windows down. Wait till they figure out he doesn't even have a radio."

"Oh, God, it really is funny. He finally got someone in the car." No one in our family will ever drive anywhere with him in the car. Momma hasn't gotten in a car with him in years. If they go anywhere together she drives her car. In the first place he never rolls the windows up.

"I thought you wanted her to stay."

"He's going to ask them to let her come next year. She's going to Switzerland with us as soon as school is out. Can you believe that old bastard? I mean, can anyone believe him?"

I started to say, Daniel, it was your place to go see her family and meet them and ask to let her come here. But I didn't do it. In the first place it was so wonderful to see Daniel smiling, to see anyone in this family happy for a moment, after this fall. Also, at least someone was taking Olivia home. At least someone had enough sense to know that a straight-A student is not supposed to be missing weeks of school or being put in a different school in the middle of high school.

Just picture them on the highway. Daddy lecturing
to them about the decline of morals and the failure of
the Federal Reserve System and the coming decline of
the world and why they should be wearing anti-
abortion armbands. Thousands of miles of road before them and no radio. Momma heard from them
last night at nine o'clock. They had gotten as far as
Alabama.

☙ 19 ❧

☙ TODAY IS THE DAY I start on the filing cabinet. The galleys to the books are rolled up in one drawer and what looks like a lot of poems. Some essays and speeches. Her diploma. She didn't even frame it. She went back to college to get her degree when she was twenty-six. She had quit to put her first husband through school. Then all those miscarriages. They could have fixed it now. There are drugs you can take. The miscarriages ruined the marriage, so she got a divorce and went back to school. That's one version of what ruined the marriage. At the time of the miscarriages I was having babies every year and so was James's wife, so that must have made it harder but she said it made it easier. She was a great believer in DNA. She was always talking about DNA. Later, about replicating something that meant the same thing, only it means the genes want to make themselves into babies and use you any way they like to do it. I don't like to think about children in such coldhearted ways.

Anyway, Anna went back to the university since it was right here in town, and she made straight A's and majored in philosophy. There was this philosophy profes-

sor she adored named Doctor Borg and that was what
he taught so she took all his courses. The rest of the
philosophy majors were thin quiet boys waiting to go to
divinity school. Except for this Norwegian aristocrat, a
beautiful young woman who had married a Charlotte
boy against her parents' wishes and run away to America with him. She was having a hard time adjusting to
Charlotte, North Carolina, and Anna befriended her.
By which I mean that she and Anna drank together and
hung around the new theater that was just getting
started, down in the black section near Seventh Street.
Who was Anna sleeping with in those days? I can't remember, if I ever knew.

Anyway, she went back to college and got that degree
that's rolled up in the filing cabinet. The day she graduated she gave the philosophy professor a statue made
out of the parts of a watch. A man made of a watch. *A
Bust of Plato,* she wrote on the card, and after she gave
it to him she came over to my house and cried all afternoon. She was going to miss talking to him so much. She
cried and got drunk and she kept telling me this absent-
minded professor joke he had told her. "Did you hear
about the professor," he said, "who filed the leaves and
burned his papers?" She kept telling me that joke over
and over. We were drinking whiskey sours and the children were running around in their pajamas doing anything they liked and later that night Spencer, my
husband, came home with a lawyer from Jackson Hole,
Wyoming, and she left with him. I think that lasted
about six months. Spencer blamed it on me and said it
embarrassed him to death.

Also, he is not crazy about me coming over here every
day and reading all this stuff with no one with me. If I had
died she would have taken care of my children. I guess
she would have. So here I am in this room with all these
half-finished books and letters and papers and essays and
poems. You should see this room. I should describe this

room. I should take a photograph of it. First I'll go get a cup of tea. That's all there is to eat in this kitchen.

Later: Her room. Where she worked. A squarish room about twelve feet by fourteen. Closets along one wall with out-of-season clothes and the suit she ran her marathon in and some old cocktail party clothes from long ago. On the shelves are paper cartons of reviews of her books. On the floor a pile of old blue jeans and sweaters and sweat shirts and boots. Boxes of unpacked books. All over the floor are little piles of half-written stories, drafts of novels, photographs, maps, books about ancient Greece. Dozens of them. Two cheap book-cases holding an *Encyclopaedia Britannica* and the green filing cabinet. An advertisement from a magazine is pasted on the side. A picture of a snow-capped moun-tain and a caption that says, LIFE IS THE URGE TO ECSTASY. Some cheap Mardi Gras beads are taped to the advertisement and a letter from some little girl named Athena she knew in New York City. I haven't had the heart to read that yet. Anna was always adopt-ing children and writing to them.

Some of mine, some of James's, some of Daniel's. The ones that got in trouble were driving her crazy last year. My nephew, James, that we had to lock up in the Baptist hospital, and any of them that were drinking or getting fat or not doing well in school. She grieved over them. She went crazy because she couldn't fix it. She brooded. I think James was the one that really broke her heart. He's doing fine now, she should have had more pa-tience, should have trusted God. But Anna didn't be-lieve in God, so how could she trust Him?

On the darkest nights since her death I think we gave her cancer. That runs in the family, getting sick over things other people do. I have seen Mother break out in hives when the phone rang after midnight and one of the boys had been arrested for drunken driving or the girls came home with their babies. Of course, once when it rang our cousin Harper Lane was dying and Mother had to go and watch him die. He was the good one, the one who never had a drink. Someone else's drunken daughter ran into him. Life is complicated even in a small agrarian state. Everything happens.

Well, this isn't getting that cabinet cleaned out. I was hoping to get done with it and start on the things on the floor.

It was so wonderful when she moved back here. I was thrilled when I heard it. I really was. I thought she would bring some glamour back to Charlotte, have some of her friends from New York down here to meet us. Go out to lunch with her old friends, let our friends get to know her. Not Anna. She just secluded herself half the time. Took the phone off the hook. Undid the doorbell. Had it disconnected. I'm grieving, mad as hell at the virus that got inside and killed her. Bugs, germ warfare. Maybe it was pollution or maybe something from that nuclear reactor she visited last year. No, this was a virus. She weakened and let it in. She quit taking care of herself and something got in and started eating her alive. Then she did what she did. What our grandfather did. Maybe it isn't true. Maybe she's in Paris or Vienna or Rome. The southern coast of Spain. A villa in Barcelona with that Norwegian sea captain she wrote that thing about. And all of this is just a smoke screen so we won't write to her or call her up or tell her what any of the children are doing.

I am a normal well-meaning woman with five spoiled-rotten children including a daughter in Memphis who hates her own body and fraternal twins who think the whole world is some private joke for *their* amusement.

"She jumped into the sea." That's what he said when he called. I was the first one he got on the phone.

"How long has it been?" See, *I wasn't even surprised.*

"This morning." She had cyanide. The police say she bought it in Charlotte before she left. She might have taken that first. I'm so sorry to tell you this."

"Was she sick?"

"I don't know. Something was wrong."

"Have they found the body?"

"I think so. I'm on my way to Kittery, there's a body there. It sounds as though it's Anna. I don't know. I'll call again when I get there. I don't know how to help you, what to do."

"I should help you. I'll come on the next plane. Where is the nearest airport?"

"Come to Boston. I'll have someone meet your plane. Leave a message with my service in New York. Helen?"

"Yes."

"She said you were the one they leaned on."

"No. She was the one that tended us. I'll come on the next plane."

It wasn't Anna. Whatever has become of her has never returned to cast its hull or bones or torn fur-lined Valentino jacket onto those rocky New England shores. Maybe she was carried up into the heavens by a choir of seagulls like Momma's old painting of the Assumption. Oh, Anna, my plane ride to meet your lover.

"I'm Philip." He stood before me. "It wasn't her. There isn't any word."

"Let me see the letter." We were blocking the other people getting off the plane and he took my arm and we walked down the hallway and out to the baggage claim.

"Do you have luggage?"

"No, just what I have with me. Let me see the letter." He led me to the parking lot and we got into his rented car and he began to drive. He reached in his pocket and took out the letter and handed it to me.

"Was she in this car?"

"Yes."

"I can feel her here."

"I know. Go on. Read the letter."

Dear Mother and Father, Helen, James, Niall, Louise, Daniel,

Forgive me and for God's sake understand. It had to be this way. I had to let the world be beautiful as long as I could. Curse the curses of man. I have loved you as well as I could and now you'll have to finish up without me.

Love, Anna

"Was there one to you?"

"Yes."

"May I read it?"

"Yes." He took it from his breast pocket and held it out. "The police have seen it. Helen, I asked her to marry me. I came up here to ask her. Please believe that." He was holding on to the steering wheel. How gentle men are when there is trouble. I was half in love with him too. Just like Anna, to find the best man in the world and have him love her back. Not like my quiet insurance executive, but right out of the silver screen and with red hair.

"I suppose we should find you a hotel. Then we'll have a drink and think it over. There will be a lot to do tomorrow." He started the car. He settled back and began to drive. It was dark as a cave in Boston, Massachusetts, that night. Not a star. Even the street lights seemed dim.

TUESDAY, 8:00 A.M.

I'm getting used to being in here now. In her room, at her typewriter, sitting in her chair. It's cold, though. I moved a space heater in. One of those new ones that looks like a radiator.

I was going to go through the poems today. It will take my mind off my problems. Lynley can't seem to find himself. He thinks of one grand scheme after the other but they don't work out. And DeDe living with that boy in Atlanta. Just living with him right out in the open. They never even mention marriage. And Stacy, I can't even think of Stacy. Some days I wish I'd strangled them in their cribs, or never had them. I don't know what we're supposed to do. It's too hard to be a parent. We can't hand over our lives to them, can't give them careers, can't go to work for them and have marriages for them. What would they do if Spencer and I died? Rootless, they are rootless except for us, Momma and Daddy and Spencer and me, holding down the fort here in Charlotte. If it wasn't for us there wouldn't be any place for them to call home. It's strange to be a mother, forever and forever called upon to sacrifice and suffer. They don't suffer for us. When Momma had shingles last year they didn't offer to go over there and sit with her. She was in such pain. Where will they be when I am that age? I guess Stacy will come and get me and introduce me to her simpleminded friends. I guess DeDe will call me up and say some smart-alec things to me. At least Lynley is bright. He's bright like Anna and Daddy. Not that being bright did Anna much good. All she had in the end was cancer and a married man.

There's always Kenny. At least he's married, even if Eugenia doesn't let him come over much and even if I'd rather never have a grandchild at all than have one out of her womb. Oh, I mustn't do this to myself. The world is out there. I must stop.

Four days later: I am better now. Imagine Anna grieving over never having children. She didn't know what a blessed life she had. How did she think she had time to write those books? All that time to think and reflect and make up things. Time to be her full self with nobody screaming or pulling at her or getting the chicken pox or being exposed to homosexuals and dope.

No one ever knew Anna. She never stayed long enough in one place. She'd come in your house and walk around looking at everything, then she'd sit you down for a talk about whatever was on *her* mind, why Jodie should get a job, how to get the kids off dope, who was an alcoholic, what was wrong, what school I needed to go to for further education, books I should read. Then she would go to the bookstore and be back in an hour with the books. Later, she'd find the books and take them home with her. She had so many parts to her, so many roads and valleys. When we were small we would celebrate New Year's Eve together. At twelve o'clock we would go out on the back porch and beat on pans and yell and scream. I remember how big the stars always seemed on nights like that, brilliant and white and my big sister, Anna, beside me, beating on the pans. We were alone a lot when we were children, the two of us, now that I think of it. Alone in a bed having chicken pox. Alone with a book she was reading to me. Hiding from James and Niall and Daniel and Louise. I don't know how this family got so messed up but I think it was the money. Daddy made a lot of money when Anna and I were in junior high. He had it by the time the rest of them were in school but Anna and I can remember a small frame house on a tree-lined street. Neighbors that baked bread. Momma making our dresses. The whir of the sewing machine. The smell of new fabric, dotted swiss and chambray and checked pinafores. Momma cooking and us setting the table and Daddy pretending to think asparagus was poison.

Wild asparagus we picked by the railroad tracks. Life was better back then. And then my grandfather died and Momma was sick all winter and the other babies began to be born. Too much of everything. After that it was always too much of everything. Too much paper, this whole room full of paper to be sorted out and put in boxes and decided upon. Here's something I found today that's pretty funny. One of Anna's diets:

    7:00   Water, one egg.
    9:00   Four-mile walk. Water. Three carrot sticks.
 10:00   Water. Herb tea.
 12:00   Water. Salad from McDonald's. No dressing.

The rest of the page was blank. She never could concentrate on deprivation, hunger, keeping her mouth shut, doing without. We used to roller skate on the street in that little neighborhood where we were happy. They had so few cars that you could roller skate on the asphalt road all day. Anna could go backwards as fast as I could go forwards and we would dance on our skates and sing "God Bless America" and "We Three Kings of Orient Are" and do figure eights.

"It is not the poverty of our solutions," she once wrote to me. "It is the enormity of our problems." She was talking about the children, about Kenny and Lynley and James, and Crystal Manning's son, King, and so many more. The sad uncertain children of our friends. They don't have anything to do. No one likes to work anymore. Except for artists. But even they have critics that say horrible things about them and try to hurt them and put them down. People are jealous of anything wonderful they see. Even Anna had to put up with that. They loved her at first and could only say good things about her, then they turned on her. She always told them to go fuck themselves. I'll say that for Anna. She called up the *New York Times* one time and told the executive editor to go fuck himself. Of course she had a bad temper. I never forgot that after she got famous and was so calm and serene looking when she would show up in public. With her famous light-hearted sense of humor and all that. Her New York clothes and coats from London and Italian shoes. Underneath I could always see that bad temper shining through. I guess it came in handy when she walked off that pier into the ocean. I guess it took getting mad to make her do it. She could have said something like, I'm not going to live very long, Helen, and I want you to know I love you. Then she could have gone on and walked off the pier and no one would have stopped her. Into water that deep wearing all those clothes and leather boots. I think they filled with water and took her down. Or maybe she just wanted to look wonderful the last time the married doctor saw her. A white parka lined with fur and dark gray slacks and knee-high boots. That's what he said she was wearing. And a scarf. I can't believe they can't find the body. I will never believe she's dead until I see that body.

Phelan Manning's cuff links on the dresser beside her bed. I was the one that Phelan loved. The year he broke his collarbone playing football, the year I was Junior Maid in the Homecoming Court. I went with him and wore his class ring and I was the one who held the other end of the streamers when he decorated the gym with his arm in that polka-dot sling he wore all fall. He never cared a thing about Anna. He said Anna was a book-worm. We used to make fun of her.

His cuff links on her dresser beside her rings. A box of pearls and a small white jewelry box full of costume jewelry and a gold bracelet that belonged to our grand-mother and a pair of Phelan's cuff links. Big squares of gold with ivory in the middle. Maybe he gave them to her. But I think he left them there. Imagine Anna in bed with Phelan. There wouldn't be any air to breathe for the ego taking up all the room.

He has the nicest shoulders, such an elegant body.

All the Mannings are elegant people. Charming and witty and full of themselves. Well, she may have gone to the coast with him to forget the married man but she didn't keep him. No one could keep Phelan, which is why I had enough sense not to marry him. He is famous all over Africa. He went into the bush after an injured lion and the story made *Sports Illustrated*. He went through a hive of swarming bees. James was with him. He said the bearers wouldn't even go where Phelan goes. Phelan never was interested in anything but sports and playing chess and hunting. Daddy told me if I married him I would be a widow all my life and he was right. So now he's back in town and living with his grandmother at the old Manning place out in the county near the airport. If these cuff links belong to him then they are worth a lot of money and I should give them back.

So I called up Phelan and asked him to come over to Anna's apartment and talk to me about Anna. He came that afternoon. It was a beautiful day, the sun shining on the lake and I had made some cheese straws and had a drink waiting for him. We sat down on the sofa and I came out with it.

"I found a pair of your cuff links in Anna's bedroom. I guess she must have borrowed them from you."

"No, I gave them to her. She forgot the cuff links to a dress."

"Where were you?"

"On the coast. Last spring. We went down to see if we still knew how to have fun."

"Did you?"

"Yes, we did. Where are they, Helen? The cuff links." I took them out of my pocket and handed them over. He held them in the palm of his hand.

"There was no one like her. No one could take her place."

"She was a coward to kill herself. It's almost killing Mother."

"Your mother had no right to ask for Anna's pain."

"She could have tried a few things first."

"Like what, Helen? Having her breasts cut off? Can you imagine Anna doing that? Now can you really?"

"No."

"I applauded when I heard she'd done it. I would have helped her if she had asked me." He stood up then. "I have to be going, Helen. How are things coming with her papers?"

"It's a big mess. I'm not getting anything done. I stay over here for hours every day and it seems I don't make a scratch on the surface. Her other executor is coming. He'll be down next week. He'll take some things back to the publisher."

"Take your time with it. That's my advice. They won't be less valuable later."

"That's good advice. Look, don't you want another drink?"

"No, not now." Then he took me by the shoulders and kissed me on the cheek and hair. Then he was gone, and I stood for a long time by the door looking out at the road.

Here's a piece of paper I found today. "He puzzled over reality in the world outside his work, it was presumably a place where people could be happy, laugh, bear children." There are thousands of pieces of paper like that. Pages torn from tablets. Sometimes I think she believed the things she wrote were true. That the people she made up were real. She made this paper world out of pieces of our lives and out of dreams. I wish Phelan would come back. I wish he would tell me all that happened. Everything they did, everything they said. Where they stayed, what they had to eat, what they did to each other and how it felt and if they went into the ocean, letting the waves play with their legs. Anna loved the ocean. Born under the sign of Pisces and now this terrible unlucky end.

Here is something else I found. "It is our disease to want to contain everything within the frame of reference of a psychology or a philosophy. After all Justine cannot be justified or excused. She simply and magnificently is; we have to put up with her, like original sin. But to call her a nymphomaniac or to try and Freudianise her takes away all the mythical substance — the only thing she really is. Like all amoral people she verges on the Goddess." [Lawrence Durrell]

James says the married man should be forgiven for not knowing she was going to do it. "Although," he added, "I think he knew she was sick deep down. I talked to him again last night. He said he knew it wasn't what it seemed. He said she was in a state of grace. 'What do you mean by grace?' I asked him. He said, 'I mean she was so completely wonderful and beautiful and wise, the way she would lift a fork to her mouth or the way she touched me. As if the whole world was transfigured and illumined.' He was going on. I think he had been drinking."

"I'm writing down some things on her typewriter. Some things of my own."

"What sort of things?"

"About the family. About the children."

"How is Lynley?"

"He's trying to find a job. It's hard to find one this time of year. It's pretty dreary."

"I hope he'll find one."

"I hope so too."

On a more cheery note, here's what's happening out in Oklahoma. Daddy has fallen in love with the whole

Indian nation. He says we should all go live in Oklahoma and not send the children to college. Jessie flew
home so she wouldn't fail all her courses but Daddy is
staying awhile. An old friend of his from Wyoming is
coming to meet him and they are going to drive back
across the country together. Mother refuses to discuss it.

Also, here's the main part. Olivia has been invited to
go to Washington, D.C., in May to compete in an international debate contest and Daniel and Jessie are going
to go and hear her. It turns out that the principal told
Daddy that she had been invited and that is why Daddy
drove her home. He is so crazy about those two little
girls he won't let them get on a plane. What is going to
happen when he wants to drive everyone to Washington? That's what I'd like to know.

Mother says Jessie is receiving love letters from King
Mallison in New Orleans. Oh, thank God my girls are
past that stage. I would rather not know all these details
but Mother will tell me whether I want to know or not.
She is obsessed with the grandchildren. She thinks of
nothing else. I don't know how she has time to get
dressed for thinking about them. How does she sleep?

THURSDAY, 2:00 P.M.

"The forces of barbarism versus the forces of civilization." That's the beginning of an unfinished essay.

I have come home to this little agrarian capital to
forgive and be forgiven. To kiss my father on the
cheek and listen to his advice. To be my mother's
friend, to stop being jealous of my brothers and
sisters. To count my blessings and bestow kindness
upon my kin. I have failed. All I do is count the
waste and make mental lists of changes all the way
back to 1961 when the first obstetrician gave us the
first bottles of black mollies. First I started taking
these goddamn diet pills WHILE I WAS PREG-

NANT because a doctor was fool enough to pre-
scribe them to me. Then my sister-in-law took them
and I aborted the first baby and hers was born to an
alcoholic mother because she would be so goddamn
hungry by the time night came that she drank to
get nourishment into her body. A mother's body is
supposed to be full and rich and fat. A mother is
supposed to feed her babies but instead I killed
mine in my womb trying to keep my weight down.
Well, it's true. Those black mollies Doctor Grayson
gave me were the start of it. No one in our family
had ever been an adulterer or a drunk or a dope
addict or divorced the father of their children. Although Granddaddy committed suicide and so did
Uncle Daniel.

I don't know what to do with this stuff. I can't let
anyone publish all this stuff about our family. The other
executor is coming Saturday. He's flying in from Boston. He'll get here at noon. Well, I'll get this cleaned up
before he comes. I'll just throw the embarrassing things
away. I will wear my new gray dress and that pink and
green scarf Putty sent me from Dallas. It's from a museum. I'll bet someone from Boston will like that.

❧ IV ☙

Helen

ཨོཾ 20 ཨོཾ

ཨོཾ HELEN LEFT the office and began to walk toward her mother's house. It was a beautiful sunny day. The bulbs were coming up. The birds of North Carolina were everywhere, flying and singing, picking up seeds in the grass. Her mother was sitting on the patio, looking marvelous in a pale green printed dress. She was sipping a cup of coffee and watching the birds on her lawn. She smiled and waved when she saw her daughter. Helen bent down and kissed her. "Anna was writing about our grandfather's death," she began. "She was going to publish it in an autobiography."

"Oh my. Well, throw it away."

"She said it was a great act of courage, to die that way."

"Oh no, it made us all sad. He didn't even leave a note. At least Anna left a note."

"Most suicides don't leave them. They're in too big a hurry, afraid they'll lose their courage. I think it's better than a terrible horrible death in a hospital hooked up to tubes. I think Anna was right."

"You don't know, Helen. It was terrible when my father left that way. He was so sick. Anna wasn't even sick yet. He had tried it before." She muttered into her knitting. Helen had ruined her beautiful morning, her lovely spring day.

"What did he do?"

"I don't know. He tried to drown himself. It didn't work."

"Well, it worked for Anna."

"Please don't talk about it anymore today, Helen. If you don't mind. It's good of you to sort out her papers. We all appreciate it. I know it's very hard on you, staying over there. Trying. Don't stay over there all the time. Protect yourself. She had too much power over you. She always had a way of making you do things."

"She isn't making me do anything. I'm enjoying it. It breaks the routine of my life. I'm writing some things myself. Did I tell you that?"

"That's nice." Mrs. Hand put down her knitting and pointed to a feeder by a kitchen window. "Look at that mockingbird. He listens to jazz on that Negro station from the college. Look at him turn his head." Helen laughed. Her mother was so serious about plants and birds. Her hair done to perfection and her little silk dress and her nails polished, sitting here watching the birds, playing jazz for them.

"Oh, he's such a darling." Mrs. Hand stood up and walked nearer to the feeder. "He comes every day. Look at them, Helen. How could there be so many wonderful colors?" She waved her hand around the yard, which was full of trees with swings and bird feeders and birdbaths and flowers and shrubs. An English garden. There were birds everywhere, redbirds and bluebirds and jays and robins and tiny rice birds that ate the pieces the larger birds dropped.

"I'm going back now," Helen said. "I just wanted to take a break. I've got to finish some things before the other executor gets here."

"What's his name?"

"John Carmichael. I've told you that. He's a poet."

"Carmichael?"

"People call him Mike. Well, I really have to go. The trust is for the children, so this has to be done right. We have to decide what to send on to her agent."

"Well, bring him over. I'm sure he wants to meet Anna's parents. Do you want him to stay here?"

"No, he can stay there. He won't have a lot of time. He's a teacher. He's taking his valuable time to do this for us."

"When does he arrive?"

"Tomorrow afternoon."

"Well, your father is going to want to meet him."

"I'll bring him over then. Maybe Sunday." Helen kissed her mother and made her escape. She followed the flower beds to the street and began to walk back toward Anna's lake. The birds of North Carolina flew before her, darting from oak to maple to hickory to walnut, feeding and singing. I hope this poet is nice, Helen thought. I would like to talk to a nice man about something I haven't already heard a dozen times. I hope he's not a disappointment.

Mike Carmichael was not going to be a disappointment. He had never been a disappointment to anyone in his life, although he was sometimes a surprise, often a surprise, a surprising man, with great energy and strange darknesses. The darkness would fall across his face and his friends would think, I never knew this man. No matter what else happened to Helen Abadie, née Hand, Mike Carmichael was not going to disappoint her. However, on this particular day, his plane was late.

Helen wandered around the airport and bought and read a *New York Times,* then bought a *Vogue* and was deep into an article on cellulite when the intercom finally announced the plane. She stuck the *Vogue* in between the sections of the newspaper and walked over to the rail to watch for him. It was easy to pick him out. Then he was beside her, introducing himself, a broad, cheerful man, a sexy man, a very sexy man. She tried to shake his hand and the *Vogue* fell out from between the sections of the *Times*. She abandoned the newspaper and the magazine, dropped them on a chair. "I'll bet you're tired," she said. "I'll bet you're worn out."

"Not at all. I want to see the papers, the stuff. I haven't adjusted to her being gone, Helen. I've written six terrible elegies to her. Really bad." He smiled and his dark eyes waited.

"For a magazine? You wrote them for a magazine?" It was all she could think up to say. He took her arm and they began to walk out through the crowded airport. He was leading her as if he knew the way. They passed a concession stand and he stopped and bought a package of cigarettes and lit one as he talked. "An elegy is a poem you write for someone you loved that died. The best one I've ever read is one line long. 'Who would I show it to?' That's the whole poem. Well, mine for Anna aren't that good." He paused. "But they aren't for magazines." He stopped and took a drag on the cigarette and looked at her again, very intently.

"I guess everyone calls you Mike," she said.

"Mike," he answered.

"Come on," she said. "I'll find the car."

She let him drive. Also, he took charge of the rest of the day. As soon as they dropped his bag at Anna's apartment he insisted on being taken to meet her parents. Mr. Hand had just driven in from Oklahoma and they had to hear all about that. Then they went to meet her brothers. They had a drink with Niall and one with James and then several with Daniel. By the time they got back to Anna's apartment it was dark and they were reasonably drunk.

"What about your husband?" Mike said. "Don't I get to meet him?"

"I told you he was busy tonight. He's an insurance executive and there's a convention in town. Besides, he doesn't like to talk about Anna. He's mad at her. He said at least she didn't try to make it look like an accident. He said that's the best thing he could say for her. He's tired of me working on the papers."

They were still in the car, parked in front of Anna's apartment. Helen opened the door and got out and walked up onto the porch and opened the door with a key. She pulled the key out of the lock and handed it to him.

"So do you love this guy you're married to, this insurance executive?"

"No, but I'm married to him. We have five children. Oh, I don't mean that. Of course I love him. It's just the way things are with married people, you know. We run a business, a five-child circus. We don't have a lot of time to be in love. Everyone's that way." She had stopped looking at him now. "I've got to get on home."

"You'll come over in the morning?"

"As soon as you want to start."

"I wake up early."

"So do I."

"Thanks for coming to get me. Taking me everywhere. I like your brothers and your folks. Nice folks."

"I've got to go."

"I'll see you tomorrow then."

"Well, goodbye."

"Goodbye." He watched her until she had gotten into the car and driven off, then he went inside and began to circle the idea of reading Anna's papers. He found a bottle of whiskey in the kitchen and poured himself a drink and, carrying it, he went into her workroom and began to poke around, making little sounds under his breath. He found a half-written story called "The Man

Who Licked Cancer's Ass" and read that for a while and then he wandered into the bedroom and took off his clothes and opened the closet door looking for a bathrobe. A white terrycloth robe was on a hanger and he put it on. Above it on a shelf was a flat cardboard box marked INTERIORS. He took it down and carried it over to the bed and opened it. He sat in the middle of the bed wearing the bathrobe and looking at the contents of the box. It contained a set of ivory Hear-No-Evil, See-No-Evil, Speak-No-Evil monkeys, a Fort Walton Beach, Florida, newspaper, dated September 13, 1968, with a fake headline that read "THE LIGHTS ARE ON FOR ANNA AND FRANCIS," a jeweler's box with a wedding ring, and a piece of white cardboard with a sign printed in the middle in inch-high block letters. AS IF NOTHING HAD HAPPENED, the sign said. There was also a packet of letters held together with a green and red plaid hair ribbon. He took out the first letter and began to read. "My lovely Anna, now we have lived through four seasons together. I have suffered August with you, and been out to watch the leaves lose their chlorophyll and held you in my arms the night ice turned the trees into gaudy miracles. 'One must have a mind of winter, to behold the junipers shagged with ice. And have been cold a long time.' We have been happy a long time. I don't want either of us to forget that, no matter what happens next."

Mike put the letter carefully back into its envelope and turned off the light and lay down upon the bed. He lay on the bed in the darkness trying to sleep. In the night it began to storm, one of the wild storms that sweep across the Carolinas from the coast. Rain beat upon the windows and the roof. Rain banged the shutters and pounded the wooden floors of the porches. Rain fell on the lake and lightning made a circus of the sky above it.

*   *   *

Mike had the packet of letters in his hand when Helen arrived at eight thirty the next morning. She had forgotten to call first. The doorbell was ringing. When Mike got to the door she was standing on the porch dripping wet and holding a grocery sack. Rain was dripping off her yellow rainhat down into her face.

"I barely was able to get here. I thought I better come on over before something happened."

"What do you think will happen?"

"I don't know. A tornado. We have them. Or a hurricane. Look, I didn't wake you, did I?" She came into the foyer and deposited her slicker on an umbrella stand. He was wearing the bathrobe and he was barefooted and he needed a shave. He hadn't combed his hair since he had left Boston the day before. "Let me make you some coffee," Helen said. "I went by the bakery and got some fresh rolls and butter. They make the butter by hand." They moved into the kitchen and Helen found the coffee maker and put the coffee on to brew. Then they walked into the living room and Mike laid the packet of letters on the coffee table. "Have you read these letters?" he said. "Francis Gautier was my favorite poet writing in the sixties. I don't know if I can read these letters. I don't know if I can do this."

"Where did you find them? I went through everything in the room. I didn't find any letters from Francis. Or anything of his. Anna gave his papers to Yale, a long time ago when you could take it off your income tax. We talked her into it. We didn't think she should keep all that stuff around. After the wreck." Helen watched the belt of the white terrycloth robe where it fell between Mike's legs. The rain poured down outside the windows. The smell of coffee was beginning to fill the room.

"They weren't in her office. There was a package on

the shelf in the guest room. I looked in the closet for a robe and it was on the shelf."

"What else was in it?"

"Mementos. Look, Helen, are you sure that coffee is all right?" He was looking toward the kitchen, from which came a burning smell and a gurgling sound. Like water falling to the floor.

"Oh, my God," Helen said, and ran into the kitchen. She had forgotten to replace the coffeepot under the spout. The freshly made coffee had dripped out all over the coffee maker and onto the cabinets and was now dripping onto the floor. She pulled the cord out of the wall and began to mop up the mess with a kitchen towel.

"Can I help?"

"No, well, I'll be goddamned. What a goddamn mess. I don't believe I did this. It's because you have that bathrobe on."

"I'll go get dressed," he said, and took the cloth from her hand and finished cleaning up the mess.

"We don't have to read those letters," Helen said. She had found another towel and was helping again. "Don't read anything that makes you sad."

"It's going to make me sad. It all makes me sad."

"I've been doing it for a month. It's about driven me crazy. I don't think I'm the same person I was a month ago. Well, at least I'm glad I didn't find Francis's letters while I was alone. She really loved that man."

"She should have loved him. I would have given anything in the world to know him. I didn't know Anna until after his death. Come to think of it, I guess I met her the winter she brought those papers to Yale. I met her in New York right after that. At a friend's. We were together a lot after that. I couldn't believe it when she asked me to do this."

"Why do you think she asked you?"

"I really don't know. She said it was because she trusted me not to let anyone put terrible covers on her posthumous books."

"There probably won't be any. There isn't anything that's finished. Everything that's here is bits and pieces of things, nothing that's done."

"That's never stopped them yet, the vultures that come and clean up writers' rooms."

"We aren't vultures."

"Not yet," he said, and dropped the towel into the kitchen sink. He wiped off the coffeepot and put another pot of coffee on to brew. "I'll go get dressed, then we can get started."

"I'm going in there and read those letters," Helen said.

"No, we can do that later. Let's start with the big manuscripts."

Many hours later the letters were still unread. First they ate the rolls. Then they drank the coffee. Then they went into Anna's office and took turns handing each other pieces of paper. Then they went back downstairs. Then they started back upstairs.

"I'll never understand it," Helen was saying. "Not as long as I live."

"There's nothing to understand. 'We owe God a death,' as the playwright said." He leaned against the banister. Helen was below him, looking up. She struck a pose she hadn't used in years, legs apart, pelvis extended, hands in her pockets. She and Anna had called it the Lilli Marlene. She couldn't believe the way this strange man made her feel, so hot, so burning and hot, the hot wild thing that made the babies, that sometimes even made Spencer seem exciting.

"It's raining so hard," she said. "I don't think I've ever seen it rain this hard."

"Maybe the flood is coming. When I was a kid I was

always waiting for the flood. I thought my old man was crazy because he didn't build an ark." He stopped and laughed and smiled at her. "One of the first poems I ever wrote was about being relieved to go work on the docks because at least I knew where a boat was, since we didn't have an ark."

"Were you poor?" She looked so serious. If he had been poor she would have an excuse for desiring him. He watched her mouth go soft at the thought of him being poor. He shook his head.

"I didn't think of myself as being poor. I thought of myself as a good-looking sexy son-of-a-bitch who was irresistible to women. Young men don't feel poor, Helen. Old men feel poor." He walked down two steps and took her arm, pulled her up to his level. "Would you mind if I kissed you? I woke up this morning thinking about your mouth, what a gorgeous mouth you have."

"I don't care much what I do this morning," Helen said. She moved closer to him. "It's Anna's fault. It's because we're over here. Besides, this rain is never going to stop."

"Do you want me to kiss you, aside from that?"

"Yes. I want you to. I want you to a lot." He pulled her into his arms and held her there and then he kissed her for a long time. Then they went upstairs to Anna's bedroom and turned down the covers on Anna's bed. I didn't expect this to happen, he was thinking. But I should have. Breadloaf or Aspen or Port Townsend, Washington. If there are writers and women in the same place, someone always gets screwed. It always ends up in a bed. Only this is Anna's sister. Jesus Christ, Anna's married sister.

I deserve this day, Helen was thinking. All I do is work, work, work and worry, worry, worry. Nothing ever happens to me. Something should happen to me once more before I die. I never even want anything to

happen. I had forgotten there was anything worth
wanting.

The afternoon rolled on by. Soon the floor was lit-
tered with Helen's pantyhose and her bra and her silk
blouse and her new gray skirt. With his sweater and his
tie and his shoes and his shirt and his pants and his
shoes and his socks. The light came in the skylights and
then the light died and it was dark and they were still in
the bed. "My God," he said. "Where have you been all
my life?"

"Having babies. I have never been unfaithful to my
husband once in my life. I want you to know that. And
don't get so far away. I'm scared."

"How many children did you say you have?"

"I have five. And now I'm doing this. I'm an adul-
tress."

"It's not going to change you because you slept with
me. It's all right, Helen. Look, aren't we supposed to be
somewhere? Aren't people looking for you?"

"Probably. I'm surprised they haven't come over
here." He got out of bed at that and found his clothes
and began to put them on. This was the sort of thing he
had expected to happen to him in the South. He wanted
to be dressed before it was time for the guns.

Later, when Helen left to go pick up her husband and
get dressed for dinner, Mike got the letters out and read
them.

Dear Anna,

It is strange to be away from you on your birthday. I
think the day you were born is the most sacred day of
the year. I woke up this morning and wanted to call your
mother and thank her for bringing you into the world.
If I am gone more than another week and you don't
come up here that is seven days and nights that we can

never get back. But I don't believe in time anymore
anyway.

I saw Dick and Shirley's little girl, Athena, last night
and we talked about you. Tell her to come to my house,
Athena said. Tell her to get in her car and drive fast. She
has a sweat shirt with her name printed on the front. A
white sweat shirt, size three, that says Athena in flamingo
pink. Hurry up, drive fast.

Frank

Dear Anna,

You were asleep when I left and I didn't want to wake
you to tell you how nice your back is when you are
asleep. The right side of your body curls around your
left leg. Did you tell me you were bowlegged when you
were a child? Or did I dream that? You should see how
your bones curve in while you sleep. How strange sleep
is. See you at four.

Frank

Mike put the letters back in their envelopes and tied
the package back together and put it back in the larger
package and put the larger package back on the closet
shelf and then stood at the window for a long time
watching the rain and smoking cigarettes all the way
down to very small butts. Then he lay down upon the
guest room bed and fell asleep. He slept until the phone
rang telling him Helen and her husband were on their
way to pick him up for dinner.

If the night was strange the morning was stranger.
Helen came over at eight in the morning and as soon as
she closed and locked the door they lay down on Anna's
blue-and-white Karastan rug from Damascus and took
off each other's clothes and made love.

"I don't even care," Helen said. "It doesn't even matter to me. We're all going to die anyway. All I think

about at night is that I'm going to get it too, what Anna
had. I'd have a mammogram every day if they'd give me
one."

"Don't say that. Don't think like that."

"I tried to talk to Spencer about it and he wouldn't
even let me talk about it. He acts like it's all right to think
you're going to die."

"It's not all right. We should rail against it, despise it,
fight back, do this." He pulled her body closer to him,
pressed her soft round butt into his legs, caressed her.
"This is our revenge, Helen. We have always known that
joy is our revenge."

"Let's go upstairs," she said. "Let's stay in bed all day."
They left their clothes on the living room floor and went
upstairs and got into the bed and made love again and
then they fell asleep and slept until one in the afternoon.

"We should get some work done," Helen said, moving
beside him in the bed. "I guess that means I'm starting
to feel guilty."

"Don't regret this. Don't regret anything you do with
me." He pulled her close to him. He was falling in love,
no mistaking that old madness. What time was it? What
day could it be? Where else did he ever confuse the
mornings from the afternoons?

"I don't know what time of day it is," he said. "That
means you have me. I think you have me, Helen."

"We ought to get dressed. I want to put my clothes
on."

"Do you want me to go get them for you?"

"No."

"I'll go put on mine. That will be a beginning." He got
up, disentangled himself, stood beside the bed looking
down at her. She looked absolutely terrified and he
loved her for trying not to let it show. "Put on something
of Anna's. These closets are full of clothes."

"I will in a minute. Go on. We'll open up a box of papers. We'll start sorting them. Don't look at me any more right now."

This is the garden, he thought. Never leave the garden to look for the garden. "How about going back to Boston with me," he said. "We could take some boxes of papers and work on them up there. I have people at the university who could help us. Will you go?"

"If I can get away. When are you leaving?"

"I have to go back Tuesday. Will you go with me? I want you to go up there with me."

"I might," she said. "I really might do that. If you really want me to."

"I want you to. I definitely want you to."

"Get dressed then."

"Okay, I will."

Fifteen minutes later Helen came downstairs wearing one of Anna's satin slips. "I found something the other day that puzzles me," she said. "I found some papers with numbers on them and I can't decide if it's fiction or about money. Look at these." She handed him the papers.

"You look gorgeous in that slip. Come here and let me feel it."

"I'm going to get dressed right now."

"Come here, Mrs. Abadie." She moved close enough to be touched and Mike began to read the papers she had handed him.

"Anna was terrible at math," Helen said. "She always said, 'Anyone can count.' It might be something about a mystery novel. She said she was going to write one, with a buried treasure."

"Were you close to her?" He put his hand around her waist, ran his hand across the soft yielding fabric and the softness of her stomach and down across her thigh. He kept on wanting to fuck her. He hadn't liked fucking a woman that much in years. He accepted it and liked it. He didn't question it or try to blame it on the weather or on death.

"Come to me," he said. "Let's go back upstairs and make love again."

"You want to?"

"Yes, why not?"

The phone was ringing. It was Helen's husband, Spencer, and he said she had to get home right away.

"What for? I'm busy, Spencer. We don't have much time to do this. I may have to go up to Boston with Mike and work at the university on them."

"Well, you can't do that. That's why I'm calling. DeDe just called from Atlanta. She's in trouble."

"What kind of trouble?"

"She broke up with Ronnie. She was really upset. She couldn't get you and the maid didn't know the number over there. You'd better go home and call her."

"Well, I can't do it now. You take care of it, Spencer. You're the one who spoils her to death. You talk to her."

"Don't make any plans about leaving town right now, Helen."

"I may have to. It's a lot of money for the children. Besides, it's my sister's work. It's something I have to do." She looked at Mike. He was smiling and shaking his head. I am so fortunate, Helen thought. I'm beginning to be as lucky as Anna was. I could go home and make love to Spencer too. My God, I'm becoming a sex maniac. Unless the children die. Then my luck would stop. Unless DeDe goes to join her aunt in the ocean. Oh, my God. "What's her number? Where did she call from? Goddammit, Spencer, I'm sick and tired of these children driving me crazy. Aren't any of them ever going to grow up? For God's sake, I can't even get this work done that is for their future. Tell me the number. I knew it was a mistake to send her so far away to school. Give me the number." She wrote it down and made a face at Mike. "That damn Ronnie. I never did trust him and he's too old for her anyway. She might be pregnant for all we know. She might be pregnant and about to abort our grandchild. She told me the last time she was here that he didn't want any children no matter what." Helen hung up on her husband and called the number in Atlanta. Her daughter DeDe answered the phone and began to recite her problems. DeDe droned on and on about the past weekend and the difficulty of living in a small apartment and the trouble she was having with her sinus.

"Are you pregnant?" Helen said at last. "DeDe, are you pregnant?"

"Yes," the girl answered. "I am."

"Oh, my God." Helen sat up.

"He doesn't want it. He wants me to get an abortion."

"Come home this afternoon. Get on an airplane and come down here."

"Okay. I'll call you back. Let me call the airport." DeDe hung up and Helen stopped making faces and shook her head.

"She's going to have a baby," she said. "I'm going to be a grandmother."

"Is there a map with this? With this mystery novel stuff?"

"Yes, in the folder. It's with the rest of the stuff. Look, I'll have to leave for a while. I'd better go find Spencer and talk to him. My daughter may be coming tomorrow."

"It's all right. Go do what you have to do."

"Daniel's planning on taking you to dinner tonight. At his house, with his daughter."

"Fine. You go on. I'll call him later."

Helen went upstairs to get dressed. Mike followed her and sat on the bed watching. She adjusted each piece of clothing very carefully before putting on the next one. He liked the way she dressed. He liked the day and the work that lay before him and this strange new woman, this mother of five with her naïveté and her candor. She reminded him of Anna in calm moments. I'll do the papers justice, he promised himself. I'll do it right.

"I can't think of a thing right now but DeDe," Helen said. "I really have to go on and see Spencer and talk about this."

"I know you do. Go on. I'll be here when you get back. God, that was a lovely morning."

"Well, I'm glad you liked it." She looked at him very seriously, she wanted to give him a sexy seductive look but she had lost the mood. She kissed him on the cheek instead and then left him and went down the stairs and out the door and into the car. It was a relief to think of DeDe, her crazy dancing daughter, DeDe. Her silly, man-crazy, spoiled-rotten DeDe. Imagine DeDe's womb filling up with a baby. DeDe didn't even know how to cook. Helen began to drive in the direction of her husband's office. All of a sudden he seemed very dear to her, his body beside her in the night and her own body swelling up time after time with his children and now, the child of a child. The daughter of my daughter, Helen was thinking. Oh, I should go by and tell Momma. I will call Momma as soon as I get to Spencer's office.

Mike was due to leave on Tuesday afternoon. In the meantime DeDe had called back four times making four different sets of plans to fly home from Atlanta. On Tuesday morning, when it was too late for Helen to change her mind and go to Boston, DeDe called one last time and said she had made up with her boyfriend, and was going to stay in Atlanta and "work things out."

*   *   *

"The little spoiled-rotten brat," Helen said. She was wrapped up in Mike's arms. She had come in the door of the apartment and gone straight to his arms. "I could have gone to Boston with you if this hadn't happened. Now she probably won't even have the baby. She and Ronnie will probably go out and abort my grandchild without even asking me about it. Oh, I am going to miss you so much."

"Someone named Phelan called. He's coming by." Mike disentangled himself. "He sounded like a nice man. He said he was a friend of Anna's."

"When's he coming?"

"Right now. He said he wasn't far away. Is he a relative?"

"Distant. Well, I'm glad you'll get to meet him. We can ask him about the map stuff. I think it might be about a book we can't find." The doorbell was ringing. Helen went to the door and there was Phelan, wearing corduroys and a leather vest. He came in and shook Mike's hand and was told about DeDe's pregnancy and then Helen handed the folder with the map to him. "What is this about, Phelan? Did Anna say anything about this to you?"

"I don't know, what is it?"

"It's a map of Summerwood and the old graveyard and figures, like surveying. Or math. I think it must be some mystery book she was writing. I want to find it if I can. It might be a valuable manuscript."

"Well, it's a valuable map." He was laughing. "Jesus Christ, Helen. This is about the coins. What a goddamn joke. It's the coins. I'd forgotten about the coins."

"What coins?" Mike moved in.

"A bunch of goddamn Krugerrands her daddy was selling her. Old man Hand is a nut for gold. He's a goldbug from the old days. He bought into gold at thirty-five dollars an ounce and if I'd done what he told me to do when he told me to do it I'd be the richest man I know. I'll be goddamned. She kept on burying them."

"What are you talking about, Phelan?" Helen took the map from him.

"Anna must have buried all those coins she got off your daddy out at Summerwood. We did it the first time one night when we were drunk. She told me she was going to dig them up but instead she must have buried some more. Well, shit, let's go out there and see what we find. Have you got a shovel around here, Helen?"

"Of course not. But there's one at the place. We can stop at the house and get one. I want to show Summerwood to Mike anyway." She stood up. Mike was smiling and shaking his head. He can't leave now, Helen was thinking. Now he'll have to stay another day and I can go with him when he leaves. She walked over to the other side of the room and put her arm around his waist. So that's how it is, Phelan thought. Well, I'll be goddamned. Anna, you should have lived to see this. We finally got Helen to leave the yard. "Let's go," he said out loud. "Mike, you got any boots with you? You might need some boots."

"I'll be okay," Mike answered. "I don't mind getting my shoes dirty."

They piled into Phelan's Porsche and drove out the highway toward Summerwood. "The goddamn coins," Phelan said. "Only Anna would go off and leave something like this. God bless her, well, just goddamn I miss her and wish she'd lived a thousand years."

"I think she forgot," Mike said. "She was thinking about dying, about her death. She didn't give these coins a thought, whatever they turn out to be."

"She gave everything a thought. She knew what she was doing every minute of her life. She could shoot as straight as a man. We used to go out to shoot skeet. Well, never mind." Phelan gripped the wheel. What goddamn East Coast Yankee could understand Anna. To hell with him.

"Phelan," Helen said. "Let's be nice, okay. Mike came all the way down here in the middle of a semester to help me. And don't drive so fast. There isn't any hurry."

Phelan gunned the motor, weaving in and out of the lanes of traffic. They turned onto asphalt, then onto a winding road that led through pine trees to the house on Summerwood. They stopped at a shed and found shovels and Phelan opened the trunk and rearranged some boxes. One box contained rifle shells. Another held six bottles of Napoleon brandy. Phelan took out a bottle and gave it to Mike to hold. Then he reached down into a corner of the trunk and found a leather case that held four dusty silver cups. He carried the case over to an old outside spigot beside the shed and washed out the cups and shook the water off and put them back into the case. "Hold this too," he said to Mike, and Mike obeyed. Phelan loaded the shovels in the back of the Porsche and tied the trunk lid down with a piece of cord. Then they all got into the car again and drove up to the graveyard. It was on the top of a flat hill, surrounded by oak trees. A breeze was blowing from the south.

"A breeze is always blowing up here," Helen said.

"That's so," Phelan agreed. "Well, bring that map and let's go dig. I hope she put them all in one place but you can't tell from the map. I'll show you where we put the ones we buried."

"You want this bottle of brandy?" Mike asked.

"Good thinking," Phelan said. "Open it up."

Two hours later, when all the boxes had been found and dug up and opened and half the brandy had been drunk and the other half spilled on the grave of one Archania Duval Hotchkiss, they sat on a marble slab and counted the coins. There were 461 Krugerrands in mint condition, 60 American Eagles and 47 Canadian Gold Leaf coins. "There they are," Helen said, "the children's legacy from their aunt."

Mike and Phelan were leaning on their shovels. "Mike," Phelan said, "would you get another bottle of brandy out of the Porsche? It's in a box in the trunk."

"We could steal them," Helen said. "They're going to do the children more harm than good." She looked up at Mike. "You don't have to do everything Phelan tells you," she added. "Tell him to get his own goddamn brandy."

"I'll get it," Mike said. "Why not? I spilled the other bottle."

"If we stole them we wouldn't have to fool with the income tax," Helen went on. "I mean, how am I going to explain this? They'll think there are thousands more. I can see Stacy right now, handing Anna's coins over to that preacher that has her hypnotized."

"I'll steal them if you will," Phelan said. "I'll be glad to help."

"Anna would want us to steal them." Helen picked up a box and took off the rubber bands and extracted a roll of coins and unwrapped them and began to take them out of their plastic wrappers. "I want to hear them clink."

"I'll get the brandy," Mike said, and walked off down the hill toward the car.

"So you're fucking this guy," Phelan asked. "Is that the deal?"

"No, I am not fucking him." She had several of the coins in her hand now, dropping them on each other like cards in a deck.

"You're going to ruin those, Helen. Those coins are in mint condition. They lose their value if you scratch them up."

"What do you think I ought to do with them?" She sat

back on the tombstone. She very carefully placed one of her leather riding boots on the very edge of the stone so that her thigh was tight beneath her skirt. She had been doing this kind of stuff so long she didn't even know she was doing it.

"When you get tired of him it can be you and me," Phelan said. He moved nearer. "Go to Africa with me for the winter. Let Charlotte chew on that." He waited. Helen didn't answer him. He stuck his hands in his pockets and went on. "It should have been you and me years ago, Helen. Your old man's got every one of you by the balls, I know that. But you could still escape. A week away from here you would have forgotten they exist. Fuck a bunch of grown children running your life. Well, I've said too much."

"Go on."

"It could be you and me. It always was. It's not too late." He lifted his shoulders, looked down at her out of his crazy black eyes.

"I wouldn't fuck you if you were the last man alive," she said. "All the people you've fucked, you've probably got every disease known to man." She lowered her eyes, then turned to look in the direction of the car. Mike was walking back up the hill carrying the brandy. The sun was past the meridian, halfway down the sky behind a bank of clouds. It was a gorgeous, a memorable day. My boots and skirt match the trees, Helen was thinking. I bet I look divine. Phelan placed one of his handmade Justin cowboy boots on the tombstone next to her riding boot. He decided it would probably be at least three months before he actually got in her pants. A tractor started up in a nearby field. A 747 crossed the sky. Phelan patted the tombstone with his boot, thinking what a wonderful world it was after all, full of so many women waiting to ruin you and make you broke and horny and happy and occasionally even satisfied. Helen tossed her hair and turned her face toward the poet from Boston who was going to take her away from it all.

"Here's the brandy," Mike said. He held it out and Phelan took out a pocket knife and cut the seal and filled the small silver cups. He handed one to Helen, then one to Mike, then filled one for himself.

"To life," he said, and raised his cup.

V

The Gods

༄ 21 ༄

༄ THE BOXES are all packed now. The only thing I
don't know what to do with is the stuff she wrote when
she was young. All Daddy did after she died was show
people the poetry she wrote when she was young. Once,
when she first started publishing, he xeroxed copies of
some poems about Jesus she wrote when she was young
and taped them over the pages in her books that had
sexual scenes in them. Mike says those books will be very
valuable some day. He thinks Daddy is a beautiful man.
Well, it's like him to think that. He's the sweetest man
I've ever known, and the kindest. Oh, God, it's so
strange to make love to him. I know I'm going to hell for
this but I don't care.

Also, he is fascinated by this stuff about Olivia and
Jessie. Daddy is going to ride on the plane with them to
Washington to hear the debate contest. He hasn't been
on a plane in twelve years, ever since a plane he was on
hit some air pockets over Mobile. He wouldn't even go
see Lynley graduate. Well, I have never given in to
jealousy and I won't start now.

They are all going to Washington together in May.
Even Mother is going. I wouldn't be a bit surprised if

Olivia won. She really is a wonderful little girl, a very very nice little girl. I only wish some of mine had manners that nice. Exquisite manners, like Daniel has always had. It might be inherited. Anna thought everything was. Of course she always went too far with her ideas. If it is inherited then they could splice some genes or something onto some of mine and I wouldn't mind. Especially onto DeDe.

The most unbelievable things I have found were the letters from LeLe. I started to burn them up to save her from getting blackmailed someday. Well, never mind that. I put them in an envelope and mailed them to her, insured, first-class mail and I got the receipt back where she signed for them but no thank-you note as yet. She was so strange at the memorial service and spent all her time with Anna's little carpenter friend. I shouldn't say that. He is at Vanderbilt engineering school now and doing very well. He is the sexiest thing I've come across in years. Some sort of aura about him. So naturally LeLe picked him out. I'm one to talk. Oh, Mike, I miss you so much. I haven't talked to you all day. As soon as I finish closing up this apartment I am going up to Boston and spend at least a month. They will just have to do without me for a while. What else?

Jessie came over yesterday afternoon in the middle of me sorting out the rest of the clothes for the Goodwill. She had a letter from King Mallison, Junior, in her pocketbook and asked me if I wanted to read it. Poor little motherless child. She had already shown it to Mother and read it over the phone to Olivia. She has half the boys in town in love with her but she has to hang on to these love letters to make up for Olivia being invited to go to Washington.

"The terrible part is that Olivia's in love with him too," she said, and lowered those long eyelashes and looked so innocent. "Oh, Aunt Helen, what will I do? I can't do this to Olivia, but I like him and he likes me. I guess I should talk to Dad about it when he comes home tonight."

"Do you want any of these clothes before I give them away to the Goodwill?"

"Don't give them away, Aunt Helen. Not yet."

"It has to end sometime. We can't keep this stuff forever."

"I would like her hats," Jessie said, and walked over to the dressing table and put on one of Anna's hats, a gray felt slouch hat for winter in the city. Her golden hair fell out below it onto her shoulders and then I began to cry and so did she and that was the end of yesterday's work. We went over to Momma's instead and kept her company until Daddy came home.

Here is a copy of the letter from King in case anyone is interested.

Dear Jessie,

I dreamed last night that you were in New Orleans watching me play rugby in the park. Sometimes the guys on the Tulane team let me play with them when they're in the park and sometimes I play with them on the Tulane campus. So you were there watching me and somehow you fell down and broke your leg and I had to carry you home on the streetcar. We got on the streetcar right in front of Tulane and you had on this white dress and I was afraid it would get dirty dragging on the ground. I took you home and put you in a bed with flowers all around it and my dad came and stood at the foot of the bed and played the guitar for you.

I think meeting you is the turning point in my life. I told this shrink my stepfather sends me to about it and he said I might be right. I want to start doing really well in school and maybe go to Tulane to law school or be an architect. I don't want to be some crazy cynical kid getting drunk at Tipitina's and having a bad reputation. Uncle Phelan said you are going to be at Highlands for Christmas. So are we.

Did I forget to tell you that I love you? I love you. My mother says men never have the courage to tell women they love them. I will never forget as long as I live seeing you in that room in that green sweater. We will be in Highlands on Wednesday night, the 22nd. I will call you as soon as we get there. I can come over no matter how late it is. Will they let me see you that late? Do I need to write to your dad and ask him? Well, I'd better go now.

Love, King

Could Anna be missing all of this? Could Anna really be dead? I know no one is going to believe this but I saw her ghost twice. Once, sitting on her piano bench, at dusk, just as the light was leaving the room, the day after Mike left to go back to Boston. She was just sitting there, laughing at me. So you found the coins, she said. And then: You better go on home now, Helen. You better go home and fix dinner for your husband.

The second time was a few days later. I came down the stairs holding some papers in my hand, a story about a character named Finn who is just like our cousin LeLe. I guess LeLe wouldn't care what you wrote about her. She told me once she had had every important man in the American South for a lover. Anyway, I was coming down the stairs of the apartment. I will miss being there with the stark walls and half-empty rooms and shadows everywhere, and I saw Anna's ghost standing behind a green velvet chair smiling at me. She was being so kind and sort of funny and it didn't scare me like it did the first time. Didn't make me want to run away. Here is how she looked, like a hologram, half real and half sort of smoky. But her face was clear, and her hands. She had them lying one on top of the other on the back of the chair. She said, Helen, I want you to be happy. I want you to have anything you need of mine.

"Was Mike your lover?" I said. I couldn't believe I said it. I didn't even know I wanted to ask that question. She just shook her head, like no, that isn't anything to bother about. Then she was gone and I turned on all the lights as fast as I could and left the house with the lights on until I came back the next day. The mind is a funny thing. I know I was just making that up about the ghosts but it tells me one thing. She really is dead. She isn't in Europe. She's at the bottom of the sea. That is done.

I'm going to Boston next month. To stay a long time and talk to people at the university about her papers. She left them to four different universities. Fickle to the end.

The only things I am keeping for myself are two things in her own handwriting. One is a page out of a Giant Jumbo coloring book, signed with DeDe's name. It is a picture of a mother dinosaur feeding a young dinosaur some leaves. Mountains in the background. I remember sending it to Anna because it was the first time DeDe ever wrote her name. The leaves are colored green, the dinosaurs are brown, the mountains in the background are yellow and orange and purple and pink and blue. Underneath DeDe's name Anna had written, "So she'll be able to think about things that aren't there."

The other thing I kept was a poem by Sappho, part of a poem by Sappho copied on a piece of yellow legal pad. "Queen, Cyprian, fill our gold cups with love. Stirred into clear nectar." It is a great consolation to me to think that people were having a good time that long ago. I don't think the human race would have made it this far if someone wasn't having fun at least part of the time.